DOWN
THE DEEP

BOY
CULTURES

TAVARUS INGRAM

outskirtspress
DENVER, COLORADO

Down In The Deep
Boy Cultures

v1.0

Outskirts Press, Inc.
http://www.outskirtspress.com

ISBN: 978-1-4327-9391-3

PRINTED IN THE UNITED STATES OF AMERICA

Chapter 1

Dre packed his bags with anger in frustration as he talked to his girlfriend Gia on his cell phone.

We can keep talking about this until my mouth falls off but that's the situation, she shipping me away said Dre.

Damn, I can't believe your ruthless mother is shipping you off to some fucking barnyard out in the middle of nowhere…she is straight bugging I mean all you did was get caught selling a little drugs which weren't yours by the way, you were just holding on to that stuff for your boy which was kind of stupid on your part…for getting caught anyway said Gia.

It's not just about that, she talking about me dropping out of school too said Dre.

Okay so she found out that you dropped outta school a few months ago to get that job at the busted ass corner store to help me raise our baby she didn't know about but I mean the point of going to school is getting a job right and she ready to just try to take your life away from you like really what kind of shit is that? Gia asked him.

You're a father now and she just can't take you away from your responsibilities …plus I need you here to help me, I am not trying to take care of this load by myself said Gia as Dre sighed listening to her zipping up another bag.

His mom Margaret was downstairs on the phone talking to his aunt.

He upstairs getting packed right now so he can be on his way, I'm not having all this mess he getting into and doing out here on these streets…he starting to act like that older brother of his and I will not let him fall in those footsteps she said.

These teenagers today, have no clue that the decisions they make now will have a lasting effect on their life relied her sister.

I'll be damned if I just let him throw his life away on the streets and I'll be visiting him in prison somewhere in a few years…maybe if his daddy stayed around and been a father to him like he suppose to be then he wouldn't be going down this route…his sorry ass checked out of both their lives a long time ago and has never been nothing but a dead beat.

But I'm all he got and I aint having it and until he turn 18 that behind belongs to me and he'll do what I say…I tried a scared straight program and that didn't seem to work obviously she said.

Sometimes you have to take drastic measures to get the message across to them said her sister.

Girl, He was all up in here with drugs stashed in my house and I kicked him out to the streets but that was my biggest mistake at the time cause he went to stay with that no good cousin of his and could do whatever he wanted over there said Dre's mother.

He knows I went through this same shit with his brother and told him not to ever let me find that mess in here or he can't stay here…I swear I see him following that same path…the path that leads to nowhere fast…want to be gangster and thug sagging with pants half way to the ground, what is that all about anyway?

I know that he smoking weed, we use to do it too back and our foolish days… but now a days these young boys are either slinging rocks or smoking it, won't have nothing or want nothing in life said Dre's mother.

Dre come stay with me, you don't have to go…she just trying to break us up you know she can't stand me said Gia.

We tried that remember, your moms caused so much drama the whole time I was there all up in our relationship and business fussing at me and you fussing at her then you both turn on me and kick me out…naw aint trying to go through that again said Dre.

So you're just going to go?You are city Dre, born and raised that's all you know... you can't cope or handle that boring ass life in the country with all those hillbilly folks I mean do black people even stay out there where you going...this aint right...you got a job...get your own place for me and the baby... we suppose to have our own by now anyway, what's the problem? Gia asked him.

I'm 16 I'm not old enough to get a place and neither are you, plus there's nowhere else I can go my mom telling all my relatives what I been doing and they don't want me anywhere near they crib more less staying there said Dre.

She did that on purpose, what kind of monster mom makes her son look like a drug dealer you didn't sell drugs you worked at a store so what she know said Gia.

Dre was silent for a moment finally deciding it was time to tell his girlfriend the truth.

I never worked at a store...I just told you that at the time because I couldn't let you or anybody else in my business he said.

Then what were you doing? asked Gia.

I can't believe that Andre has had all of this going on behind your back said his mother's sister.

I'm still shocked too...he just turned 16 and already got a baby by this little mouthy hutchie momma from around the way and I'm just finding out not by him but his cousin who I overheard him talking too said Dre's mother.

Oh my, do you think that the baby belongs to him?You know how these fast tail girls are out here pinning the tail on the donkey said her sister.

I seen the baby already and I know it's his, got his head, eyes and everything.

Babies having babies don't make no sense, He dropped out of school a while back after I begged to get him back in after he threatened and tried to fight the principal who I'm good friends with and they were going to kick him out, now he hanging with that scheming rambunctious girlfriend of his and hustling in the streets pushing weight said Dre's mother.

That's terrible said her sister.

Yes I know and he went to jail shortly after caught with drugs he was holding for one of his homeboys supposedly and was willing to take the rap for it like a little ol do-boy or something.

Grown ass men using boys to take the heat all they gotta do is show them their nice car with 23's or whatever they called, flash some money in the face and put them on to the game and they go for it she said.

I was selling for Flip Dre told Gia on the phone.

Flip? He like one of the biggest drug dealers in the city so that's why you was hiding all those stacks telling me that store manager was paying you under the table to unload trucks…I should have known that was a lie said Gia.

You were too busy holding out your hand anyway…I was taking care of you and the baby and spending mad money on you that's all you knew and needed to know said Dre.

Turn out he was selling for him too got me all in court embarrassing me like that…he was a straight A student making the honor roll and dean list then he start hanging with those no good boys in the streets and watching these rap videos that got his mind all messed up and twisted.

Then people asking me what have I been doing or where I was at while all this was going on and I liked to cussed them out but I prayed like I usually do…that's why I'm sending him away for a while to get his mind right and away from all this city trouble…show him the life of a drop out…yeah his girlfriend tried to sweet talk me into letting him stay and talking about how the baby need him and I hanged right up on her…she going to be the reason why he'll be in jail if he stay around here said Dre's mother.

So you were selling? Why couldn't you tell me that? Gia asked him.

You know how your moms is and I wasn't trying to have her in my business and you tell her everything even though you say you don't, plus she don't like me and took whatever she thought I had while I was there so she would have had her hand out right beside yours and if I didn't give her what she wanted...wouldn't surprised me if she threatened to tell the cops or something said Dre.

She do like you Dre in her own way,she didn't tell your mom you dropped out of school and was living with us did she?asked Gia.

16 and already a father and don't know nothing about being a daddy, well you do all you can do to raise them right and they want to act out because they feel like they come from a broken home.

Reason why all these bad kids feel justified to do the things they do, I might not have been able to save his older brother from that life but I will save him by any means necessary and that little trap he fell in dealing with that girlfriend of his aint enough to keep him here and doing whatever it takes to take care of that baby but it won't be that way so Miss Gia can kick, cry, tell him what a bitch I am and scream to she lose her breath but she might as well say goodbye to him for now said his mother as the door bell ranged.

That's his uncle here to pick him up I'll call you later she said ending call and opening door.

I don't know what I'll do without you Dre... please don't go I'm going to lose my mind and the baby keep right on crying, see he know something wrong said Gia.

You both gotta be strong for me...I'll be back soon I promise said Dre.

Like how long? asked Gia.

I don't know like a month or 2 said Dre.

So you just want me to wait for you and put my life on hold... Ugh, alright...so I mean how much money you got on you...I know you just not going to dip off without leaving me and the baby some ends plus I know you got a stack or 2 put up somewhere all the smart sellers do said Gia.

Man, I told you my mom found it and confiscated it and not giving it back to me and wherever she got it…its not here because I tore this place up trying to find it said Dre.

She need to give you back your money it's not hers…this is not fair everybody just trying to run our lives and tell us what to do just because we not 18…guess I'll be robbing banks and holding up stores while you gone to take care of the baby then said Gia.

Naw stop talking crazy for real, you going to stay in school and let my mom and your mom help you take care of the baby.

Get a job and what you have to do while I'm gone…hold it down for me baby alright said Dre.

Okay…I'll try…I love you so much Dre said Gia.

I love you too said Dre.

Dre! Dre! Get off that phone and come down here! shouted his mother from downstairs.

Man that's my mom's…I'll call you back when I'm on the road alright said Dre.

Ugh that witch…smh,alright…call me as soon as you out that torture chamber…love you and I promise not to give it away while you gone that's my word said Gia.

Alright smiled Dre and ended the call then walked out his room and stood to the top of the stairs.

You about ready to go boy said his mom.

Yeah relied Dre in a attitude type tone.

Yeah? Boy…said his mom with a stern look.

Yes mam said Dre.

Don't get grown cause you just started smelling your must and you around here popping out babies told you I don't play that disrespect stuff period, your uncle here she said.

Yes mam I see him said Dre.

Then speak she said.

Sup Unc said Dre.

How you doing Andre he said.

Been better replied Dre.

Sup Unc?thats not even real words some of that old street slang right there…you sounding more like foreign garbage every day I tell you she said as his uncle smirked shaking his head looking away.

I could have caught the bus there or wherever it is you sending me said Dre.

Naw I wanted to make sure you get there, you have a tendency to get lost said his mom.

How you going to just ship me off in the middle of nowhere, I got a baby here that I need to take care of said Dre.

Boy we already talked about this and I know the situation but that baby will be taken care of just fine while you're gone and I'll be paying your cell phone bill while you're there so you can keep in contact with that girlfriend of yours go gather your things you got a long trip ahead of you she said.

Really mom? You're sending me out to the country? Out of all places…that is mest up I might as well go to jail or something said Dre.

You go down there trying to be a billy bad ass and act crazy, your next trip I'm sending you away to a place a lot like it and I'm not playing now move it she said.

Andre your mom is only doing this for your own good said his uncle.

Naw it's for her own good said Dre walking back to his room.

Go up there and help him get his stuff in your car, you might not like the country but it's as big as this city that you run around day and night and you won't be able to get in trouble out there too much she said.

Chapter 2

Dre took the grueling travel with his uncle for hours on end.

Man, I'm hating this move already, I haven't been able to get a signal for the past hour all the way out here…yo its straight dead out here and I'm not even seeing buildings and cities no more but big ass corn fields and trees this is crazy and it stink out here so fucking bad… damn chicken trucks, cows and road kill…I can't fuck with this… yo Unc, please turn this whip around and drop me off to the nearest city…I won't tell if you don't…I'm not going to be wearing overalls, flannel shirts and straw hats its hoodies and fitties for me all day…she really think throwing me out in the country going to have some big impact on my life…epic fail said Dre.

Sorry nephew, but I got strict orders by the boss lady to drop you off to your destination and make sure you get there on their door step…she going to be calling there in a little while to make sure you there anyway so try to take this as a learning experience and make the best of this situation for right now…you don't see it right now but she's only trying to teach you a lesson…she only wants the best for you and don't know how else to get you to see that right now said his uncle.

So she sends me all the way out here so she doesn't have to deal with me, what is that? I got too much going on up there to be trapped down this place…got a son that I need to be home with taking care of…how I'm suppose to do that from here out in the wild…telling you I'm never forgiving her for this ish said Dre.

The what? asked his Uncle.

Nothing just a saying…my hood would straight up laugh at me if I told them that I got stuck down in the country on a freaking farm or something…when I get back I'll just tell them that I got sent away to a boot camp or some shit and got sent home for kicking everybody ass up in there including those ass holes that scream in your face and order you what to do said Dre.

His Uncle laughed. Don't want to lose your street cred huh? He asked.

What you know about that Unc? grinned Dre.

I was young once so don't think that wasn't a word when I was your age ripping and running the streets…I know how important all that is when your age but when you live as long as I do you just don't care about any of that stuff or living up to a reputation or anyone's expectations said his uncle.

I don't really care about that either but just how you got to be out there man and I'm not going out like this telling them I went on summer vacation to the plantation said Dre.

Comon it might not be all that bad as you making it seem, I spent quite a few summers living out here and I gotta say it can be a quiet and relaxing place to get away from the city said his Uncle.

Yo I don't care about quite and relaxation I'm 16 and I want noise and fun, I want to see busy crowds on the street and traffic everywhere, parties and hot dog stands hell even a hobo or crack head doing something crazy in the middle of the street for a couple dollars or a hot meal but now I'm all out here out of my element…man hope I don't pick up the accent these people have said Dre.

You might even come to tolerate this place before you get back, you won't be bored out here it's plenty to do said his uncle.

Yeah like work…all day long…I'm just waiting for the roads to turn into dirt roads so I can officially say I'm out in the middle of nowhere and up shits creek without a paddle said Dre.

Well they do have boats and paddles out here and creeks said his uncle.

Not funny Unc, not at all said Dre.

The city isn't the only place you have family, these are your relatives out here too and you can finally spend some time and get to know them better said his uncle.

Ye, they never bother to come to the city the same way we never bother to travel all the way down here…we don't want too nor care too…I know for a fact that the town they stay in is like a 100 miles from their house and the population probably under 50…no buses,trains or subs anywhere so I'm guessing you get around on bicycles and horses…picture me on a horse or fishing said Dre shaking his head.

Damn nephew, you complain more than my wife do…suck it up you a big boy now you can deal with it just make the best of it…whining won't pass the time any faster said his uncle.

Yeah that's what this whole stay going to be about…making the best of a bad situation so how much farther is this farm on a hill at asked Dre.

Coming up right in front of us said his uncle.

Dre glanced ahead and saw a 2 very nice 2 story house up a hill in the distance.

Alright, so this how my country relatives living that's what's up… diamond in the ruff said Dre.

Your Uncle owns a large piece of this land 4 to 5 acres I think said his Uncle.

Damn…farmer Unc must be holding down some major stacks then so now I know who my grandfather left the fortune too…dad should have followed his lead and maybe he'd have something to own like this…I know he's your half brother but he doing it…you and dad must have fell off somewhere down the line said Dre.

Nephew…you don't know what I have said his uncle.

I know you live comfortable but whatever you got big, hiding or holding on to your wife or kids going to get it all anyway…well if you fall off before she do…what good is having a lot of money if you don't spend it while your living said Dre.

I think the city life got you spoiled and lazy thinking that things can be handed to you easy or fast money passing that dope…you need some hard work in your life and the true value of a dollar when it's made the honest way said his uncle.

I got street smarts said Dre.

That's helpful but book smarts can get you farther in life said his uncle.

I got them too said Dre.

You haven't been using them that well in a while…dropped school remember said his uncle.

Man you don't understand I had a lot going on…yo we pulling up now anyway so no need to even go into discussion about it said Dre.

You too young to be having business anyway…you really look stress the fuck out too laughed his uncle.

I am and it's not funny said Dre cracking a smile.

They pulled up to the yard as his uncle beeped the horn.

Here we are your home sweet home for the next few months said his uncle.

Where the farm animals at I know they around here somewhere… see there go some chickens in a goat in the fence way out in the back… aw hell…this is really how it ends for me said Dre.

His Uncle, Aunt and cousin came out of the house and down the steps waving as Dre waved back at them mumbling under his breath.

Wow…they sho is friendly looking folk sho hope I don't cause them no trouble he said in a country voice.

Boy get your clown ass out of my car and go greet your people said his uncle taking off his seatbelt as they both got out as Dre grunted a bit under his breath looking at his phone that still had no signal.

His Uncle greeted them first hugging them as Dre kind of peeped out his surroundings and frowned his nose a bit at the air.

How was the travel? Uncle Richard asked them.

I been trapped in a car with a 16 year old boy for 8 hours who turns up my radio blasting Big Ross and Plies crying and blowing kisses to his girlfriend for hours on end on his phone use your imagination he said.

Man stop trying to play me Unc, I was not crying you tripping said Dre.

Well long time no see nephew, hear that you getting into all sorts of things back in the city and got your mom hair falling out, she wanted me to take you in down here to get you away from it all and talk to you said Uncle.

Hey Unc, Is that possible for you to have called out in done that because I'm not even getting a signal out here said Dre.

Oh we don't use cell phones out here nephew, hell we use Dixie cups said his uncle.

You are joking right? Dre asked with a serious expression.

They all looked at each other and laughed aloud. Boy just because this the country don't mean we live in the stone age…I stay buying all those fancy devises and gadgets to keep your cousin here happy…we spoil this girl rotten he said.

Boy why you all marked up like that? Uncle Richard asked observing Dre's body.

Their tats Unc, how we express ourselves in the city said Dre.

Seem like too much ink on a human being and a waste of a lot of money drawing all over yourself like that but I guess its what your generation consider cool where you come from said his uncle.

Darius…is that the name of your baby you just had? asked his cousin Erica.

Ye said Dre thinking to himself: Damn, aint no telling how much of my personal life my mom already told them:

How is your mother doing? Aunt Marylyn asked him.

I'm sure she's doing a whole lot better now that I'm gone and here said Dre.

Yeah probably so…Erica this is your cousin Dre he's all growed up now and the last time you saw him was when you 2 were 5 or something said his Uncle Richard.

Hey Andre she said with a smirk on her face.

Sup said Dre hearing the door open to the house and a guy walked out down the steps over to them and seemed to be checking Dre out sharply.

He was 6'ft 2, brown skin with corn rolls, dark facial features, 20 years old but looked a bit older for his age and a nice slender muscular frame in a wife beater, blue jeans with rips in them and work boots. He looked just like that singer De-Angelo to a tee.

Andre this is Trevor, he's family and been living with us since he was 14 and the most steady pair of hands to have on the work load… Trevor this my nephew Dre said his Uncle Richard.

Trevor took off one of his gloves from fixing something in the house and held out his hand.

Nice to meet you said Trevor.

What up said Dre shaking his hand and he had a firm and strong grip as he notice a collie come up beside him.

I see you got a lassie said Dre.

His names Charlie, had him since I was 12…we kind of found each other and he been by my side ever since…dogs are more loyal than people sometimes you know said Trevor.

Ye I know man…I had a pit-bull back home… street name was killer, too bad they couldn't meet said Dre.

Trevor gave him a slight glare but hid it with a grin shaking his head.

So how do you talk on phones out here? Dre asked him.

You can usually go out there in the field across there and wave your phone like a magic wand into the sky and you bound to get a signal but you gotta stay in that spot…good reception comes and goes out here and you learn to live with it or without it said Trevor.

Oh alright...all the way out there...so what's that funk in the air like barnyard animals or doody fields or something yo? Dre asked him.

I know it's not that city pollution or car smog your use to breathing, but you get use to it after while...funk dies down around dusk just in time for you to get some sleep...not too bad but the funk is bi- waste products turned fertilizer so we can grow all kinds of food out here to feed and support cities like yours you know said Trevor.

Dre nodded and thought to himself. This dude got a real smart ass mouth...not liking homie already:

Well it was nice meeting you little man and maybe we can talk more after you settled in I'm going to go finish fixing the sink said Trevor walking back toward the house.

Alright let's get you unpacked and show you around your new living quarters said his Uncle.

Alright...nice crib...means place Unc said Dre.

I know that, damn how country do you think I am he laughed.

Chapter 3

They helped Dre bring his stuff into the house then gave him a tour of the house from the living room to the big luxury kitchen and dining room area they had, wash and laundry room then finally going upstairs.

Dre this is going to be your room, I prepared it for your arrival... this use to be your cousin Antoine's room before he left off to go to college and move to the big city to be a stock broker.

Although your father wanted to him to stay and run his farming company with him and still holds a little resentment about it to this day that he chose the city.

Antoine seems to have built a nice life for himself up there and all that truly matters is that he happy said his Aunt Marilynn.

To be clear I'm not angry anymore or harboring any resentment to Antoine wanting to make his own life choices, just would have been nice if he chose to stay and carry on the business I been running and that's been in our family for 3 generations now.

He is free to live in the city and have the fast life to his heart's content but stock is a risky market and I have a feeling he'll come back to fulfill his family obligation when he goes broke poor and down on his luck... god forbid said Uncle Richard.

Nope, his pride and ego will never lead him to running back or begging for help you 2 are just alike and why you have this complex father son relationship said Erika.

Dre meet the future therapist said his uncle.

So do you like your new room? Dre's Aunt Marilynn asked him.

Dre walked in the room and looked around. Ye its Cool...very spacious...thanks he said looking around it.

Trevor's room is right next door and this is the bathroom that's connected from both rooms by doors, it's a nice size so I'm sure Trevor won't mind sharing it with you just make sure to use the locks when your occupying it so you want have any awkward walk ins… the other 2 are on the other side of the house…one belongs to Erika of course you know she being the girl and needing her own privacy and the third is beside the guest room and our master bed room but we have another in there too said his Uncle Richard.

Gary I prepared the guest bed room since I knew you were going to spending the night after that long travel and I heading back first thing in the morning but not before breakfast she said.

Of course, I'm not about to get back on that road with an empty stomach he laughed.

Dre walked up to one of the large windows in the room. Wow… nice view…see a lake over there past the woods from here he said.

Yeah where we go to do some fishing from time to time, we got neighbors that stay on the other side of it said his uncle.

Word, so your closest neighbors is miles away wow…when I look out my window they right there and half the time looking all at your house from the porch seeing what's going on over there just being nosy…I hate nosy people said Dre.

His Aunt giggled to herself.

I'll be getting dinner ready soon so just make yourself comfortable and get yourself unpacked and washed up and meet back down stairs she said as they left out his Uncle Richard stayed behind in the room with him and handed him a piece of paper.

Here you go nephew he said.

What's this? Dre replied looking at it.

Your weekly schedule all mapped out for you during your stay… breakfast is first thing in the morning at 6 sharp, at 7 you and Trevor are going to one of the factories to pull up and load crops their running short of help tomorrow and I need you to start immediately and don't worry about not knowing what to do its very simple and Trevor will show you the ropes of how the processes are done, I'm very sure a city slicker like yourself learns fast and not afraid to get your hands dirty pretty boy...work starts 8 sharp you get a break at 12 and again at 3 and usually finish up around 7...6 at the latest once you get the hang of it but I'm sure you'll slow Trevor down a bit at first..come home wash up for dinner, no hats or phones at the table take a few minutes to catch your breath and sleep all to do it again the next day... you work Monday through Thursday and you'll find the earnings and payment well worth the time and work...as requested by your mother half those earnings are to be deposited every week from your check and home to take care of your baby and what's left goes to the girl... according to her so expect a automatic dock of pay said his uncle.

Alright Dre replied gathering the light speed instructions.

Friday is a day of rest sort of speak you can kind of go about your way and enjoy your free time whatever you want and I'm sure Trevor will show you all the nice spots in town to have a little down time but should I need you for anything I prefer you drop whatever plans you have to assist me...the weekends we usually get together to go in town to various community activities, festivals or over to the lake but again whatever you choose to do with that time is up to you though I trust it will always be spent productively just how we do it here...I know summer vacation in the city for young man like you from the city and summer in the country are 2 different things because work here really begins in the summer....don't worry a little hard work won't hurt that strong young back...why do you think Trevor look so cut it sure aint no gym around here I'll let you get settled and I'll see you downstairs it's nice to have you here he said walking out.

Dre looked at the paper than back at him and twisted his lip walking over and sitting down on the bed thinking to him self then laid back for a moment.

Damn...this is a comfortable ass bed though he said to himself.

That night, they all had dinner together and Dre's 2 uncles did most of the talking mostly about their younger days as older men often did. the food was really good and he hated to admit it that it was slightly better than his moms cooking…judging by his Uncle Richards big blubbery gut he was rocking, that his stomach really loved it too… Dre noticed that Trevor was cutting his eyes and looking at him on the sneak a couple times as the dinner past but Trevor didn't say much to him since he had arrived but he figured it was because he was the new person in the house and it's just normal for someone to be curious or suspicious about strangers but whoever he was they treated him just like family and like one of their own sons.

But Trevor was looking at him in a way he never seen a dude look at him…on the streets staring at somebody like that got you cussed out or knocked out.

Yo why the fuck he keep looking at me like that, it's so fucking-I don't know but I don't like him feeling me out like that he want to ask me something than ask me but right now I'm not even trying to get to know nobody like that but maybe that's just how they observe people down here or something Dre thought to himself.

Hey man, I like that bling you rocking said Trevor.

Thanks man said Dre.

Is it real gold cous? Erika asked him.

I rock nothing but that real, you see my neck green said Dre.

I can't tell because you're neck all inked up soldier boy said Erika.

You always did come at me with that little smart mouth huh cous said Dre.

I haven't forgotten when I came down there when I was little and you got my new dress soak and wet with your water gun but it was Kool-Aid in it you were so mean when you were a little boy and bad… guess a lot hasn't changed since then huh said Erika.

Not really but a little said Dre.

Yep and when I was crying and told your mom she smashed that butt up and through that house and I sit back and laughed so hard said Erika.

Well I haven't got a whipping since I was 10 said Dre.

Lies your mother said she stopped hitting you with a belt and using her hand just a year ago said Erika.

Trevor laughed a little and went back to eating.

A little later that night after dinner, Dre was about to give Gia a call to let her know he had arrived and settled in.

Dre went back downstairs into the kitchen where Trevor was sitting at the table writing in his notebook while his dog ate at the end of the kitchen.

Hey man, I was wondering if I could get a flashlight…I'm going to go walk out across the field and pray for a signal so I can hit my girl up said Dre.

Alright hold on man said Trevor going back to writing for a while longer and even taking time to think to himself before writing again as Dre looked at him in frustration a bit…You could tell me where it is and I could just get it didn't mean to disturb you with what you doing said Dre.

You good, I'll get it said Trevor finally getting up then walked to a closet in the back of a kitchen and opened it turning on the light and got one off the shelf and walked back out.

Here you go man said Trevor as Dre took it thanks man he said walking out.

No prob said Trevor looking at him and sat back down at the table finishing what he was writing.

Dre walked outside to the porch light on across the vast darkness in the distance then glanced up at a bug zapper buzzing above his head then turned on the flash light and walked toward the field going a little ways out there and holding his phone up walking around trying to get a signal.

Comon baby, daddy aint got a whole night to pick up a fucking signal in this dead zone…e.t. phone home I don't give a fuck just work for me baby in this fucking battery straining place said Dre.

Trevor came outside with his dog and walked to the edge of the big porch and stood grinning as he watched Dre in the distance of the field shinning his light around raising his phone.

Hey man remember what I told you, wave it like a magic wand toward the sky trust me it works for me and when you get that signal hold the posistion!yelled Trevor.

All this just to make a fucking phone call mumbled Dre.

Thanks man!Dre yelled back to the house as Trevor took out a cigarette and lit it up pulling it then blew into the night air then sat down atop the platform of the ledge.

Dre waved his phone around and got a signal and he almost gasped.

Man, about damn time- he said freezing in place like Trevor told him then called his girl Gia.

Hello said Dre.

Omg what happened to you calling me back, I was waiting and you just hung up on me earlier today and I been trying to call you all day said Gia.

Naw I didn't hang up my phone was in bad tower areas that got worse the deeper we got down here and kept cutting off and out here where am at you gotta walk a few blocks from the house just to get a signal I been trying to call you for the longest…man this shit is so crazy and oh shit-wtf is that?! I think a raccoon just ran across me… fucking vermin and shit all over this place trying to sneak attack me said Dre.

Aw my poor boo boo, I miss you so much already and I'm feeling depressed…I started looking at videos we made together with the baby and listening to a few of our favorite songs and couldn't help but cry hell me and the baby was crying for daddy…so heartless of your mom to break up our family like that…I still can't believe she threw you on the doorstep of old MacDonald said Gia.

How Darius doing? Dre asked Gia.

He just finally went to sleep…I talked to your mom shortly after your departure…in fact she called me said Gia.

What she say? Dre asked her.

That venomous harpy was already telling me about how we going to work this thing out with her keeping the baby while I'm at school and all that and telling me how could I get knocked up by you like that and didnt take responsibility of sexual protection when you didn't have the sense to use it. Wish she get over it already…nag like for real…why she so stuck on us like she don't have a life of her own to contend with said Gia.

Yo real talk Gia don't disrespect my mom's calling her out her name like that, I'm pissed at a lot of shit she did but knock off that a bit…she still my mom's you know what I'm saying said Dre.

Oh I know boo, I was just giving her harmless pet names that's all…I didn't mean nothing bad about it, like I call you my boo bear and I'm your snookie…now my feelings hurt I can't believe you just snapped on me like that…guess you already pushing me off and don't love me really now…you changed so fast on me omg and you haven't even been down there long said Gia.

Shut up you know I love you but I need for you to try to get along with my mom's for the baby sake and who knows if your relationship get better and you start to grow on each other than she'll let me leave this place of punishment said Dre.

Yep thats true…cut down your stay there and come back home… just tell her how much you love her and appreciate this opportunity to get your mind right and be like how much you miss her and home after a while…moms always give in to that stuff when it comes to their sons…just promise me you won't snap being out in the middle of nowhere and go crazy in the meantime said Gia.

I'm good…I can handle this…shit can't break me, My Uncle already got me starting this job first thing in the morning and I barely got here…whatever though as long as I don't have to sit around this house bored as fuck…so I got you and the baby and I'm sending money every week down there straight to you said Dre.

Word that's what's up! my boo been down there a few hours and already got a job, at this rate you'll make corporate boss in a month and stacking up them fat checks for us because I know the country pay good money they not driving tractors and sweating all day for nothing…yah now I'm so happy I love you and when you make enough your shooting right back down here and we going to run away you me and the baby…fuck the world said Gia.

I love you too said Dre.

Trevor was at the end of his second smoke when Dre had got back into the yard as he glanced over at him.

Hey you get to talk to your honey? Trevor asked him.

Ye…thanks for that tip man about the phone and magic wand shit laughed Dre a little.

No prob said Trevor looking back out across the yard.

Yo can I get one of those smokes? Dre asked him.

How old are you man? Trevor asked him.

Just turned 19 man said Dre.

Lies, your Uncle and Aunt said you were 16…sorry man but I don't want to be the cause of you having any bad habits or being a bad influence on you while you're here… said Trevor.

Ye I feel you man…said Dre slowly walking up the porch to the house taking a deep breath.

But if I was to leave my smokes right here and you happen to take one and I didn't see you that's a different story…just make sure you do it out there where they can't see you said Trevor looking away as he slid the pack down the ledge looking away.

Dre smiled and took one out.

Thanks man, thanks a lot I need one for real said Dre.

Trevor put his lighter on the ledge.

Just drop that by my room when you get back in…night man he said going into the house with his dog following right behind him.

I guess he may be alright after all Dre thought to himself.

Chapter 4

Dre couldn't understand that for a nice big house with working central air conditioning that they didn't believe in running it on these already slightly warm nights but he just stripped down to his boxers and lifted both huge windows in the room bringing in a breeze added with the ceiling fan and that was more than enough to be comfortable and it took him a while to fall asleep taking in the strange noises in the country night air from the crickets to the sounds of an owl outside in the distance but beyond that it was so quiet with no noise from miles around no vehicles on the roads or anything and it was eerie because he wasn't use to these kinds of surroundings compared to the city so he just put his ear plugs in and listened to music on his iPod and fell asleep in no time.

He awoke to a loud buzzing sound in the room as he blinked his eyes and looked at the alarm clock set for 6 am sharp that was loud and irritating as hell as he looked around at the day light now shinning in into the room as he smacked his lips and closed his eyes and laid back down on the pillow hugging it.

Man damn it's 6 o'clock all ready he mumbled as he decided to close his eyes for a few more winks but the rooster outside somewhere on the back property barn area of the house kept right on screaming to the top of its lungs and with the windows open it was as if he was right there in the room.

Alright already shit he said finally getting up and throwing the cover off him and walking across the room to the bathroom stroking his hard dick with sleepy eyes as he opened the bathroom door to Trevor walking into it from the other side at the end of the bathroom almost at the same time with his bare athletic chest and dark grey jogging pants not doing much to hide the morning wood that he had as well as both instinctually did a quick inescapable glance at each other's privates than made direct contact that stayed there.

Oh damn man; my bad you go ahead said Dre turning back.

Naw you good man and stepped in first, by all means go ahead if you just taking a leak or something I usually go ahead first in get my shower out the way in all then it's all yours from there said Trevor.

Ye I just gotta take a quick leak said Dre.

Trevor nodded as he closed the other bathroom door back.

Dre took his dick out and stood in front of the toilet about to take a piss when he heard Trevor's voice.

Don't forget to lift up the seat man said Trevor.

Ye I did that said Dre lifting the lid up then took a long piss as he closed his eyes taking a deep sigh preparing him self for whatever day laid ahead for him.

A little while later, the entire house met downstairs at the table for breakfast which was a new and strange experience for Dre because he wasn't use to family getting together for breakfast or dinner for the fact even if they were his relatives…they were talking, laughing and preparing for the days events but breakfast was just as good as dinner and just as big… he was looking forward to come down to the table from that day on.

How you feel about having that tough city back broken down for country labor nephew said his Uncle Richard.

I'm good I can handle it, looking forward to getting my hands dirty and getting into it said Dre.

I like your spirit nephew, Trevor is going to give you a run down on how the work is done and guide you along the way but once you got it down packed you'll get through it fast and getting as much done in one day as possible that's what gathering the crops is about on the acres outside the factory you 2 going to this morning said his uncle.

Ye I got you man, nothing to it said Trevor.

Fast hands and steady movement is all you need out there...Trevor usually go back and forth between the factories for my friend Dave and mine but he's running a little short of help this week and progress is coming along a little slow so he's helping out there today and probably another day this week because I don't have too much work going on there right now and more than enough help so you will most likely be working at Dave's by yourself sometime this week said his uncle as Dre nodded.

You must conduct your business well Unc, maybe Dave's workers coming to work on your side because you pay a little bit better under the table after scoping out how he drop checks out there and to make up for taking his extra hands you selling me to him in a modern slavery day setting said Dre as his aunt laughed aloud in a way she couldn't hide like he made a really smart point.

You leave the business to me nephew and focus on doing a good job and getting nice checks at the end of the week...you here to work and stay out of trouble...you leave the business thinking and expertise to me said his Uncle with a slight grin.

Cool that's all the motivation I need said Dre.

So Trevor are you finished that boat project you been working on for the past few weekends? Dre's aunt asked him.

Well I plan to finish it sometime this weekend and give it a fresh new coat of paint before we take it out to the lake sometime said Trevor.

Yo you mean like a real boat? Are you building a boat man? Dre asked him.

Actually I'm just really restoring it man, but it's kind of a old classic boat Uncle Richard really likes so I told him I'll just polish it a bit instead of him buying a new one...sure he could but he has a special love for it since its been in the family for a hand full of years now said Trevor.

Cool said Dre.

Wouldn't hurt to have an extra pair of hands the weekend's end to get it done faster, so how about it, want to help me? Trevor asked him.

Depends, are you the type that takes pride in their work? Dre asked him.

You ever paint before? Trevor asked Dre.

Does graffiti count? Dre asked him.

Nothing to it, you just grab a brush, wet it up and swoop and swob...taking strokes back and forth and going back over them said Trevor.

Alright, I'm in said Dre as Trevor smiled nodding.

So what else do you build, or whatelse can you build? Dre asked him.

Just a little this and that, nothing major said Trevor.

Trevor's being modest, he can build a boat from scratch and the paddles too and he has one in the barn back there that he takes out when he goes fishing with dad or when he's wants some alone time... you'd think that he was the son of a craftsman said Erika.

Yeah we all have our hobbies, what was yours back in the city? Dre's Uncle asked him.

Playing basket ball, macking on girls, going to parties, macking on girls...laying pool or rolling dice and macking on girls said Dre.

All that Mack daddy business got you a baby, that's going to slow those activities down a bit said his Uncle.

Yeah just a bit... but I grew up fast...kind of seen it all and did it all so I got my priorities in line, not saying I'm going to wife her or marry her but I'm going to make sure she taken care of and my son and still do me said Dre.

As a young man should, just learn from premature situations that have occurred in your life thus far and progress from there said his uncle.

In other words cous...keep that thing wrapped up next time said Erika.

A little while after, Dre was upstairs and finally figured out why Trevor was eager to take a shower fast because he had almost used all of the hot water and he had to take a moderately cold bath then was in his room just putting on some pants as Trevor knocked on his door.

Its open said Trevor.

As Trevor walked into the room with a nice fitted shirt with the logo of the plant they were going to and a hat on. Hey man we should get ready to get on the road in a few but you definitely don't want to wear any of your good clothes out there with all those expensive labels you probably be rocking or that cap so I bought you some work gear…you got some old pants and shoes you can work in? He said handed him a shirt and a hat.

Ye I do thanks man but I think I'm just going to put on a wife beater said Dre taking them.

Cool, might want to pull up your pants and get a belt because at certain points you're going to have to make jumps on and off the machine at certain times to run and pick up the scattered crops that got past your hands as it goes down the field and hop back on it but let somebody know what you about to do so they can cover your side automatically until you back in place said Trevor.

Got you man said Dre.

Alright, I'm starting up the truck and I'll be waiting outside…I got gloves and everything we need and auntie fixed us some break grub so just come straight out he said leaving out.

Dre looked at his pants and his ass sticking out from his sagged pants.

Damn this dude definitely rushing me out of here…see he like to be on time and definitely focused on his grind he thought to himself.

Soon they were in Trevor's truck and on the road and this dude was burning it Dre thought it must be nice to be on the country roads with no speeding signs or police really to restrict your movement as he told Dre how it works at the factory.

So we hop on these big plowing machines at the factory it's about 4 of them stretched out to different parts of the acres all moving and plowing crop fields at the same speed as it chuck them into the giant shovels you're going to be passing them to other workers behind you who will be separating the good and bad leaves and piling them into crates behind us...the field is like some ways across while workers in the field following behind grab the ones that fly off into the field cause we collect every drop and leave nothing behind so if we have to slow down to collect them you run back and grab them all fast then when we get to the end the workers there collect the piles and load them on trucks usually takes about 5 minutes or more than were going back up to the next section and do it a dozen more rows down...by noon we take a 15 minute break for food and drink and depending upon the field were covering we move inside to the factory where they basically dump loads of crop leaves to the floor and your loading them into other crates while removing the few bad ones that got pass said Trevor as Dre nodded taking it all in.

At 3 we have another break for 30 minutes in the factory break room, after that were back on the fields doing the same process till about five...six at the latest then from there we just go around to the storage areas and push the crop crates into these giant storage containers about a dozen of them and were done for the day said Trevor.

Got it man said Dre smoking a cigarette staring out the window and conversation was silent between them a few minutes longer.

So how long you been living with my relative's homie? Dre asked him.

Since I was 14,the man I lived with and your Uncle were good friends and I been doing this kind of work since then so when he died and I was left alone I maintained the residence I was at till a storm rolled in and the worst was approaching and your uncle came by and told me that it was going to be a bad one and that I should come to their house because they have this storm shelter I resisted at first and was going to hold my ground even though this house was a bit old and ratty but he convinced me to go with him and if I did…don't think I would be here today…he automatically offered me a place to stay and welcomed me into his family and I been there ever since…didn't plan on staying there long but like I said they became real family to me so I chose to stay said Trevor.

Word…that's what's up said Dre wanting to go in deeper and ask him where his real parents were but decided that it was too soon to get in his personal business like that and would tell him in his own time.

Trevor was quite again after answering his question and didn't seem like much of a talker to Dre so he decided to keep it going because maybe he was one of those quiet types that talk when spoken too.

So am I going to have to walk a few miles from the house every time I want to make a call laughed Dre.

No not always some days you get lucky and can pick up good reception from the yard said Trevor smoking a cigarette and looking at the road.

When I gave you your lighter back last night I saw all those drawings on your wall…you got mad skills said Dre.

Ye, that's another hobby of mine…paint sometimes too on those really bored weekends where I don't have anything else better to do said Trevor.

I figure you make some good money doing all this, so what do you send your money on all the way out here in the country? Dre asked him.

Myself…I stack it up man…I plan on buying my own piece of land and build a house on it eventually said Trevor.

Cool that sound like a plan said Dre.

I see country people know how to invest their money…in the city we do our hustles to stack up and get by but always have to keep it going…constantly on that sell 24/7 or end up assed out or until you get caught by the cops thought Dre to himself.

How old are you? Dre asked him.

I just turned 20 a few weeks ago said Trevor.

So tell me man...you ever smash my cousin Erika since you been there...be honest grinned Dre.

Naw man never said Trevor.

Why not she a pretty girl and its right there so what's the problem said Dre.

Besides that disrespecting your Uncle's home that he opened up to me I don't see her like that at all...she like a sister to me man and that's all I ever seen her as not denoting the fact she's not a pretty girl because she really is but some lines you just don't cross and your Uncle made that clear long ago and I respect that said Trevor.

I feel you, so where all the chicks at in this town or wherever one at near here said Dre.

Why you want to know little man you already on lock down and have a relationship smiled Trevor.

Yo I'm out here for the next few months or whatever so yeah...I don't know if I can wait that long to get laid...so me and girl taking a break right now...she just won't know about it, besides I'm too young to be all serious like that and I'm betting her ass feel the same way back there said Dre.

I hear you Trevor grinned at him.

So when we off Friday what's there to get into or do for activity? Dre asked him.

Friday I can take you in town and show you around...that night it's going to be a party going on there...dancing, drinking, music and plenty, plenty of girls said Trevor.

Word...that's what's up...so they won't be playing that hokey pokey or nothing like that, will they? Dre asked him.

Naw man...I don't think anyway but you will be in my hands when were out and I told your Uncle I would watch over you so can't let you drink man he will be doing a breath test when you get back in and I'm not going to get hanged for it said Trevor.

Yep, so you going to have moon shine and the whole nine and I can't even get a sip of it.

Damn said Dre.

Naw you can have a little just know how to cover it up so he don't know and if you get caught then I aint seen nothing when you were doing it at the time and you will have those un-curfew weekend privileges revoked so choose your actions carefully...I know he want me to supervise you and I'm going to watch over you but not trying to be the cause of you wanting to have some kind of fun or do what you want out here because this aint the city and it can get bored and shit to somebody like you to be held down just keep it at a cool level and I won't say anything said Trevor.

Got you said Dre.

Chapter 5

You got a girlfriend? Dre asked Trevor.

Got a few running around here and there that I have fun with from time to time but not a steady one right now, but there was this one girl I was dating for a minute… Trixie Johnson…pretty ass red bone that I fell in love with and we were in a serious relationship for about a year in a half that I broke up with a few months ago…slick bitch, I spoiled her rotten and gave her whatever she wanted and she just took my heart and stepped all over it man… caught her kissing another dude in front of her house when I rolled up over there un-announced when I got suspicious of her blowing off our plans or coming up with excuses for me to see her at certain times…the most available bitch I knew for years suddenly got so fucking busy…Shorty was busy alright…busy with another dude said Trevor

Damn yo that's fucked up laughed Dre a little.

She trying to exlain to me that was her friend that she was tongue kissing like that as if I was really going to believe that…hard for people to lie good when you catch them on the spot and even then they still trying to lie when you seen it with your own eyes…I was so fucking mad man, I jumped out my truck and kicked his ass and kissed her ass goodbye and that was that but she call and see me from time to time so apologetic for doing me dirty like that cause that other nigga dropped her ass a few weeks after me busting her that day for some other chick I hear said Trevor.

Yep karma's a bitch said Dre.

She been wanting us to get back together but I felt I couldn't trust her anymore after lying and playing me like that after I committed a whole year and some to her and I had plenty opportunities to do the same shit she did my dude but I didnt and I wasn't going to invest anymore time in it after all that so I told her that it was over over and she said for real for real? I looked her in the face and say yep, for real for real... so currently I'm breaking from anything serious at the moment and just enjoying being single and free...females can be sneaky as hell sometimes and play the game just as hard as us if not better said Trevor.

Word... damn, I feel you on that...got quite a bit of ratchet ass females running around back home but there are some decent good girls out there and I know I got one that's waiting patiently for me to come back said Dre.

That's what's up man you should hold on to that and cherish her said Trevor.

Ye...I've seen those 4-wheelers Uncle got out back, gotta take them out for a ride at some point said Dre.

Ye we can do that said Trevor.

Cool said Dre looking at Trevor's arm as he drove.

So how did you get those small burn marks on your arm man? Dre asked him.

It got burned in this accidental fire a long time ago...we pulling up to the spot now where we take the workers to the plant said Trevor as Dre glanced over at a small station where a crowd of Mexican workers were posted outside smoking cigarettes and talking.

So he got a army of immigrants for his work force and paying under the table cheap to keep their illegal alias secret huh, I bet you none of them even got a green card either... but it's no different in the city though when they have big construction projects or certain task needed to be completed there you can usually find a stash of Mexicans in the back of places waiting for any kind of work that's why you see loads of them on the back of trucks or on vans going to make that money...Immigrants taking all the jobs man and I see they roll as deep down here as they do back my way said Dre.

Their cooperative efficient hard workers, that's all the boss cares for…it's about business said Trevor.

I know, instead of hiring construction workers for a hefty fee to build new shit in the city they just get them to do it for half that happily…who can out work them anyway…they were genetically built for labor for real and love it…more than that they want to stay which is why they risk their lives getting here from across the border digging underground tunnels and smuggling away on boats and broken doors through stormy seas and shit but I respect them because they stick together and support each other as a people not like ours that most of the time wont to tear you down or put dirt on your name…so I guess I'm on that unfair salary that I know they get here huh…tell me I'm wrong said Dre.

Trevor grinned shaking his head. You smart you know that but naw…truth be told they work twice as hard for twice as less than the standard worker should make in this type of field…but eager workers come a dime a dozen and doesn't matter how you get the help or what the manager offer to pay as long as the work gets done and at the end of the day it's about business and yeah it's dirtiness and crooked shit in every venture…but Uncle talked to Dave and you good… consider your check to be standard he winked.

That's what's up because anything less would be uncivilized, not breaking my back nickel and diming…that's the case I'll take my ass back to the city where the money come better with the right connections said Dre.

Trevor pulled up in front of the place.

Grab your stuff and let's go he said taking his bag as they both got out of the truck and walked toward the office as Trevor raised his hands speaking a little Spanish to them as they replied back to him smiling and speaking back.

Are you bi-lingual man? Dre asked Trevor.

Naw I'm straight said Trevor.

Naw homie, what I'm saying-said Dre.

Yo it was a joke I know what you mean and yeah I speak a little, been working alongside of them for years and even have a few friends that I shoot pool with in town and some drinks so yeah you kind of learn a little of it said Trevor knocking on the door to the office and opening it going inside of the place as Dre followed him.

Hey Good morning boss man, time to get another work day started just like old times said Trevor.

Morning to you too Trevor, glad you could come help me out a little out of favor from your uncle who stole you from me by the way a long time ago...told you whatever that old man was paying you I could triple it...I really liked having you around here...Samuel and yourself went on plenty of hunting and fishing trips with me and cook outs at me and my wives house...good times back then... said Dave.

Yeah and I enjoyed being a part of your work force and you were a really cool boss, it was nothing personal you know he became family to me after all the events that took place and the rest is history but today I'm here because my Uncle doesn't have much work for me to do on his end and I know you could use a little and I bought a extra pair of arms with me...this my Uncles nephew Andre said Trevor.

Yeah he told me that you'd be coming to stay with them for a few months and he wanted to put you to work immediately... real work... so you can put some money in your pocket to stack up over the summer and take back to the city with you to spend on all that nice expensive stuff they have there laughed Dave.

Yep I told him to bring it on, I can do it said Dre.

Nice to meet you Andre, names Dave he said shaking his hand.

Nice to meet you too said Dre.

I'm sure Trevor here already told you the processes and how it all works, don't really take special training or any resume to submit... just workable arms and legs and a steady pair of strong hands to jump right into it and get it done...the work day is long but not hard and well worth it by the end of the week…so Andre what is a young city boy like yourself doing all the way down here in the dust of the country…paying your dues here for debts in the city huh said Dave.

Ye something like that sir said Dre.

Well consider yourself officially hired and on my pay roll Mr. Andre, here you go said Dave handing Trevor one of his truck keys.

Thanks and enjoy that central air blowing in here on you in this nice office I'm going to steal from you one day said Trevor leaving out as Dave laughed.

As they both walked out. You sitting up front with me Trevor told Dre.

Alright let's load up and move out Trevor told the group as they begin loading up in the back of the truck.

Cool…I'm riding shotgun in the chicken truck said Dre as Trevor grinned to himself shaking his head.

What? You know that's what it is or what it used to be anyway said Dre.

The work day went along well and Dre got the hang of it fairly quickly while Trevor did his job and glanced over from time to time to observe him to make sure he was keeping up.

Dre glanced over at him and saw a certain smile or pleasure on Trevor face as if enjoying seeing a city dude getting in deep to that real country work and even threw in a few joking gestures during the crop plow…the way Trevor worked he could tell he was use to this and actually going through it like having fun but he definitely wasn't but he didn't want Trevor telling his uncle that he was slacking or slowing them down so he worked his hardest as if he was having just as easy a time as he was going up and down those long field acres that seemed endless as the hours past and watching those Mexicans running down the fields behind the machines gathering scattered crop leaves and cheering as if it was a game to them.

Damn…so this is how the slaves felt…where the fuck is the

Underground Railroad about now…I guess the first day is always the hardest he thought to himself wiping sweat off his forehead.

At 12, they took a break for a snack and drink then Trevor gave Dre a smoke that he was most certain he wanted.

You good man? Trevor asked Dre who was looking extremely worked already.

Ye…I'm straight man said Dre.

You doing good man he said patting his chest walking over to one of the machine drivers and talking to him and then they were back in the crop fields for a couple more hours finishing up then went back to the factory for their 3 o'clock break and washed their hands in the bathroom as they both sat down at a table in the break room for lunch.

I told you that it wasn't hard man, already got through half the day and just some hours left until we done here and roll home said Trevor.

So this how that country grind is done huh Dre asked Trevor.

Yep… all day long but you doing it just fine big city Trevor grinned as he turned his attention to his food and ate.

After break, they worked on the inside of the factory pretty much dumping the gigantic piles in front of them that they had gathered outside just to put them into new containers inside.

After 5, they were taken to another one of the smaller acres compared to the ones they had been through that morning and around 6 headed to the final job loading the crates from the factory into the storage units on the other side of the factory and were finished for the day loading up and headed back to the office where they got into Trey's truck and headed back home around dusk.

Job well done today big city said Trevor.

Dre smoked a cigarette on the ride home and put his fittie cap over his face falling asleep.

Chapter 6

When Trevor and Dre got back to the house that night they both went upstairs to get washed up for dinner and Dre made sure he got his shower in first before Trevor could use all the hot water like he did before by putting his stuff in it before he left the house that morning.

Dre finished his shower and wrapped his towel around his waist then unlocked the bathroom door connected to Trevor's room and walked back into his room sitting down on his bed and laid back across it relaxing his arms behind his head closing his eyes for a moment, this was the first day he had ever worked this hard and damn right now he couldn't even move or wanted too.

Damn, I would kill for a massage right about now he thought to himself.

Hey you finish in here man? Trevor asked him.

Dre looked over at him. Ye man just let me get my stuff out the way he said getting up and moved past Trevor gathering his stuff and went back into his room.

It's all yours homie, enjoy the shower grinned Dre as if saying it to get pay back for the cold shower he stuck him with that morning.

Trevor took off his wife beater as he stood in front of the mirror then observed his facial hair and plugged up his shaver.

As Dre gathered what he was putting on downstairs he cut a quick glance at Trevor.

Damn dude is pretty cut he thought to himself just being the non-gay thoughts of a straight guy observing what he was seeing but went back to what he was doing.

Trevor unbuckled and unzipped his pants and closed the door.

A little while later downstairs at dinner, His Uncle was eager to ask them how the work day went and Trevor gave Dre a good review.

So how was it for you boys out there today? Real manual labor wear you out nephew asked his Uncle Richard

Big city did his thing and mastered it all pretty quickly…we should get through tomorrow pretty quickly said Trevor.

Big city, must be his new nick name for me thought Dre to himself.

Good, after tomorrow I need you back with me at the farm Trevor because I'm putting out pesticides to the fields so you'll be on your own working at the plant nephew…Trevor will take you there in the morning and pick you up in the evening said his Uncle Richard.

Alright cool said Dre.

Trevor tells us that he's taking you into town to show you around and then taking you into a gathering with the young crowds that night said his aunt.

Ye I'm looking forward to it said Dre.

You mind yourself out there nephew, you can stay out as long as you want with Trevor.

I know he only associates with good company and it's the weekend and I'm not setting any curfews after a hard week of work a boy disserves to go out and have a little fun…after you do what is required of you here the rest of your time is yours said his uncle.

Thanks Unc said Dre.

But the night comes with its restrictions your still 16, no smoking or drinking said his uncle.

Oh naw, I don't do that smoking or drinking said Dre frowning his lip.

There was a unexpected rang at the doorbell as they looked at each other.

I wasn't expecting us to have company drop by tonight for dinner were you? His aunt asked his uncle.

No…I'll get it he said getting up from the table and going to the door recognizing who was on the other side and smiled laughing to himself as he opened it.

Well look what the wind blew back in to the country, long time no see Brent he said shaking his hand and hugging him and inviting him inside.

Nice to see you too Mr. Richard, Sorry to drop by so late and unexpectedly but bad signaling in this area you know… I actually came into town earlier today to handle some family business concerning one of my dad's estates and I knew you'd be busy through the day manning your farm and I was on my way back out and decided to drop in to see how you and the rest of the family were doing said Brent.

I'm glad you had us in your thoughts, I talked to your dad a couple weeks ago and he said he was coming down here to one of his estates said Richard.

Yeah he was going to but he got tied into some important business venture for his company last minute back east and sent me to handle it for him said Brent.

Alright, well my self and the family were just having dinner and I'm sure Trevor will be glad to see you said Richard.

I didn't mean to disturb you said Brent.

Your fine man, I know they'll be as glad to see that you stopped by as I am he said putting his hand on his shoulder and walking into the kitchen.

Look who dropped by for a drive by visit before shooting back out of town said his Uncle Richard as Dre glanced up and saw this young mixed guy walked in with a jacket and cowboy hat on.

When Trevor saw him his face lit up a bit as he got up and smiled.

Brent, longtime no see he said shaking his hand and hugging him patting his back.

Has been a long time, how have things been going down here he said smiling at Trevor and giving him a particular eye contact.

Good man, no complaints just work as usual said Trent as Brent grinned nodding.

I hear that… same back my way man he said still in the hand shake that he broke away from sneakily and quickly then smiled turning and speaking to the rest of the family.

Brent this is my nephew Dre, he's from the city and staying for the summer to earn some money but mainly as punishment… Dre this is a friend of the family Brent who was Trevor's best friend back in the day and worked with us for years before his family moved away to run the big city company that was left to his father by his granddad said his uncle.

Hey how you doing man said Brent shaking his hand.

Sup man said Dre.

How are the wife and kid? Dre's aunt asked him.

There both doing very fine thanks said Brent.

Please sit down for a while and join us for dinner said his aunt.

Oh no mam I don't want to impose said Brent.

Nonsense, you're about to be back on the road for a long drive back and you need some food in you…sit down you know you loved my cooking especially my baked apple pies said aunt.

Yes I did indeed smiled Brent sitting down beside Erika.

During the dinner Dre noticed Trevor and Brent talking to each other and there was this unmistakable tension, awkwardness and strangeness in their communication and at times uncomfortable as if they were talking into some kind of code at times when asking each other's questions but Dre recognized it because he once had this same awkwardness when he saw someone he had a certain history with and could be wrong but was for certain that it was very similar…. something happened between these 2 in their past that they were not talking about or what no one else knows but them.

After dinner, Trevor, Brent and Dre's Uncle talked in the living room for a while and when it was time for him to go both he and Trevor went outside and talked on the front porch for a while then walked over to Brent's car to finish their conversation.

Dre came outside to talk to his girl before going to sleep and walked across the opposite part of the yard trying to get a good signal while glancing over at them and saw that the conversation they were having must have been passionate in some way almost like one he and his girlfriend would have at times and made him even more curious what had happened between them but it wasn't his business so he just went back to focusing on to what he was doing and finally got a signal and didn't even have to go a mile off into the field this time.

Hey what's up baby said Dre.

Hey Dre…so how was your first day at work? Gia asked him.

Pretty good…just glad the day over so I can get some sleep to do it all over again tomorrow…so how Darius doing? Dre asked her.

He doing just fine, he just sitting here chilling with mommy watching a little TV that's all said Gia.

Cool…yo, who was that talking in the back ground just then? Dre asked her.

Who? Gia asked playing dumb.

They was whispering something to you just then you know I got them cat ears said Dre.

Oh yeah that's my cousin Jeremy said Gia.

I never heard of him said Dre.

That's because he from my dad side and we don't talk like that but he in town over my aunt's house and stopped by after forever to just see me that's about it said Gia.

Right, so where your moms at? Dre asked her.

She work evening shift from 6 to 6 remember said Gia.

So what are you 2 doing? Dre asked her.

Just talking and chilling but I'm so glad your day went well and I'm not going to hold you up on this phone too long because you have to get your rest and I gotta change the baby and put him down to sleep said Gia.

Are you trying to get off the phone or something? Dre asked her.

No but I do have family over who I haven't seen in a long time said Gia.

So what that gotta do with me, I haven't even had a chance to talk to you all day because I was busting my ass in a fucking hot ass field and me calling you now is a sudden inconvenience to his visit…is that your cousin or your play cousin…I haven't even been gone a day good and you already on that bullshit said Dre.

Boy what are you talking about? dont even go there or trip because it's nothing like that for real and I see you all stressed out and shit after a hard day of work and I understand but you can't be taking that shit out on me with all your accusations so just get at me when you get rested up and talking sense said Gia.

Yeah sure I might as well, you not trying to ask me what my day was like or showing any kind of fuck so see you later and enjoy your company said Dre.

My cousin said Gia.

Right…hold it down later said Dre.

Boy aren't you forgetting to tell me something said Gia.

Dre paused for a moment. Love you he said.

Muah night said Gia ending call.

Sneaky az mumbled Dre glancing over at Trevor who exchanged a long hug with Brent who patted his back and said something in his ear as he nodded then both shook hands and he got in his truck and left down the yards trail as Trevor stood there for a minute lighting up a cigarette until he vanished out of sight down the highway in the distance then walked back to the porch with his dog and sat down finishing his cigarette and looking down as if in deep thought as Dre walked across the yard back to the porch.

So I see you got lucky and got a good signal in the yard tonight said Trevor.

Ye…got lucky…can I take a couple hits of that? Dre asked him.

Trevor handed it to him as Dre took a couple puffs then gave it back to him.

Thanks man, laying it down for tonight…night said Dre walking into the house.

Night man said Trevor rubbing his dog's head.

Dre finally relaxed in his bed and closed his eyes.

The end of day one…shit he said to himself.

Chapter 7

After the end of the work week, Dre was finally glad when Friday arrived and he was off and didn't have to go back till Monday morning and Trevor was taking him to town to give him a tour and anything was better than just sitting around the house out in the middle of almost nowhere so he was eager to ride out as he took some pants out his closet and put them across the bed deciding which pair to wear when Trevor knocked on his door.

Come in said Dre as Trevor walked in. I'll be ready in a bit, you ready to go? He asked.

Ye just about man...hey do you have any good barbers around here, I need a slight trim and an edge up...I know I'm all the way out here in the country and don't have to worry about seeing people all like that but I'm not walking around here all fuzzy and busted up for a few months said Dre.

Save your money man, I can do you right quick said Trevor.

So you can cut hair? Dre asked him.

Yep...who do you think do my edge ups Trevor asked him.

Ye, that is pretty sharp...cool, Think you can do it before we go? Dre asked him.

Sure, let me get my clippers and freshen you up said Trevor walking out.

Appreciate that man said Dre after him.

Trevor gave him a slight trim and edge up. Done man he said.

Dre admired himself in the mirror looking at it.

Ye that's what's up man...you got skills...thanks said Dre.

No prob said Trevor.

I'm about to hit the shower right quick then I'll be ready said Dre.

Cool said Trevor cleaning the floor than gathering his stuff and leaving out through the end of the bathroom connected to his room and closed the door as Dre took off his clothes and looked in the mirror for a moment and lifted his arm pits then looked at his dick hair.

Damn…looks like I'm looking really 70's now said Dre going into the room and getting his personal clippers from one of his bags and shaved his arm pits down then shaved his dick hair low but decided to leave his small chest hair that was growing the way it was and looked at it for a moment and was pleased as he turned around and looked at his ass that was slightly hairy and a bit bushy.

Guess I don't really pay attention too much back there he thought to himself then locked Trevor's side of the bathroom then turned around in the mirror and shaved his ass and alongside his cheeks.

Damn, never did that before…this feel a little weird as fuck… bet I'm not the first straight dude to do this though he said to himself.

Dre took a shower and put on his wife beater sagging pants and fitty cap on then met Trevor downstairs to leave.

You 2 have fun and Trevor if you don't mind can you pick me up a few things from the store on your way back here asked Dre's Aunt.

Sure no problem said Trevor taking the list and putting it in his pocket.

Thanks…Um Dre baby…how are you going to walk with your pants hanging almost to the ground like that…pull them up sweetie you have a belt and you're not even using it she said.

I'm good auntie, this isn't just sagging it's that city style swagger and how we just wear our pants said Dre.

Alright…if you say so she said going back into the kitchen.

Soon they were both on the road headed to town that was ten miles from the house.

So where you hiding that pot you got stashed around the house somewhere? Trevor asked him as he pulled on a cigarette he was smoking.

Pot man? Dre asked him.

Yeah you know what I'm talking about, weed, smoke, trees, marijuana... whatever you call it there in the city, I know for the past few nights you had a ladder up to your room window and sneaking out down it and going into the shed to blow some said Trevor.

How you know that man? Dre asked him.

I know that the ladder been moved and Uncle nor I hasn't used it in a while and you didn't close that shed good after you left out the night before and you left those little butts and some ashes in a can on one of the shelves...I know my surroundings like the back of my hand and know when something's been moved or touched...better work on covering your tracks and doings up a little better or Uncle could find out and you'd be in it...mad you didn't invite me to your little late night smoke chokes said Trevor.

Word, you smoke? Dre asked him.

Ye man go out there myself from time to time to blow something, I got my connections out here to get a hold if it...that good shit all those white boys smoke down here said Trevor.

Real? That's what's up...I'm running low on smoke supply already anyway said Dre.

Yeah same here, I can call one of my friends and get some before we head back home and we can go out there and blow on some late nights said Trevor.

Yeah definitely man...I'm so glad you living with my peeps real talk said Dre.

Trevor grinned to himself.

Shortly after they arrived into town and rode through it as Dre looked around.

Wow...this actually look like a miniature town that would be in my city said Dre.

What did you expect our town to look like? A country cowboy town with dirt for roads and briar bushes rolling through the town said Trevor.

Ye I mean something like that,shit I never been all deep in the country like this and expected some itty bitty novelty type set up said Dre.

Yeah this place may be way different from the city but despite what misconceptions you have about here…we just as much out of the Stone Age as you are smiled Trevor.

Ye, But yall just entering into the 21 century by the looks of it just saying laughed Dre.

Man fuck you big city laughed Trevor.

Trevor pulled up to a spot in town and gave Dre a tour around town.

Yo man why everybody down here stare at you in the face like that, back in the city people don't do that shit we just keep moving… tempted to cuss a few of them out and tell them what the fuck they staring at for real man…its rude said Dre.

Cool it man, just how people in the country are…you stand out man and they know that you not from around here and just checking you out…that's all they don't mean nothing by it…so let it ride said Trevor.

Okay well at least you put that in perspective for me…I didn't know said Dre.

I think we can learn a lot from each other…I never been to the city before said Trevor.

Whole new atmosphere man, people down here are more friendly and generous in the country but up my way they street yo best way to put it and you can't help any of the begging mother fuckers you going to meet…here yall don't have that because people work here…scammers and thieves are in plenty too…here it's about helping each other but up there it's about taking care of self…the worst you have here is drunks but we got crack heads and pill takers running around naked and dancing in the streets…crazy life man and never a dull moment always something going on and if you don't see it you can find a video on your phone somebody took on a subway or in a fast food restaurant said Dre.

Wow...sounds kinda awful said Trevor.

Yeah to you but it's always been home for me and all I ever known said Dre.

Heard rumors about the city and how it is that way, I'm not too interested in going there...I love the peace and quiet here said Trevor.

Ye probably better that way man, in the city they got this awful name for people in the country said Dre.

What's that? Trevor asked him.

Coons, cornballs, bammers...some of them think you country people easy to trick on and shit said Dre.

So what you think about us so far? Trevor asked him.

I'm still learning but so far you seem cool as hell to me and I'm thinking you good people said Dre.

I am good people and you better be good people...I can be the best dude to hang with and get to know but cross me and be on some shade tree shit and we got issues said Trevor.

Same here so we calling the city slash country boy alliance from this day forward and for the rest of my summer here said Dre.

No doubt said Trevor giving him dap.

You like pool? Trevor asked him.

Ye I do said Dre.

Comon I'm taking you to a pool hall on the other block...see what kind of game you got big city said Trevor.

Ye let's do that man said Dre.

Later that afternoon when they got back to the house, Dre helped Trevor paint the boat in the barn.

Trevor glanced over at Dre painting one end of the boat.

Your doing a good job said Trevor.

Thanks man, painting is kind of fun said Dre glancing over at

Trevor in his overalls with one strap hanging on his bare chest and shoulder with clearly no underwear on beneath them.

So not that I was staring or looking like that but I notice that you like to free ball while you work huh? Dre asked him.

What that mean? Trevor replied.

Letting your junk and everything else swing in the breeze beneath outer wear said Dre.

Oh... Yeah, feels more natural to just let it swing as you put it, do you free ball? Trevor laughed at the new catch phrase Dre had just told him.

Only when I sleep at night said Dre.

Oh...just make sure you keep your door lock at all times then,wouldn't want your aunt or cousin walking in on you asleep or doing other things in the nude like chocking the chicken...be pretty awkward you know said Trevor.

Thanks for the heads up said Dre glancing over at Trevor again.

Yep Trevor replied.

Choking the chicken Dre smiled to himself shaking his head.

What was that? Trevor asked painting on his side.

That phrase you used just then pertaining to jacking off, you called it choking the chicken...funny grinned Dre to himself.

Ye, maybe you'll get to help me wring some chicken necks when its time to slaughter them for food, you get a grip around their scrawny little throats and chop them off with an ax said Trevor.

Word, how barbaric said Dre.

Hey we gotta eat big city and with us being the top of the food chain, better to be chopping then on the cutting block said Trevor.

True, plus I love me some chicken, not just a southern thing Dre replied back.

Aw, something else we have in common said Trevor.

Hey man you got something right here said Dre pointing at his own face.

What? Trevor asked him touching his face as Dre walked over.

Right here said Dre swopping his chin with the paint brush.

Oh slick said Trevor touching chin.

Now you got a goat beard get it said Dre.

Yeah, just like you have this said Trevor swopping it across his cheek then across his sleeveless shirt.

Oh its on now said Dre dipping it into the can as Trevor laughed backing up.

Comon big city, I declare paint war said Trevor as they chased each other around laughing flinging the paint brushes at each other.

Chapter 8

That Friday night, Trevor took Dre into town to this barn looking building where a small crowd of young people had gathered to blast music,dance ,drink,smoke and hang out and there were few adults not so much supervising their activities but kicking it with the young kids and the little party that they had going on there and Dre had found a pretty young girl name Aubrey to talk to as she took a quick shinning to him and pretty much all under him not allowing any other girls to get close to that but he was mad cool with it...since she was one of the prettiest ones up in there.

So how old are you Dre? Aubrey asked him.

I'm 18...what about you? Dre asked her.

I'm 17...but I don't look or act like it...I'm very mature for my age and consider myself a real woman among these ditsy little girls running around here she said.

Cool...you mad pretty for real...I didn't know the country had chickadees made like you said Dre rubbing his hands and checking her out.

She giggled covered her mouth. Whatever you just saying that...so you here from the city for the summer? Aubrey asked him.

Yep...staying with some relatives and seeing what life is like on the other side said Dre.

Oh really...that's cool...so you a city guy huh...I like city guys yall got that swagger and I really dig that said Aubrey.

Word...so you liking what you see huh said Dre.

I know we just met but I can catch feelings really fast when I'm digging somebody and feeling the vibe that we seem to have said Aubrey.

So are you feeling me? asked Dre.

Ye I really do…so are you like a gangster or something and have you ever shot or killed somebody before? Aubrey asked him.

I'll say this much, I haven't been proven guilty of anything if I have said Dre.

Omg…I think it's so hot when guys are really hood and they have a hardcore edgy smack a bitch up type attitude and a unpredictable dangerous side to them…I been to the city a few times and I dig the guys up there these bumpkins can all kick rocks because they lame as hell chasing chickens, hunting and fishing and all that shit is there idea of a good time…I want to be a city boys ride or fly chick for real said Aubrey.

Its ride or die chick said Dre.

Yep that too…I'm so glad I snatched you up first…I just want to touch you and give you a kiss but I'm so shy…I'm so excited and feeling this vibe we have so much…but your swag is so overpowering and it scares me a little.

Cause I know you a bad boy with game from the city breaking hearts left and right and I'm a good girl like for real I don't smoke or drink or do anything…I'm kind of nervous said Aubrey.

Why? I don't bite…I nibble said Dre.

Omg you making me um-stop…you just got me feeling all bothered…I can't even explain it…I been waiting for a guy like you to come along…can I tell you what I want to do to you in your ear? said Aubrey.

Ye Shorty go ahead said Dre as Aubrey whispered it in his ear.

Word…damn, check please he said as she laughed falling on him.

Trevor was drinking and talking to a girl name Shayla he kicked it with a few times in the past.

I see your little city friend got my girl all on his balls, she is definitely stuck on him…poor little virgin he going to tear her little naive ass apart…I know her, she looking for a boyfriend and not some fly by night fuck like I'm sure he has in mind… bet he just like you…

all about fucking and ducking…why you aint call or talk to me lately like that…I know you be busy working and all but you know I been feeling you for the longest and trying to get to know you on a serious type level ever since you dumped that tramp Trixie but you give me no play said Shayla.

I told you already, I'm not looking to date right now I'm taking a break from all that and keep it real…you and me don't even have a connection or click on a feelings level like that… we just do what it do and go our own way…I take you to the back trail woods and beat it down and take you home until we feel like freaky again and that's all it is…you know that said Trevor taking a sip of his drink.

Smh, you trying to be a heartless hit it and quit it nigga because of that Trixie bitch and you taking it out on all other girls now…you were always the good guy and that hoe turned you out…whatever I don't even care and want your ass like that anyway just give me that tongue and that dick from time to time and we good…you go your way and I go mine…I can be just like a nigga too said Shayla.

That's what's up said Trevor.

So what's up can I get that dick and mouth tonight because I'm horny as shit, aren't you horny? Let me check….yep you are indeed… that country boy dick stay hard… so what's good for tonight…hope it can be me said Shayla.

Trevor pulled a cigarette. I got my little partner with me and I told his Uncle that I'd watch over him he said.

That's cool, shit we can all hang out together…I mean we don't have to jump straight into fucking we can hang out a little back at my mom house she gone for the night…he can keep my girl Aubrey company and I can keep you company so let's set it up and ditch this tired ass party its getting dull now anyway and aint no sexy niggas really showed up like I thought said Shayla.

Alright cool…let me holla at my boy and let's get ready to leave said Trevor getting up and putting his cup down.

That's what's up daddy she said smacking his ass as he looked back at her she blew a kiss as he walked over to Dre.

Dre, let me talk to you right quick said Trevor.

No you can't take him away from me...we having so much fun said Aubrey holding on to his arm.

I'm just going to talk to him for a sec and you can have him back Stretch Armstrong damn said Trevor.

Shut up Trevor she said letting go.

Be right back said Dre.

Okay I miss you said Aubrey as they both walked off.

Damn nice to know the girls as easy here as they are in the city what's up man? Dre asked him.

Trevor put his arm around his shoulder and whispered in talked in his ear.

We packing up to leave man, I'm going to Shayla's spot to hang out for a bit so you can finish chilling with girl there said Trevor.

Alright cool, she kind of getting annoying and I'm ready to go ahead and lay her down and knock it out said Dre.

I come prepared said Trevor put some condoms in his pocket on the sneak.

Good looking out so who the thick girl with the really pretty face you been macking on all night said Dre.

Fast food if you get what I mean said Trevor.

I feel you hope that one move just as fast too, about to give her some of that city boy slab said Dre.

What about your girl and being true? Trevor asked him.

Yo I been working hard and horny all fucking week and my dick need to push one out asap before I explode and my girl about 900 miles away probably got her hands on her ankles like I don't know... like they say in Paris bra if you can't fuck the one you love, fuck the one you with said Dre.

The saying doesn't go quite like that said Trevor.

Well you get it lets make it happen said Dre.

A little while after, they all met back up at Shayla's place to hang out and playing cards for a bit.

I'm tired of playing cards...I want to do something else now said Aubrey.

Yeah me too said Shayla looking at Trevor.

Not that nasty, I'm talking about another fun game said Aubrey.

Girl, you and your damn games well go ahead and tell us what it is because we don't got all night for this kid shit and time is going by so fast now...this grown folks time up in here said Shayla.

Let's play spin the bottle, have a little truth and dare fun up in here said Aubrey.

Spin the bottle? Dre asked him.

Yep it's a game that's really fun and you can make it as dirty and freaky as you want too with truth or dare questions...way to heat it up Aubrey let's play spin that mother fucking bottle said Shayla getting up.

How you play that? Dre asked him.

It's simple we sit on the floor in a circle and spin the bottle and whoever it point to we ask you truth or dare and if you say truth then you have to answer honestly what question we ask you and if you say dare than you gotta do whatever we dare you to do no questions asked..Comon everybody sit down said Aubrey sitting cross leg on the floor as they all sat down in a circle.

I'll spin the bottle first said Aubrey.

Why you get to go first hoe said Shayla.

Bitch we going around a circle so shut up she said spinning the bottle around as they all watched as it pointed to Trevor.

Mr. Trevor...hmm...truth or dare said Aubrey.

Truth said Trevor.

Is it true that you have a really long tongue? Aubrey asked him.

Why you worried about what Trevor got, I should have never told your ass about that said Shayla.

It's just a game and a question girl you know how it's played…so is it true Trevor said Aubrey.

Yep Trevor replied.

Prove it let me see said Aubrey.

Trevor stuck his long tongue out his mouth.

Oh wow giggled Aubrey clapping.

Yep that's all mine tonight too, my turn said Shayla spinning the bottle around and stopped it to Trevor.

Well look at that, Trevor I dare you to fuck me right here on this floor in front of everybody right now said Shayla.

You stupid bitch,you messing up the game that's not how you play it…you can't stop the bottle with your hand said Aubrey.

Damn baby girl it's just a game and you getting all serious about to fucking cry…you straight silly and you starting to get on my nerves too go to sleep little girl and leave the grownups to play said Shayla.

Cow said Aubrey.

You so lame you couldn't turn a man on if you had a switch with your little virgin ass,your mouth aint no virgin though…remember Steven and Rick …2 on 1 back of my house and I was look out said Shayla.

Shut up and stop trying to play me in front of Dre, don't make me start on you miss run around town said Aubrey.

Lies said Shayla.

Yo Yo are we playing this game or not said Dre.

Yes we are and Shayla lose a turn for rigging the game just then… your turn Dre said Aubrey.

Dre spun the bottle around as it pointed to Aubrey as she laughed clapping. Yes!

Yo this girl a witch, she made that bottle point to her said Shayla.

Shut up bitch, go ahead Dre said Aubrey.

Alright…truth or dare said Dre.

Dare said Aubrey.

I dare you to get up and show us your tidies said Dre.

What? Omg I can't do that said Aubrey.

That's the game bitch remember so play it, now take them mosquito bites out and let the mother fucking room see what the hell you got said Shayla.

Omg...this is so crazy said Aubrey covering her mouth and getting up.

Yo she fronting trying to act brand new, she know she did this shit before and that innocent little girl shit is all an act Shayla told Dre.

Aubrey raised her top up showing her tidies real fast and put her shirt back down sitting down covering her face.

Omg...why did I play this game said Aubrey.

You got some nice tits you should be proud of them said Dre.

Thanks...said Aubrey with her face still covered up.

Fuck her...Trevor boo... your turn spin that bottle said Shayla.

Trevor spin the bottle around as it ended up pointing at Shayla.

Ha! That's what's up she said.

Truth or dare said Trevor.

Dare said Shayla.

I dare you to deep throat that coke bottle said Trevor.

Shit no problem she said taking it and sticking it down her throat deep as Dre put his hand to his mouth in amazement as she took it out.

You aint said nothing nigga, that's the best you got putting it back down on the floor said Shayla.

Let's get her icky germs off it said Aubrey polishing the bottle with her shirt.

Okay my turn again said Aubrey spinning the bottle around as it ended up pointed at Dre again.

I believe the universe trying to tell us something Dre...truth or dare she smiled winking at him.

Umm dare said Dre.

He a risk taker, I likes that said Shayla.

I dare you to show me your dick said Aubrey.

Can't wait huh Shayla asked her.

Shut up now do it Dre...you saw my breast now I want to see some nuts said Aubrey.

Alright no problem, might want to turn around Trevor so I can give the ladies a show said Dre getting up unzipping his pants.

Go ahead said Trevor looking away.

Dre pulled out his dick and showed it to them.

Damn...the city got it like that? Fuck... I must be shopping at the wrong sausage factories how old are you again? said Shayla.

Don't worry about it said Aubrey.

Dre put it back in and sat down as Trevor turned around.

Okay wildebeest your turn again said Aubrey looking at Shayla.

Shayla spun the bottle around as it pointed to Trevor.

Got you nigga ha ha...truth or dare said Shayla.

Dare said Trevor.

I'm a freaky ass bitch so I got a freaky ass dare...I dare you and your home boy to kiss said Shayla.

Say what? Trevor asked her.

Man hell naw you fucking mest up in the head said Dre.

Yo play the game and follow the rules now both you niggas lock lips said Shayla.

Not doing that said Trevor.

Hell to the no...next question...I'm not gay said Dre.

Who the fuck said you have to be gay and shit...it's a fucking game boy if you dared me to make out with this nasty bitch Aubrey I'd do it...don't mean I want her ass...if you 2 niggas straight and solid and secure in your sexuality than you should be able to do it unless you hiding something...you don't do it than you gay and you gay too Trevor which would explain a lot...so give each other that peck you faggot ass niggas and prove me wrong...go ahead said Shayla.

Naw laughed Trevor shaking his head and looking away.

Dre rubbed his hands nodding and looking away.

Just as a thought some mother fucking secret butt loving, dick swallowing girls said Shayla.

Dre looked at her then at Trevor.

Alright he said.

What? You going to do it said Shayla.

Just a fucking dare right and I know I aint got no sugar in my tank...what about you Trevor said Dre.

Not a drop said Trevor.

Then swab spit mother fuckers while I finger myself said Shayla.

Dre leaned across as Trevor did as both kissed as quickly as lightning and jumped back fast as Dre wiped his lips.

Yes sir buddy now that's how a true straight nigga do it said Shayla.

That was so cute said Aubrey.

Whatever...game over let's get on to something else said Dre.

Chapter 9

A little after an hour later, Trevor and Dre were back on the long dark country roads on their way home and Trevor was going at a speed of 90 smoking a cigarette.

Damn man, you hauling ass back…I thought we didn't have curfew said Dre.

We don't man but day break is in a few hours and I want to get home and get some sleep so I can finish up my boat project by tomorrow…I just got this schedule thing and like to get things done at specific times said Trevor.

Ye I know I saw that calendar stacked with mad shit on it hanging on your wall…nothing wrong with having your priorities in line… yo man when I saw your smash buddy take that whole fucking coke bottle almost to her tonsils I figured out fast that I was going after the wrong bitch tonight…skills like that are coveted in my book and you the man…got them serious straight up country freak girls on your dick so how was it said Dre.

Just when we were about to get into it man, she tell me she on her period and shit so I just told her to suck me off and that mouth aint no joke…sprayed every ounce all over her face and she licked it off her face like it was honey and sucked the rest off my dick swallowing every bit of and squeezing the head for whatever was left in it… problem with her is when you get her on one it's hard to get her off it said Trevor.

Damn that's what's up said Dre.

So what about you and the Virgin Mary? Trevor asked him.

Yo is that chick really a virgin dog? Dre asked Trevor.

Yeah man, I heard of quite a few dudes who tried to get it and never did…you had some of them pissed off in there when they seen her all over you like that said Trevor.

Ye let them be pissed…ready for somebody to start popping off on some hating type shit on me…I'm new here but I'm not that guy you want to try said Dre.

Man…we was getting into it good…kissing her neck and sucking her tidies and squeezing them heating her up and pulled the dick out and put it in her mouth and that shit was so fucking horrible dog…she was biting it and scraping it man indicating lack of experience and when I was yelling out she must have thought that she was doing a good job and speeded up gripping the fucking base of my dick like a vise so when I did finally pry her ass off I told her was she going to let me break that v card in and she was looking in my eyes man telling me that she want me to be her first…want to be with me and to promise to not take it and break her heart…I saw it all in her face and what she really wanted from me beyond my dick…I started to remember the conversations we had through the night that I didn't at first because I was too busy throwing that game on her to skit them panties…a girl with daddy issues looking for the love her father didn't give her and the one that was never there for her…something I understand…it started fucking with me hard said Dre.

Trevor shot a quick glance over at him as he was driving.

She was shaking from being nervous and excited man and trying to get me to fill that empty void in her heart rather than between her legs…I had her right there man all I had to do was take it…legs wide open and she was pretty as fuck you saw her…I couldn't do it man…I couldn't be that guy as horny as I was…not the one that fucking told her what she wanted to hear because truthfully I just wanted to bust a nut and I would have been done with her…I got a girl and a baby already and I'm down for a summer fling but not trying to start a relationship and get hearts and feelings involved…I know what I'm down here for and beyond that I just want to fuck man…city girls…some of them I'd piss on them if they let me but she different maybe it's her country girl genuine kindness and naivety that made me pity or show some deeper respect for her but I told her that we should wait and tonight wasn't the night said Dre.

Oh word...wow kid I didn't know the big city mack had a heart of gold said Trevor.

Don't get it twisted man took everything to not unleash the beast on her ass...tonight I go home to bust one the old fashion way but at least it's one I'll have without guilt...at least you got yours off said Dre pulling his cigarette.

Yeah and it was damn good too man, but I'm feeling like I got a lot more left in this to get out before I finally lay it down said Trevor.

Man yaw play some crazy ass games here in the country...fucking spin the bottle shit...that was kind of fun up to that part where they dared us to do that bullshit...fuck what was up with girl...super freak az...shit at least your lips were soft and not crusty in shit if I had to do that gay funk...didn't wipe my lips cause your breath was nasty man...just couldn't look like I was into that shit like that because I wasn't said Dre shaking his head.

Trevor laughed a little to himself.

When they got back to the house, Dre closed his room door and locked it then strip butt naked, grabbed some Vaseline and laid back on his bed stroking his dick and balls and was already rock hard before he even got started.

He closed his eyes pumping it harder and faster and in Trevor's room he was doing the same thing stroking his dick fast and hard with his lamp light on holding up a porn magazine of a naked girl in it.

Dre continued his jack off session a while longer and as he begin to reach his peak he begin to stiffen up clenching his toes hard as he busted a huge load all across his chest in massive squirts while stroking it super fast pushing every drop out...it was beautiful...as he took a deep breath and closed his eyes for a moment while Trevor was busting just as big a load as he had earlier.

Dre got up and walked across the room into the bathroom as Trevor was coming in from the other end and both saw each other's full naked bodies with their dicks still hanging and nut sprayed all across their chests and this should have been an embarrassing moment for them but it wasn't at all they just grinned looking away from each other.

I guess this is just something were going to have to deal with from time to time homie…no escaping it…it is what it is though… said Dre.

Yep…I guess so man said Trevor.

Dre took a cloth from the rack and turn and left out.

Night man he said closing his end of the bathroom.

Chapter 10

Early Saturday noon, Dre awoke to the bright sun shining in the room and felt like he had slept longer than he usually do in the morning and felt well rested and was still naked as he looked at the goofy alarm clock his Uncle had given him and it was after twelve as he looked at it again to make sure he was seeing the time right and wonder why no one bothered to wake him up this late into the day even if he had turned off the alarm when he heard a knock at the door it was a certain knock that Trevor did.

Hey you up yet man? He heard Trevor say from the other side of the door.

Ye…just waking up man hold on said Dre rubbing his head and eyes then got out of bed and looked around and put on some jogging pants then opened the door.

Morning, you going to sleep all day man smiled Trevor.

Naw but everybody don't wake up at the crack of dawn especially on days they don't have too…why didn't anybody bother to wake me up for breakfast or something…bet you already had brunch too said Dre.

Big city hungry huh, Forgot to tell you on Saturdays breakfast isn't as mandatory as it is throughout the week…weekends get pretty busy even with work not necessarily involved…so much activities and things everyone likes doing and if you're not down when its prepared than you just miss it and grab a snack or something when you do get down…Surprised you slept as long as you did…figured you be up downstairs watching Saturday Morning cartoons and eating cereal said Trevor getting a piece of lint out his head as Dre swatted at his hand rubbing his eyes.

I don't watch cartoons man, do I look like a kid or something to you? asked Dre.

You are still a kid big city said Trevor.

I'm 16 said Dre.

You are smart and mature for your age I can see that but in reality you still a kid growing up said Trevor.

Word homie? So you just think I'm some bae bae kid from the city that you baby sitting or something said Dre.

I didn't say all that...but if you want to get out of the house today and enjoy some of the country side festivities with Auntie, Uncle and your cousin you should get up and get dressed soon...I'm going to finish my boat project for the day so no reason you stuck around here bored but I promise you the weekends ahead to be a lot better...got some things planned out and some places I want you to go with me if you interested said Trevor walking off and stopped to the door.

Oh and Auntie told me to tell you your sweet heart Gia has called for you 4 times from the home phone since this morning and just now...so probably should get back at girl said Trevor closing his door as Dre yawned to himself and stretched his arms and walked into the bathroom.

After a little while, Dre got dressed and came downstairs and saw his cousin Erika braiding Trevor's hair as he looked at a hunting magazine she sat on the couch watching life time movies.

About time...too late to say good morning so I'll say good afternoon said Erika.

Sup people he said glancing at the TV as he walked into the living room.

You shouldn't watch lifetime movies cous, that stuff rots woman's brains and puts bad thoughts in their heads said Dre.

You leave my lifetime alone and I'll leave your Wire alone, I saw your box set of that and the Corner in your room said Erika.

I know this your house but stay out of that room and out of my stuff said Dre.

Boy please I was not going through your little gangster garbage, I just bring clean towels and cloths to your bathroom when you leave out of here for work and leave things in a mess…you too Trevor she said bumping his back with her knee as he grinned to himself.

Do you think they just magically appear there Erika asked Dre.

Oh…thanks said Dre.

Umhm, your welcome big city said Erika going back to braiding Trevor's hair.

Where's Unc? Dre.

Making his rounds and checking on his animal farm and stable out back and feeding them…sometimes I think he loves those horses and goats more than me with the love and attention he showers to them… he doesn't tell us but we know after the long work week the weekend is devoted for them he just squeeze us in to that schedule…speaking of which were going to the country side festivities this later this afternoon…its fun kind of like a cheap county fair without the roller coasters but a lot of fun activities and contest to get into…Trevor is going to be locked in that work barn Uncle and he built together finishing the restoration of that boat can't wait to see it and he prefers to be left alone to his devises so I'm guessing you're going to come with us unless you want to stay behind and fit the horses with new horse shoes uncle got from Blacksmith Tom…be nice for you to bond a little more with Sugar, Pepper jack and Rage said Erika.

Naw,the only shoes I'm putting on today are my jordans, I think I'm going to attend that outing with the rest of you…see what the country's weekend of community fun is like said Dre.

Great although I have to take you horse riding out there with me one of these days, there's nothing better than straddling a powerful steed as he gallops gracefully across the acre's trails and the wind in your hair…trust me, I'll teach you how to ride one and you have nothing to fear… their actually very gentle and majestic creatures and I've been riding one since I was 10 said Erika.

Sounds like something that could be fun said Dre.

Dre's aunt walked from the kitchen into the living room with the phone.

Hey Dre baby, Gia has been calling you on the phone all morning while you were fast asleep and not too long ago…again…when you were upstairs and I told her that you'd be down in 20 minutes and she said she'd hold on and wait for you to get on the phone because she was washing clothes anyway and not doing anything else…very persistent…this one she smiled handing him the phone.

Thanks Auntie said Dre taking the phone and going to the outside back porch.

Hey what's up said Dre.

About time Dre, I'm calling you and they keep telling me that you sleep and as it got later and they kept telling me that… I thought that they were lying or you were still mad and didn't want to talk to me but anyway…hey boo I miss you so much and I love you…so sorry we had that little argument that night but you was tripping hard and it wasn't nothing like what you was thinking…keep telling you that you got a good one and you need to have more trust in me and faith in us…I kept stressing out over the fact that we all mad and irritated with the distance killing us and I could never forgive myself if you got hurt doing that dangerous hard country work and that was our last conversation…I just needed to hear your voice like for real said Gia.

Thanks I love you too and I'm good, just making this work for me and for us you know said Dre.

Yeah I know…so like I know that you got paid Thursday right… just asking because I still haven't got that money yet that was supposed to be sent down here for me and the baby because we need things and I cant make moves without it… and the weekend here….still haven't got it yet so I mean what's going on with that because I need to buy diapers, new sleepers and the whole nine said Gia.

Oh don't worry my Uncle took care of that for me and wired the money down there so you and the baby should be getting it soon…not sure what the holdup is but it's on the way said Dre.

Oh okay good…wait hold up-Why is your Uncle making transactions with your money…that's your pay check and why didn't you make sure it personally got to where it was going…I told you its best to handle your own money and keep your people out of your business because they might be trying to get over you or snatch some in their own pocket because they think you young and count worth a shit… keep you worked hard so you too exhausted to even check on your money status you feel me? asked Gia.

I can count pretty damn good and I trust my Uncle he breaks it down to what I make and what gets taken out for what and what I get in my pocket…I might be staying here but he not charging me for housing, feeding and sheltering me so I doubt that he would be snatching up what I do make to put in his own pocket… like I said its being sent there to you so hold on and stop rushing shit you going to get it said Dre.

Dre don't even make it seem like it's about me getting the money, the baby needs it and okay I was just asking that's all…just making sure aint nobody taking what's ours said Gia.

How Darius? Dre asked her.

He doing really good looking more and more like you every day… I'm emailing some new pictures we took a couple days ago to your laptop said Gia.

Cool, can't wait to see them said Dre.

So what you been doing down there in your spare time when they not working the blood out of my sexy little boo said Gia.

Not shit really…playing hide and seek out in the cornfields you know stuff like that said Dre.

I believe that too…don't even let that horrible place phase you… just make that dough and hit the road, build them stacks so we can hit those tracks said Gia.

It's not all that bad...not saying I'm really liking it here now but it's an adjustment from the city big time...don't think the rest of my time will be as bad and miserable as I thought it would be said Dre.

Why you say that...find some country ass bitches down there to pass the time with or something said Gia.

What? Where did that come from? What happened to love and trust and having faith in us...you need to get it together and practice what you preach said Dre.

So is it girls down there? Like pretty girls? Gia asked him.

Haven't seen nothing yet that looks as good as you said Dre.

Good answer said Gia.

Dre walked back into the kitchen and gave his Auntie back the phone.

Dre you know I don't mind giving Gia the home number here because I know how bad service can be on your phone all the way out here most times but she calls you every 20 minutes to an hour ever since she got this number and I would greatly appreciate it if you tell her that your family has other people and important calls coming to this house too so she can't be tying up the line like that...I know they say cherish the ones you love with every breath that you take but she need to kind of get a handle on that...I'm not trying to be one of those evil aunts who trying to control the phone and who calls here because I'm not like that at all but I'd like it if she'd just you know slow her roll a bit and let you breath just a bit you not going anywhere you'll be here...I have to agree with your mom on this...she gotta get a grip said his aunt.

Alright auntie I'll let her know laughed Dre.

Later that afternoon when Trevor stayed home to finish his boat project, Dre and the rest of his relatives went to the country side festival that was very similar to a county fair with the largest gathering of crowds in the country he had seen so far...Dre rather enjoyed the various activities going on there, the rides and games like mallet banging, ring toss, water gun and dart board competitions, hitting the target bulls eye and knocking the guy talking mad smack to the pitchers into a giant barrel of water and countless more games there winning his cousin Erika quite a few prizes and after a while they walked around observing all the other things going on there...best pie baking contest and the foolery activities like bobbing for apples contests and most hotdog eating contest...they had music bands and talent shows for the kids and the best part to Dre was the grill food when he and his cousin Erika sat down to eat.

Wow this is actually kind of cool said Dre.

So you're enjoying the country side festival, I'm glad that big city is finding some sense of entertainment in our down in the deep miscellaneous activities asked Erika.

I guess that nick name Trevor has for me is going to stick huh said Dre.

Well it does have a certain ring to it, so what are your plans for the future once you go back home to the city...are you enrolling back in the school to finish your education or be a part time or stay at home dad? because there's nothing wrong with that if that's what you want to do...long as you're taking care of your child and not gang banging in the streets or selling drugs and stuff like that...its important to be there for him in his life and be a positive influence and role model in his life said Erika.

Yea I know...didn't plan or expect to be a father at this age but things happen and all I can really do now is try to be the best person I can be for him and shut down all that other stuff I was doing or felt I had to do to provide for him including things I weren't suppose too... at least it would be a step up because my dad didn't do anything for me really nor even being there...I'm not stupid though I realize having a baby at 15 and now being a father at 16 puts a whole new perspective in my life and I'll be robbed of my best years but I made my bed and now I have to lay in it simple as that said Dre.

As long as you learn and grow from your experiences or situations is all that really matters said Erika.

Ye…I know I been a handful for my mom to deal with the last couple years and I didn't intentionally put her through all of what I been doing but I have a lot of resentment from the past and being let down during the most important moments of my life, than I got anger issues that I'm working on…think being down here will give me a lot of time to think of what I'm going to do next with my life when I get back which is probably the point of why my mom sent me here…I know I want to get back in school when I return back home and work toward my dreams and goals that I gave up on for a while in the mean time I think that being here will be a good learning experience for me said Dre.

I think so too said Erika.

So what are your plans for the near future? Dre asked her.

Horse trainer; guess I just have a deep love for animals like mom who is a veterinarian said Erika.

Cool so what about dating? Do your father allow you to have boyfriends at the age of 16 or is he strict on that said Dre.

I'm a farmer's daughter not a nun and yes my father let's me date just makes it extremely hard and miserable on the guy…I swear thats the only think that really bums about being the girl in the family…over protective said Erika.

Dre grinned.

So what do you think of Trevor? Erika asked him.

He's a pretty cool guy to know and hang with…he's good with me and seems to be just like family to all of you said Dre.

He is, I think of Trevor as a big brother you might say and he is as close and bonded to this family as he is distant at times but that's just how Trevor has always been…the kind of guy he is…strong silent type…sometimes he's the big talker chatting it up and spending time with us and then there are those times when he goes off on his own to do whatever interest him and be alone but everyone has their private and personal time…he just been through a lot in his life and I don't know…guess I feel like he thinks that no matter how much he knows we care about him and love him like family that deep down he feels that we can never be his real family but I wish he didn't think that way or have that distance especially after all the years of him staying here and being with us…he's never been a stranger not even from day one said Erika.

So what about his real family or his parents where are they? I mean I wanted to ask him about that but he never really wanted to go into talking about them really so I left it alone said Dre.

He lost them in a house fire when he was a bit younger, he doesn't like talking about it and want share it with anyone really…the only person he really talked to about it too is my dad because they seem to have this great father son type bond and my dad tells us that he's particularly sensitive to that issue and its best for us to never go into with him…you know some wounds never heal or at least take a lot of time said Erika.

So that's how he got those small burns on his arm that I asked him about on my first day of work when we were riding together and he just kind of skipped the subject said Dre.

It's a closed subject, for future reference…its just better left alone…plus Trevor has a tendency to go into these depressions and start drinking a lot…guess it's his way of coping with the reality that their really gone and he has no other family really but us…so if he starts to distance himself and want to be left alone than just let him be and he'll come back soon after as good as new…though I think he really likes you and might share his space with you…he was telling us this morning at the breakfast your sleepy butt missed that he had all these weekend plans for you both…teaching you how to hunt,fishing,camping…stuff I know your city side ass probably not interested in but for your sake at least pretend to like it…he's a good guy…doesn't admit it but has a sensitive side too and if you hurt his feelings cous…I'll hurt your everything else said Erika.

Dre laughed. It's not like that I'm generally interested to do all these things and hang with him said Dre.

Good…thanks for all these prizes you won for me said Erika looking at her teddy bear.

Your welcome said Dre taking a sip of his drink.

Chapter 11

Sunday Morning, 8 sharp, the family had breakfast together and were getting ready for church which was the one place he hadn't been too in a long while although his mom was very church oriented and he attended every Sunday when he was younger it was when he got a little older that she had to push him to go or he wouldn't be around because she would literally drag him out of the house to go if he was there.

Dre's Uncle and Aunt had bought him a dress shirt, tie, shoes and pants the day before at a store in town after the festival and Dre wondered how church was in the country compared to the city and were they even going to something that looked like a church or was it a giant barn that they had church in...either way he couldn't get out of going here even if he wanted too...where would he go not like he can run down the street to a friend or relative's house all the way out here in the middle of nowhere.

Dre stood in the bathroom mirror straightening his shirt and trying to fix his tie that his Uncle taught him how to do when he was a little younger but it had been so long that he had to get dress for anything that he couldn't get it right properly.

Dre went to the other end of the bathroom connected to Trevor's room and knocked on it.

Yo said Dre.

What's up, its open said Trevor from the other side as Dre opened it to Trevor standing in front of his room dresser mirror fixing his own tie and looked back at him.

Hey man...think you can do my tie for me...been a while since I got dressed up grinned Dre.

Sure man, come on over said Trevor.

Dre walked over to his dresser as Trevor stood in front of him and begin to tell him the tie trick as he fixed it for him then straightened his collar for him as Dre turned and looked at him self in the mirror.

Thanks man said Dre.

No prob...you look nice man smiled Trevor.

Thanks you too said Dre walking back out.

Soon they took the family van and were on the road to church.

Trevor and Dre sat in the very back of the van beside each other as Dre cut his eye over at Trevor and just looked at him for a moment without his notice from a side view as if just checking him out he was holding his bible and looking out the window across the vast country fields then Dre looked downward and turned back to look out the other window and after a bit laid his head back and closed his eyes.

After a hour drive they arrived to what looked like a mega church and Dre was surprised when he saw it like it was ripped up from one of those fancy churches by a twister like in the wizard of oz and dropped down right in the middle of the country because there was no road parking lot but it was packed and crowded with diverse members Black, White and Mexican families and one thing he could say is that country people looked rugged in work gear but they could really get dressed up when it counted.

After church, His Uncle and Aunt stayed and talked with some of their friends and introduced Dre to them and they talked to Erika but Dre noticed that Trevor had slipped out and vanished slickly probably going back to the car avoiding this family moment for whatever reason but pretty sure the obvious reason his cousin Erika had told him that Trevor although knowing that he was very much a part of his Uncle's family in his heart on some level knew that they weren't really that and it made him feel a little bad for him...Dre knew he had his family issues but Trevor lost his parents tragically so his situation couldn't compare to his and at least his was still repairable.

When Dre was walking outside he saw a group of pretty girls standing around talking and smiling with little waves and giggles at him as Erika came up from behind him and took his arm forcing him to walk with her to the van down the steps.

What? said Dre.

Don't even think about it, this is God's house and you won't get your mack on here said Erika.

When the family left church they went to a eatery together as they did every Sunday than returned back to the house and shortly after they had settled in Dre's Uncle took he and Trevor into town to get supplies and essentials for the house and the animals on his back estate.

Well I really appreciate you boys help and you still have the rest of the afternoon and evening to do whatever you like just make sure if you plan on hitting the road to be back before dinner said Dre's Uncle as they both walked back toward the house.

You want to ride with me? Trevor asked him.

Cool where you going? Dre asked him.

I'm headed into town to go by a couple of stores and then going to pay a visit to a relative of mine that stay a little ways from here but mostly it's a task run so if you don't feel like traveling that far out I understand said Trevor.

Naw its cool man, I'm rolling out with you said Dre.

Cool well let's get cleaned up and head out then said Trevor.

They both were soon on the road and first stop Trevor made was to the gas station as he filled his truck up as Dre sat inside and looked at him through the rear view mirror as Trevor stood in his wife beater waiting for it to finish looking around nowhere in particular then suddenly looked directly at Dre looking at him as Dre quickly switched his eyes to front view then Trevor went inside the store and got back in the truck and tossed him a pack of smokes that he didn't ask him to buy then put a box of cigars in the glove department and they were back on the road.

Trevor went into the liquor store and bought a few bottles then went into town and did some shopping of food and supplies like for the house then rode out to a small neighborhood and got out to a guys house who he talked to at the door who he gave some money too and handed him a bag of smoke most likely that he sniffed and grinned slapping five with him then got back in the truck and drove a little ways that led to a long dusty trail and Dre was curious where he was going or who he was seeing because he barely talked much during the whole excursion and finally at the end of the trail they came up on a trailer a really rough looking one like the kind trailer park trash stay in and he wondered who he was visiting there as Trevor beeped the horn to an old man opening the door and grinned waving and left it open for them.

Can you help me bring this stuff inside? Trevor asked him.

Ye I got you said Dre helping him gathered the shop and bring it into this guys house obviously he made all these runs for this old dude he thought to himself.

Trevor introduced Dre to him then talked to this guy who was interested in wanting to know what was going on work wise and how he was doing then they sat down to the table with him to play a game of cards and drink a bottle of the liquor as Trevor took a cup from the bag he had purchased and poured it half way and slid it to Dre while smoking a cigarette.

I know you thirsty and that's all you get big city he said as they continued with their game of cards for a while then after the old guy got a buzz he happily took a bag containing soap and bathroom essentials and left the table to his back room bathroom.

You ready to smoke? Trevor asked him.

Ye definitely want to do that right about now said Dre.

Cool, imma roll it up in here and then were going to smoke it outside…make sure to take off your overtop so we don't carry that scent back to the house with us got some spray in the car and some mints but probably best to wash up a little up here to be on the safe side you know just enough to get it off your hands and body said Trevor as Dre nodded.

Trevor went outside and got it out his truck and rolled it up on the inside but Dre still didn't ask him about who that older guy was yet and didn't think that it was important to ask, all he knew was that it must have been a associate or something to him then they both went outside and took off their wife beaters and threw them in the truck then Trevor hopped on the back and took a blanket and unrolled it down then both sat back on it and smoked the blunt passing it back and forth and laid back on the truck beside each other just puffing and passing.

So what you think about it? Trevor asked him.

It's straight...damn said Dre sitting up coughing a bit.

Trevor laughed. Yea that's that good shit right here man...all I fuck with he said.

Dre finally had to ask him: Yo, who that old dude in there? He asked.

That's my uncle said Trevor.

So you have other relatives out here? Dre asked him.

He's the last of my relatives out here...My Uncle Tim, he use to work for Dave...guy you working for now but he got fired because he was stealing shit...robbed his secret safe at his office and when Dave found out by replaying his surveillance rather than pressing charges and shooting his ass dead he just fired him and told him never to come back on any of his properties or he a dead duck and as for the money he went to Vegas and gambled his ass broke and came crawling back where Dave was waiting for him at his house with a shotgun...I was working for Dave around that time too...I was 16 at the time and convinced him to not hurt my uncle and told him I would work off to pay what he took but Dave wouldn't let me make that sacrifice cause I was good people...probably why he let him off with that warning said Trevor pulling the blunt.

Word man, damn that's fucked up said Dre.

I started working for your Uncle and convinced him to hire my uncle who needed the work and despite what he had done to Dave he gave him a chance…your uncle believed in giving people second chances but come to find out he would fuck that up too…he would drive the tractor and plow the fields for your uncle and various task around the farm but was stealing shit there too so your Uncle got rid of him without hesitation…no one would hire him after that anywhere down here…he had burned too many bridges…so he winded up living out here in this dump his ex wife left to him after she died and basically got no income other than odd jobs here and there he get…but despite being a major thief he did look after me after my parents- were gone…so I just return the favor and help him out anyway I can…he the only blood family I got here now so I come by once in a while and look out said Trevor.

Wow homie…you talking about me having a heart of gold…where I'm from nobody would go through this amount of kindness to help somebody and you just shopped all out for dude up and down the road and riding all the way down here…you straight amazing man…hell if I was a female I would date you nigga laughed Dre.

You'd still be too young for me grinned Trevor.

I fucked a bitch twice my age before, If I'm so young then why would you let me drink and smoke this shit then said Dre raising the blunt.

You know how to say no; obviously you wanted it said Trevor as Dre passed it to him as he pulled on it.

No argument there man said Dre.

They finished the blunt and soon were on their way back out for home.

Dre saw Trevor give the guy obviously a fat envelope which clearly had money in it who was very gracious and hugged him patting his back as Trevor got in his truck.

Take care Unc yelled Trevor raising hand and drove off.

Chapter 12

The weekend came around again and Trevor went to a piece of land owned by a family related to Dave to mow their massive lawn and trim the hedges around their house and bought Dre along to make some extra money as well.

As they drove down the long trail leading up to the house, Dre saw a bunch of workers taking lemons down from the trees and gathering them into large wooden baskets as he smoked a cigarette.

Hey,I notice half those guys lemon picking that work at the plant with me, I see they stay working even after the work week over... Ye,make that money my friends!yelled Dre waving as they looked up and smiled waving.

You ready to make a little extra big city?Trevor asked him.

Damn, don't you mean a lot extra, check out the lawn on this massive property, we might need back up said Dre.

No sweat, I got the front and you got the back said Tre.

Yo,why I gotta get the back,it look like a jungle back there,let me get the front where I can be in view of things incase its bears or something lurking about back there said Dre.

Alright big kitty, I got the back then grinned Trevor.

Big what? I thought I was big city? Dre asked him.

Naw, its big kitty today, you a pussy cat scared of a little tall grass out back said Trevor.

No I'm not, give me a mechedi and I'll give it a run said Dre.

Plenty of sticks back there if something shows up said Trevor.

Oh ye? Not good enough said Dre as Trevor smiled to himself.

Trevor and Dre mowed the massive lawn of the house,cut down the weeds, than trimed the hedges.

They were nearly done when the lady of the house daughter Annabelle stepped out with a nice cold glass of lemonade and stood on the front porch smiling at Dre who glanced up and smiled back at her tipping his hat then took it off and walked to the front of the porch.

Good afternoon smiled Dre.

Hi there, my name is Annabelle, I'm so sorry that you boys had to endure chopping down this awfully big yard of ours, though I must confess it has been such a pleasing sight seeing young built boys mowing our big lawn that has need a good grooming for some time now, daddy has been away on business a lot lately and we girls just don't pay too much attention to the unkempt growth of this estate, so glad you could give it a man's touch smiled Annabelle.

My names Andre and your very welcome, hard work doesn't bother me, I like getting my hands dirty smiled Dre.

Oh my how lovely, Your not from around here are you? Annabelle smiled at him.

No, I'm from the big city, down here deep in the country for work, you're a very pretty girl said Dre.

Thank you Andre,I bought you boys some cold beverages to cool you down from this summer heat though I must say I find myself with quite a thirst and fever all of a sudden Annabelle smiled at him.

Oh really said Dre taking a glass and drinking some.

Thank you Annabelle said Dre.

My pleasure,so tell me Andre, more about where your from,what things you like to do,what kind of girls you into said Annabelle in a seductive type of way.

Girls that are pretty like you said Dre.

Oh really tell me more said Annabelle.

Annabelle! Annabelle! Get in this house right now and let these boys work and stop parading your self around the help like some cheap tart said her mother at the front porch.

Ugh, yes mother, it was nice meeting you Andre, I do hope to meet again,I'm going to leave this lemonade out here for you and your friend Trevor…I'll see you later Andre she waved going into the house.

Later Anna Dre grinned finishing the drink.

Her mother looked at Dre.

How is the work coming along Andre?

Were just about done mam said Dre.

She nodded and left the door as Trevor walked over to the porch.

What are you doing? Trevor asked him.

Their beautiful daughter Annabelle bought us cold refreshments, how thoughtful of her, have one said Dre.

Trevor took one and drunk it.

Damn, she is a dime…the most beautiful snow white princess this side of the plantation and daddy's gone out of town,might have to circle back around here at some point and get better aquinated with Anna said Dre.

Trevor finished the drink and put it on the tray.

Good luck with that big city, but if I were you I would leave that piece of tempting candy alone,her daddy shot the last guy in the ass who he caught in her bedroom from what I heard and her moms a pretty good shot too said Trevor.

Oh…well I'm good then, too far a travel back out this way anyway said Dre.

Trevor grinned and patted his shoulder. Back to work,were almost finished here he said.

Another week past, Trevor would take Dre to work at the plant then go back to his Uncle's farm to help him then pick him up in the evenings and take him home but he was starting to wish Trevor was working there with him because it would be nice to have somebody to talk too during the break days that talked English but toward the end of the week when he got back to the house before he could even get a shower in his girlfriend Gia called him and Aunt informed him that it was important.

Hey what's up just getting in…what's going on? Dre asked Gia.

Hey so okay to be absolutely clear the money you were sending was meant to come straight to me…m-e- me right? Gia asked him.

Yeah why? Dre asked her.

Alright so please explain to me how it managed to get in the claws of your mother, that's right she got your money and holding it hostage and telling me that she's not going to give it to me but use it to buy the baby what he need and throw me a little if any left to spare…telling me to write down a fucking list of all the things to get like I don't need you shopping for me and my baby, give me the money and I'll do my own damn shopping…omg this is so crazy…why you do that for? Gia asked him.

I didn't give it to her, I told my Uncle specifically who to wire it too but obviously he and my mom been talking and she told him to wire it to her instead…I mean I didn't know she was sneaky like that said Dre.

So how could you let that happen, I told you that they were going to be rolling dice with your money…why didn't you just do it yourself…I can see now why everybody just flip you all over the place cause you just sit back in chill while everybody doing all the thinking and decision making for you like for real this is ridiculous said Gia.

Shut up, let me call my mom in and see what's going on hold on said Dre.

Yeah you do that, click her ass right on in so we can have this whole conversation together and get this right because I'm not going to be sitting here while she try to control my shit while she got you at the same time…manipulating ass…ooo so fucking mad right now said Gia.

Oh god, I don't even feel like dealing with all this right now I'm tired said Dre taking a deep breath.

Somebody is going to need God, if they stealing our money said Gia.

Hello said Dre's mother.

Mom, what's up said Dre.

Hi baby, how are things going down there...your uncle told me what a good job you doing there working...that's good to hear that you down there doing what you suppose to do and out of trouble for once she said.

Mom, I got Gia on the phone right now said Dre.

Who-oh....she said smacking her lips.

So what's going on with the money, she saying that you got it and won't give it to her and the baby Dre told his mother.

The money is right here and I told her that I would be managing what is sent down here so I know exactly what is spent on what and I'm rationing out the money myself and told her to write a list of the needs and miss thang didn't like that because she want to get that money and get her hair and nails done she said.

No disrespect Miss Johnson but I have a name said Gia.

Like I said miss thang mad because I cut off that shopping spree she wanted to do, I talked to her last night and not once did she say anything about shopping for the baby but I do recall her-wait why am I talking at you-let me rephrase that since you on the phone-I do recall you talking about her bad you needed to get your hair done and nails fixed...you won't be sprucing yourself up on the baby's expense no mam said Dre's mother.

Okay so I'm a girl, I need those things done to keep myself up...I wasn't going to use that money to do that it's for the baby said Gia.

How was you going to do that because you told me that you so tired of being broke and need a job, of course you were going to use the money to get it done said Dre's mother.

So what! Gia yelled back.

Dre talked to your mom and tell her to give me that money because she did not make it and didn't work for it, that money belongs to me and the baby I conceived with you...she won't there during conception so she don't need to be all in this now…we got this said Gia.

Oo Girl no you didn't, cover me in the blood Jesus…she said talking in tongues.

I almost forgot I was a Christian for a second and going to go straight ham on you little girl said Dre mom.

Dre tell her! Gia yelled.

That's my son! You tell your own what to do not mine…Dre please talk to your girlfriend and tell her to stop disrespecting me like she was raised by a pack of wolves…I'm not having it and I'm tired of it now said his mom.

Dre! Gia yelled back.

Man just shut the fuck up for a minute said Dre as Gia was silent.

Umhm…thank you, but don't be cussing like that around me I told you about that Dre said his mom.

Mom can you please stop bickering back and forth with her like that and be the grown up for a second said Dre.

Oop said Gia snickering.

Excuse me? Boy who do you think you talking to like that are you crazy? asked his mom.

Naw man I'm just saying-said Dre.

Man? Do I look like man to you and you aint saying nothing, you might be working but I got power of attorney over all your shit including you and this money I got in my hand right now…I tell you what keep talking to me like that and I'll come down there said his mom.

Yeah right, you know you aint coming all the way down here, you wouldn't even come for your best friend funeral said Dre.

Yeah you right because I didn't have time, I was trying to keep your bad ass in check while you ripping and running the streets and all snugged up with her…I love my new grandson to death but this was definitely too soon she said.

Mom can you please give Gia the money, I want her to buy the things our baby need and I know she will do that and whatever is left

I want her to spend it on herself…that's what I want done with the money I'm making said Dre.

So it's just the blank with what I say or do right? Dre's mom asked him.

No mom, I love you but Gia is the mother of my child and I love her and him too…I want to make her happy and my baby taken care of and right now I can do that from here…I'm doing good…I'm working hard and staying out of trouble that's what you wanted for me to do and I made you happy so make me happy by giving it to her so she can handle business…don't want to fight between you too and we stuck together now so let's make it work said Dre.

Alright I'll do that…hello you there girl you got quiet on us said Dre's mother.

Yeah I'm here just listening and alright I'll be waiting said Gia.

Love you mom and I'll talk to you later said Dre.

Love you too Dre she said ending call.

Ha! Way to represent for your girl and stand up to her…I love you so much right now said Gia.

Do what you suppose to do for our son, talk to you later…time for a shower and dinner here said Dre.

Okay muah love you said Gia.

You too said Dre ending call and walked back into the house and went upstairs.

Gia looked at her cell.

You too? He never said you too…he suppose to say I love you too…Oh well he just probably tired and worn out from work in the dirt she said going over to the baby crib and shook it a little.

Hey boo wake yo ass up because you and momma going shopping she said picking him up and hugged him laughing and kissed him.

We won! We finally beat the wicked witch of the west! Go Gia! Go Darius! Go Gia! Go Darius she said.

Chapter 13

It was in mid-way through the 3rd week of the first month, that Dre's Uncle got a call from Dave from his office on the farm informing him that Dre had gotten hurt operating one of the machines in the factory where he had moved him to outside of doing the field cropping.

How bad is it? Uncle Richard asked Dave.

Well he got quite a gash on his lower inner right arm and won't need stitches but he was treated here and we bandaged it up for him and I'm sure it will heal up in a couple weeks...he's a tough kid not even really phased by it or anything said Dave.

Damn it Dave, you know operating the machines in the factory is a bit more complicated than field cropping and it takes some kind of training or experience to run them...I should have been told that he was moved to that floor and he shouldn't have been there period said his Uncle Richard.

But he told me that he told you already that he was running the machines, he been doing it since last week and he told me that he wanted to do it...I had him watch one of the guys who was showing him how to operate it for a couple days and he was doing just fine... accidents like this happen Richard rather you've been operating them for a week or a year you know that...he's alright said Dave.

That's not the point, he should have never been in there said Richard.

Well he started slowing down progress in the crop field a bit when I started doubling the labor to make my mark of shipment this month and he gets that way late into the afternoon so I moved him inside to something that might be better suited for him...I mean he is still young and a great worker but it just might be too much for a boy his age…he's in the break room and I told him that it would be best if he took the rest of the day off and this week to recover…maybe you can come over and take him home so he can rest said Dave.

Thanks I'll be sending Trevor that way shortly, I'll talk to you later said his uncle ending call and taking a deep breath.

What's going on, big city alright? Trevor asked him.

Yeah but one of the factory machines he was operating slashed his arm a little…If I knew that Dave was doubling the day labor to make his marks I would have taken him out of there…working my nephew to death…go pick him up and take him home said his Uncle Richard.

I'm on my way said Trevor leaving out.

When Trevor got to the factory, he went inside and got Dre who had his arm bandaged up to his wrist and walked back to his truck.

So how did you get that scratch big city, the boss pretty wife came by and distracted you while you were operating the machine? Trevor smiled at him.

I saw her a couple days ago, she is fine but naw man…I don't know it just happened so fast…shit happens you know…I just got a boo boo, still could have completed the rest of today said Dre.

I admire your tenacity but you have to know when to take a break, you been doing too much…you fell asleep on the toilet and left the door bathroom unlocked…comon you were wore the fuck out said Trevor.

Yo you saw me on the toilet man said Dre.

Ye no big deal man, I didn't even come all the way in I saw feet that's all and backed up then heard you snoring a few minutes later laughed Trevor.

I was tired man…its not just work but then I get back to the house and talk to my baby's moms for a little while and I just want to fall out said Dre.

Kept up the pace you've been doing lately and you would have… you can't take that kind of country work not yet big city…your back gotta be broken in so you can get use to it…like I had to once said Trevor.

Dre glanced up at the back of the truck to see Trevor's dog.

I see you bought Lassie along for the ride said Dre.

He always been my riding buddy until lately, he got jealous that you been taking his spot so I had to let him know that there was room for all of you in my big ass truck…and his name is Charlie said Trevor.

Hey Charlie wish you could talk so this would be fair but I call shotgun said Dre getting in the car and put his seatbelt on.

You had lunch yet? Trevor asked him.

Nope was ten minutes to reaching one before I got slitted said Dre.

I'll hook you up back at the house then said Trevor.

You know the worst part about working at a job where you get paid under the table? asked Dre.

What's that? Trevor asked him.

No worker's comp said Dre.

Trevor grinned then started his truck and drove off as they talked along the ride home.

I'm glad you got passed that slave mentality way of thinking and your fear of field work and a white boss man that has a super country accent…know it can be unsettling but Dave's not racist or anything… I've known him for most of my life and his best friends happen to be black not to mention his wife said Trevor.

She's mixed but yeah that still counts and you make a valid point, Dave's cool I actually talked him into getting me in the factory to make a little more than I do out there…every little bit helps said Dre.

You know that since your fine and your injuries aren't critical, your Uncle is going to yell you out for not telling him said Trevor.

Yep I know and I'm prepared for it but not just me I'm earning for so I'll take it said Dre.

Dave is doing double labor weeks now for right now and you aint specifically made to handle that much on a weekly basis said Trevor.

Double labor doo doo…so a load stacked on top of one no biggie said Dre.

Your Uncle told me that he was going to take you out of there and it's too dangerous to put that kind of pressure on you…he's going to have you working with us from now on said Trevor.

As long as I'm getting paper I'm good with that said Dre.

He also would like if you don't mention it to your mom, no need to get her all worried about it when you're okay said Trevor.

Shit this just a flesh wound and I wouldn't even tell her anyway… you know the idea of being big city…I'm made of bricks and you from the country so you're the one made of sticks and straw grinned Dre.

Ye right, you want me to show you said Trevor playfully hitting his head and driving.

Well big city meet the big bad wolf who's going to huff and puff and blow your ass down said Trevor.

What's your sign man? Dre asked him.

My what? Trevor replied back.

Your star sign, like zodiac homie said Dre.

Don't know too much about that star reading…no one ever asked me that…hell, I don't even know said Trevor.

I think I do you said that your birthday was too weeks before I got down here so that would make you a Taurus…the bull said Dre.

I'm a bull huh…I like that…so what are you in the zodiac thing? Trevor asked him.

Aries baby…the ram said Dre.

A ram huh we might butt heads eventually then huh said Trevor.

I don't know…guess we'll find out what happens when an unstoppable object meets an immovable force said Dre.

I promise when that happens, I'll be as easy on you as possible alright? Trevor asked him.

Naw be rough nigga,I like it better that way…don't hold back and show me what yuh got cause I'm going to show you best believe it… the same way you give it you should be able to take it too said Dre putting on his fittie and laying back in the seat.

Trevor looked at him unsure what he was saying but just grinned and nodded and looked back at the road.

Soon they got back to the house.

You want me to carry you inside clumsy said Trevor.

Ha ha funny…not said Dre.

Well your Auntie and Erika won't be home for a few more hours so you'll have the place to yourself…I gotta go back and finish helping Unc for the day…so what can I get you to eat before I head back out said Trevor opening the door and punching in the home security code.

I'm good yo, might just fix me a sandwich and open some chips or something said Dre walking in and flopping down on the sofa and closed his eyes for a moment.

Damn been working so hard forgot how good it felt just to not do shit said Dre.

Yeah you need to relax man…so you going to call your girl and tell her what happened and talk to her? Trevor asked him.

Hell no, I don't even want her to know I'm off work…I love her but damn I need some me time…even from a distance feel that chocking smothering feeling…I just want to breath for a few…that don't make me selfish do it? Dre asked him.

You tell me said Trevor.

Why you answering a question with a question? I'm asking you said Dre.

I don't know…I do believe that we all have the right to be selfish a little sometimes…if you give your all to someone there's nothing left for you unless they returning something back to balance it out… if someone takes and takes they have to be the also be the one to give it back too or your left feeling empty said Trevor.

Dre looked at him and twisted his lip as if thinking hard.

Hm…I never considered it that way….that is actually a damn good answer…good job country boy said Dre.

All day big city…so you good, anything else I can help you out with before I head out? said Trevor.

Dre looked at him. You've done quite enough already homie… thanks for carrying my wounded ass home…see you this evening he said.

Alright be easy said Trevor twirling his keys around turning and left out the door as Dre took some sofa pillows and laid back on them and turned on the TV when he heard the door open back up and Trevor came back in and stood near the edge of the wall.

Oh and forgot to say that I'm glad your injury is just superficial and you didn't get hurt worse said Trevor.

Dre nodded. Thanks homie appreciate that he said as Trevor nodded and left out.

Chapter 14

Later that night after dinner, Dre sat on the living room sofa reading a magazine and looked up and saw Trevor coming down the stairs walking through the living room not even looking once in his direction and go across into the kitchen and as soon as Trevor couldn't see him looking at him from a side angle he just peeped him on the low in his wife beater and blue jeans until he was out of sight then looked back at the magazine trying to sort out complex feelings inside of him that were starting to manifest and was starting to make him very uncomfortable around him and more so because he thought Trevor was picking up and knew this on some level.

Suddenly Erika came out of nowhere popped Dre in the back of the head.

Eh, what was that for? Dre asked her.

That's for being a workaholic and willing to kill yourself to make a few more quarters an hour, you tell that gold digging girlfriend of yours to pick up the slack and imma smack you a few more times when you least expect it just because you disserve it for being a hard head...running around breaking yourself to exhaustion because she want the latest fashionable handbag...don't let me talk to her said Erika going upstairs.

Dre grinned shaking his head and heard his Uncle Richard talking to someone on the phone and having a good conversation and a few laughs with them.

Dre got up and pretended to go into the kitchen to want something because he wanted to see what Trevor was doing...when his uncle turned and caught him half way.

Hey nephew guess who I'm talking too said his Uncle.

Who? Dre asked him.

Yo daddy, he said what's good with you said his uncle.

Oh…alright said Dre.

You want to come over here and speak to him for a moment? Dre's Uncle asked him.

Naw I'm good…was on my way back upstairs to go to sleep said Dre.

Sleep? You been sleeping all day knocked out cold yo auntie told me you was sprawled out across the sofa when she and your cousin got home…boy come over here and take this phone and talk to your father said his uncle.

Dre looked at his uncle and sighed to himself then reluctantly came over and took the phone.

Yeah he said.

Yeah? You come to the phone with an attitude, whats your malfunction said his dad.

Tired said Dre.

So I see you staying with your Uncle and Aunt for the summer, giving your mom a hard time back in the city ganging and slanging on the streets…cant blame you I already been there and done that you wasting the best years of your life with that foolishness you need to get your act together said his dad.

Say what? I need too? Alright Dre relied back.

I think you in the best place you need to be right now and your people going to take care of you…heard you got a baby too…what you like 15?asked his dad.

16…yep, I got a baby…guess the apple don't fall far from the tree huh? Dre replied.

I mean damn though you suppose to learn from my mistakes not go behind me and repeat them said his dad.

So are you saying I was a mistake? Dre asked him.

What? I didn't mean it that way stop twisting my words talking that nonsense...I been meaning to stop through and check you out when I was in your town a few months ago said his dad.

You were in town and didn't even call or come by? Dre asked him.

Kind of an in and out thing...had some business to take care of and had to head back...wish I had more time I would have kicked it with you said his dad.

Kicked it with me? Cool...no big deal I'm use to you not really being there anyway so not like I was expecting to see you...I probably wouldn't have been around either to see you...I be busy said Drew as Trevor looked over at him listening.

Feel you on that son...I stays on my hustle and grind too...but for real I'm going to come visit you when you get back home...play some pool have a couple beers...you are old enough to drink right? Dre's dad asked him.

I just told you I was 16...are you drunk or something or can't hear? Dre asked him.

Fucked up a bit...stressed out said his dad.

I don't know what for...not like you have 2 kids you deal with or talking too like that...how the fuck you going to visit me when you never visited my brother when he was here and I know you aint doing it from prison....but I'm sure he don't give a fuck just like me said Dre.

His dad paused. I tell you what you 2 are the most disrespectful *** damn kids I have ever seen in my life...make it hard for me to do anything for you...keep up that attitude and you'll be right there with your brother in prison said his dad.

Nigga you aint done shit for us and don't need you too said Dre as everyone in the kitchen looked at him in his heated argument silent and shocked.

You just do what you have to do to take care of your son and cut out all that crazy shit...I'm not going to apologize for shit in the past your mom wouldn't let me be there...she was and still is a cold calculating manipulating bitch and she turned you both against me-said his dad.

No you did that yourself…I don't care what you say about her… she was there you loser…have fun passing out in yo own piss dude I'm out said Dre handing his uncle the phone.

I apologize for my language he told his aunt and uncle and left out the front door and stood on the porch and leaned down on the ledge shaking his head thinking to himself and moments later Trevor came outside and stood beside him leaning on the ledge and not saying anything but took a smoke from his pack and gave it to him then lit it for him and lit himself one as they both smoked in silence then after Trevor was done with his smoke he said a few words and went back into the house.

Were going fishing the weekend, test out how good the motor boat I restored works said Trevor looking at him.

Ye…said Dre as Trevor patted him on the shoulder.

Don't lose no sleep over that…you better than that he said going into the house and closed the door.

That Night, Dre laid in his bed relaxing his arms behind his back just thinking to himself and not really tired finding it hard to still shake off how pissed he was and the nerve of his father giving him advise after being damn there absent his whole life then he saw the bathroom light turn on from beneath the door and a knock at the door from his end.

Yo said Dre.

Are you up man? Trevor asked from the other side of the door.

Ye still up man…come in said Dre as Trevor opened the door.

If you don't mind could I watch that DVD set you was talking about…the Wire? Trevor asked him.

Kind of curious what's that all about and its interesting from what you told me…see how it is in the city said Trevor.

Alright cool said Dre getting up and turning on lamp then got up and opened the dresser and took it out and handed it to him.

Season 1...best to start from the beginning in case you get hooked on it said Dre.

Thanks...I'll give it back to you when I'm finished said Trevor as Dre nodded as Trevor went back toward the bathroom.

Eh,I'm not sleepy at all can I watch it out with you...kind of hard to not want to join someone watching one of my all time favorites said Dre.

Sure comon said Trevor nodding head as Dre went into his room and stood as Trevor put the DVD in and laid down on his bed as Dre just stood with his hands in his pockets just staring at the TV.

You just going to stand there watching it like that, you can sit down man said Trevor.

Oh alright...didn't want to be all in your space like that said Dre sitting down at the edge of the bed at the end.

Eh said Trevor as Dre turned.

Get out the way I can't see through you said Trevor.

My bad said Dre who came up on the bed just half way of his body and laid his head down with his fist rested against it just looking at the TV then kept looking down on the bed as if nervous or uncomfortable about something playing with the cover with his fingers.

You want a pillow? Trevor asked him.

Dre looked back at him. Ye thanks he said taking it and rested his head on it and was quiet then did something very strange as the minutes past he moved his arm a little closer over just barely touching Trevor's leg and moved his right leg closer to his.

Trevor studied it and thought to himself: Damn...he a kid...look older for his age but he still a kid...I already know what he want to do...I can't do it...please don't make it hard for me:

Chapter 15

As the night continued Dre seemed to break out of the uneasiness he felt lying on the same bed as Trevor and gradually begin to talk and move up until he was lying right beside him conversing about what they were watching and actually making eye contact again and Trevor begin to feel an unexpected urge stir in him and his dick begin to get hard as he shifted his legs to hide it and had to get him out of there.

Wow…very good watch so far man, I'm digging it but think I better call it a night so I can get up in the morning and work on the farm with your Uncle said Trevor.

Alright cool…think I'll grab a little more shut eye too…night man said Dre getting up and walking into Trevor's bathroom door and closed it back as Trevor sigh thinking to himself and got beneath his covers and closed his eyes.

The Next Morning when Trevor got up for work and went into the bathroom he saw that Dre's end of the bathroom door was open as he went over and just took a peek out and saw Dre lying butt naked on his stomach with a leg partially hanging off the bed asleep as he turned back and quietly closed the door.

As the days past, Dre begin to feel both confused and ashamed of the way he was feeling but couldn't shake off this curiosity that was starting to burn in him and the more he suppressed it the more it bothered him and Trevor already picking up on this kept a clever distance from him and only dealing and interacting with him when he had too but it was Friday and they were both going fishing together tomorrow like Trevor had told him and neither would be able to avoid each other then but Trevor figured that this would pass and the only reason he was sure Dre wanted to get down with him was because of the way he started acting because he acted in the same way when he was his age and curious about experimenting with Brent and more than that the outcome you have to deal with.

You risk ruining an friendship and form a complicated relationship with each other and the people around you start to sense it, If he engages in this he betrays the family who love him and took him in and he repays them by screwing their nephew behind their backs in their house, Dre could like the encounter and starts to develop feelings or not like it thinking he wanted it and create a awkwardness for the rest of his stay and the big thing…he's 16…there's no way I can fuck a kid…best to just leave it alone and pretend that whatever is happening is just all circumstantial and never go beyond that.

Dre spent most of his time alone in his room when he didn't have to be around family but now he was getting frustrated and tired of whatever this was suddenly going on between them and where it came from but got tired of Trevor not conversing with him like before and went to go find him.

Damn what the fuck happen all of a sudden? We were so cool up till now…what changed between us? It's that fucking fat ass dike fault for setting us up like that…when your girls doing that its different but when your guys that's a whole other story…we just don't play like that period…weird ass country games…fucking spin the bottle shit…had me kissing a nigga like a fag…twisted ass bullshit and I did it…I'm not gay…Is he gay or hiding something…he the one that started acting fucking weird and avoiding me so what he hiding… Dre thought to himself closing his eyes then opening them and got up leaving the room and started looking around the house for Trevor then went outside and saw his truck still in the yard and glanced over at his cousin Erika sitting on the porch swing reading a book.

Hi there she said.

Sup said Dre walking up to the front of the porch and stood raising his arm on the post and just looking out into the distance across the yard in silence as Erika looked up at him and studied him.

If you're looking for Trevor he's around the back said Erika.

Oh alright but naw…I just came out to get some air said Dre.

Okay said Erika going back to reading.

So you ready to go fishing with Trevor tomorrow city boy? She asked.

Ye should be interesting…never did that before he said remaining quite a while longer.

After another short moment Dre finally spoke aloud.

Guess I'll look around the farm at the pets he said walking toward the back section of the house as Erika looked at him and grinned to her self and shook her head and went back to reading.

Dre walked toward the back end of the estate and came up to a fence and sat on it watching Trevor in the distance playing Frisbee with his dog then playfully let him wrestling him to the ground as he finally got up to his knee and rubbed his head then glanced over at Dre looking at him and stood up and raised his arm.

What up city! He yelled aloud as Dre nodded and raised 2 fingers then Trevor finally walked over to him.

So what's good…you alright? Trevor asked him.

Ye I'm cool said Dre.

We leave tomorrow at 12 said Trevor.

Alright…I'll be ready said Dre.

So how's your arm healing? Trevor asked him.

I just wrapped it with a new bandage this morning…its healed but that scar still there…its ugly man…don't want nobody looking at it said Dre.

Let me see it said Trevor.

Naw said Dre.

Only girls are scared to show bruises and scars, take that shit off and stop looking handicapped around here said Trevor.

Shut up nigga…said Dre looking at him then at his arm and unwrapped it taking it off as Trevor took his arm looking at the long scar.

Are you bitching over that? You need to rock that shit like a battle scar said Trevor taking the bandage from him.

Dre looked away for a moment then back at him. Are you and I good? He asked.

Yeah of course we are…why you ask that? Trevor asked him.

I don't know man just feel like- just asking that's all…said Dre.

Yeah man we definitely cool...just think I've been doing a little too much with you lately, being a bad influence with all the smoking and drinking… just want to get away from doing all that with you and do activities with you that are more appropriate…you know what I mean…for a little bit I guess I forgot about the fact that you were 16 but you act mannish as hell said Trevor.

Yo what are you talking about? I was doing all those things long before I met you said Dre.

Still doesn't make it right though…I just built this respect and relationship with your Uncle and he trusts me to watch over you and I don't want to compromise that in anyway…damn, if only you were a few years older than I wouldn't be feeling guilty as fuck you know...I see a lot of you in me at your age said Trevor.

Ye I feel you bra…damn, just my luck…a recovering bad apple with morals and values…you disgust me said Dre as Trevor laughed a little.

Damn what a pity…just to be clear you weren't forcing me into doing anything I didn't want to do…Alright so I guess it's good old fashion wholesome country fun from here on out...I'm not giving up cigarettes though man gotta have some kind of pleasure…so was that all it was…why you were kind of avoiding me lately? Dre asked him.

Trevor looked at him for a moment and nodded but wasn't entirely convinced he was being honest.

Well to be clear once again…no matter what it was we did, I wouldn't hold you accountable…I always take full responsibility of my own actions and it wouldn't change anything between us…quiet as kept like it all has been thus far you know said Dre.

Trevor looked at him as if trying to figure out if he was finally saying what he thought.

This kid is bold…either being curious has taken him over the age or he has done this before thought Trevor.

Time to test him by implying something on some level and see if how he gets down thought Dre.

I just like you man real talk and you cool people…I love my girl like I said before but like I said also…I'm down here to have fun and see what's up should something unexpectedly pop off and we both know and understand what it is and all it can be then we good you know…I'm into trying shit if you are…thats just the kind of dude I am you know said Dre.

Yeah I feel you man said Trevor not thinking too much into his comment and looking off.

Alright confirmed…he not gay…had to do that…I just was curious thought Dre to himself.

So how does a guy blow off some steam around here beyond the obvious said Dre.

Blow shit up replied Trevor as Dre looked at him strangely.

Soon, on another section of the acres Trevor stood holding his shot gun smoking a cigarette.

I knew you country people hid some your big firearms somewhere around here nice toy said Dre.

Thanks was a Christmas present for my 13th birthday…I know that it might seem dangerous giving a kid a powerful firearm at such a age but my father let me shoot my first one when I was 12…your Uncle is a big gun collector…during deer hunting season we hunt game for sport…I'm very certain that you've held a gun before big city but have you have fired one? Trevor asked him.

No but I had one for protection, my cousin gave it to me and when my mom was snooping around my room and found some stuff that she didn't want their I was lucky she didn't find it so I got rid of it...I had a glock nine millimeter said Dre.

You ever held something like this said Trevor.

Naw...can I? Dre asked him.

Trevor handed it to him. Yeah be careful now...he said.

Dre held the semi heavy weapon in his hand. Damn...feel like fucking terminator with this shit in tow he said.

You want to shoot it? Trevor asked him.

I can? Hell yeah said Dre.

This is a old model Remington but still powerful, if you don't hold it right you could knock your shoulder out of joint from the force of the back fire...packs a pretty nasty punch from the front and the back side...I'm going to teach you how to hold one of these and shoot it he said.

Trevor went to the back of his truck and took an old large vase out rolled up in a cloth then walked across the field and placed it on top of a fence post then turn and walked back and stood beside Dre then told him how to hold it properly straightening his arms and aiming.

Go ahead he told him backing up as Dre walked forward and took aim as Trevor watched to make sure he was holding it properly then lit a cigarette and watched as Dre fired shattering the old vase to pieces.

Yeah! Damn that's what's up said Dre.

Trevor smiled walking over. Did that take some of your edge off? He asked.

Ye that definitely did the trick...I want to blast up more shit that was fun said Dre.

Trevor went to his truck and took out another vase and sat it up on the post then took the old Remington from Dre and locked 2 more slugs into the barrels and snapped it lock walking forward and took aim then fired shattering another vase.

Old faithful got some power said Dre.

Maybe during deer hunting season and you have a weekend...you come back down here and join us said Trevor.

Ye cool...I never thought I'd say this but I would definitely make it a priority to come back here to spend a weekend said Dre as Trevor grinned to himself.

Chapter 16

That Saturday Noon, Dre and Trevor packed up all the equipment and fishing poles they would need for their outing then hooked the boat moving trailer to Trevor's truck and were set for their trip to the lake.

Trevor and Dre walked out of the house with a full hand of other things they would need.

Damn, Auntie packed a big ass picnic basket…we got the hook up, just hope that Yogi and Boo boo don't show up to jack us for our shit man said Dre.

Trevor laughed a little to himself. Yeah man, apparently there's no such thing as a light snack in this house…you may get bored as shit at times out here but one thing you won't ever be is hungry he said.

I can't believe my Uncle backed out on this outing at the last minute to go finish some things at the farm…this is the weekend and all he wants to do is do work or something like that…man he never takes a break to just relax or have downtime does he? Dre asked him.

No not often, that's just the life of a farmer…work work work said Trevor.

Well all work in no play makes up for a dull day, let's hit the road and ride that boat said Dre getting into the truck.

Alright, liking your enthusiasm already man said Trevor getting in.

As soon as they had reached the wooded trail that led to the lake Trevor was met by some people he knew who were just leaving out who were already feeling good from a couple beers.

Hey Trevor, I see you taking the boat out for a swim…you picked a good time because they really biting out there today whose your buddy there? The driver asked him.

This is Dre, he's staying with his Uncle and Aunt for the summer…Dre this is our neighbors from across the lake Dean and his brother Tony said Trevor.

Hey what's up Dre told them.

Your Uncle tells us that your all the way from the big city huh, nice to finally meet you Dre…hey me and my brother are headed into town to get some supplies for this big gathering and cook out were having this afternoon, wives are back at the place right now setting up the party spot so after your both done fishing you can drop by and kick back with us going to be plenty of food and drink so feel free to have at it…going to be more than enough to share said Dean.

Thanks, I think well drop by and check it out said Trevor.

Alright you fellas enjoy the fishing and we'll see you there said Dean as they drove off.

So those are your big party neighbors across the lake huh said Dre.

Yep that's them said Trevor driving down the trail.

Once they arrived to the lake they backed the truck up and unloaded the boat at the ramp then drove it out to the middle of the lake and settled in to fishing.

Man, almost twenty minutes have past and I haven't hooked a single thing yet…this is the hardest fish I ever had to catch if you know what I mean and you already landed like 3 big ones…I'm thinking they like your bait better or something said Dre.

Your bait is fine, just be patient man…they'll come to you…their just playing hard to get right now said Trevor.

Gotcha said Dre who was getting bored of the silence between them and decided to ask him more about the guy Brent who had stopped by the house weeks ago and he seemed to have some kind of mysterious past with and the hug before he left was way past bromance and more so a romance…

So that guy that stopped by the house weeks ago name Brent, you 2 are good friends huh? asked Dre.

Yeah, years back he use to live with his family right on the other end of your Uncle's land and we worked together on your Uncles farm and in our down time we hunted, went fishing, camping, hanging out at the bar spot in town playing pool and picking up chicks… all that… we had some good times man and one day his father got news that he inherited his father's construction company when he died so they packed up and moved away to the big city to run the family business… they still own some land and estates down here that his dad refused to sell to this day because your Uncle has been trying to talk him into it for a long time so he can use it to expand his farming business but it seems his efforts weren't in vain because he told me that Brent's dad is finally ready to settle and offer him a price for it.

But anyway the family would come back once in a while to visit and Brent had a house down here on his father's land so he use to come back in forth and stay there and we'd get up like old times but after a while he stopped visiting…went up to the city and fell in love with a city girl who he married and has a kid with now so that's where all his time is focused around now when he's not helping his dad's business… we still cool though…just moved on with our lives said Trevor.

Oh okay cool…said Dre.

Yo…I think I got something my fucking line is finally dangling… yeah…feel that mother fucker squirming beneath there….Oh shit this one's got a fat ass said Dre.

What are you waiting for man, reel that sucker on in said Trevor.

I'm reeling it in man, I'm reeling it…got a tough one…ye,keep fighting… but your ass mine now said Dre pulling his line up to a giant fish on his hook.

Oh damn man, check out the size of this big fucker…think I just landed the big daddy of the pond said Dre.

That's a very good catch big city…see I told you, good things come to those who wait said Trevor.

Yes sir… so it seems…now I got my little smile on my face for today said Dre looking at the big fish.

After while, they rode across the other side of the lake to the boat dock outside the back of Dean's house where crowds had gathered for a cook out and tied it to the post then walked the rest of the way there and were greeted by Dean.

Looks like you finally made it, how was fishing out there? Dean asked them.

We did damn good Dean, they were biting just like you told us and looks like we're going to have a big fish fry tomorrow evening at the house said Trevor.

That's what's up, well join the rest of the crowd and kick back one he said handing Trevor a can of beer.

Thanks said Trevor.

Are you old enough to drink? Dean asked Dre.

Isn't 16 legal drinking age down here? Dre asked him.

You damn right, had my first drink with my pops when I was 15 and comon I was your age once so I know this probably isn't your first time throwing back one but I'm not trying to get you in trouble with your uncle passing out cold ones to his nephew minor but I won't tell if you don't…shit this the weekend, enjoy it said Dean handing him one.

That's what's up said Dre popping it open and drinking it down.

Look the kid guzzles it down like a pro, knew it wasn't his first time comon join in on the crowd said Dean as they followed him up there Trevor heard a loud familiar voice from the crowd it was his once in a while screw buddy Shayla already drunk and talking shit to a couple other guys.

Yall mother fuckers kill me talking about how much meat you packing, prove it then take that mother fucker out right now and let me see that big ass country dick you been bragging to me about for the past hour…what? Go around the yard and you'll show me? What you need time to get it hard or something? Just unzip your pants right now and give me a sneak peek aint nobody watching like that…just as I thought you all talk go get me another drink Mr. tiny…I can tell there isn't much there just by looking anyway but for real though I can't see it? She said glancing up and saw Trevor and Dre.

Hey Trevor! Hey Um-Drew what's going on Shayla spoke unsure if that was the correct name.

It's Dre he said.

Yep I thought it was that, so what's good with you 2 said Shayla.

Just rode in from the lake, was out there fishing said Trevor.

Oh really, why you out there hunting fish when you got the catch of the day standing in front of you…look at you with your cap, wife beater and cute little fishing shorts on my sexy fishermen…damn you know you going to have to take me on side of the house in that shed that got out back before you leave and give me what I been wanting… that damn big black rod that curve like a hook…got me all hot and bothered right now just thinking about it when you working the shit…you straight murder this…eh Drew what you did to my girl Aubrey said Shayla.

What you mean? Dre asked her.

I don't know what you told her that night but after refusing to pop her cherry telling her something about having respect for herself and saving it for love…bitch had an epiphany and went to go join a convent she said she going to be a nun and dedicate her life to a man that she knows truly love her God…I told her that's what's up and good luck with that though personally I aint giving up my life to be no fucking nun…I gotta be where the men at and I can't getem rocking those ugly black and white uniforms I'm sorry…can't do it said Shayla taking another swallow of her cup of beer.

Word, that's good for her said Dre.

Huh? What you mean and why didn't you break my girl off? I know you were feeling her and shit and she pretty so what was the problem why didn't you knock it down like a true g city boy? asked Shayla.

Because I valued the fact that she was saving herself for the right dude and at the time it just wasn't me said Dre.

Unhm so you say but I don't know about you big city…you got a pretty girl trying to give you the business and you all soft dick and preacher man on her…you sure that you even like girls because I got this suspicion that you might be a little…you know…plucking chickens on the other team said Shayla.

What? I aint gay…fuck you talking about said Dre.

Okay cool calm it down just wondering, think you too cute to be wasting all that dick like that and you got this strong hint of pretty boy in you…so now that innocent Aubrey gone what's good…you me and Trevor can do the damn thing yall up for that 2 on one said Shayla.

Isn't that your sugar daddy Sam over there talking with Dean and them? Trevor asked her.

I mean yeah but so what, his old ass aint hitting on nothing and all he can do is give me that money he got and be lucky I let him feel all over the tidies and ass from time to time…Imma give that crusty ass a heart attack and take all his shit watch my word…but right now he watching me hard, I'm going to send him up to the store to get him away from here in a little bit and we can get it popping…want you both to double this mouth she said walking off.

Damn yo girl a straight up freak and she is kind of cute…I guess a little head doesn't sound too bad…that's all I want from a big girl anyway said Dre.

Trevor grinned at him and shrugged in agreement.

As the gathering continued, Shayla got more drunk and started running her mouth even more.

How about me, Trevor, Aubrey and Drew-damn I mean Dre got together back at the house and played some cards and then played a game of spin the bottle and shit got really freaky…before we knew it I was deep throating coke bottles, Aubrey taking out her tidies flashing everybody and Dre whipping out his dick and little guy here is packing some serious something down there and then I dared Trevor and Dre to kiss and them niggas did that shit... like got all into it tonguing and everything...we couldn't pull them apart for nothing once they started said Shayla.

Yo why you lying like that laughed Dre.

Really? Trevor asked her.

I'm just playing...they actually freaked the fuck out at first trying to hold on to their man hood and shit but I coheres them mother fuckers into doing it and they had a quick spit moment...I stays turning out niggas though...just how I get down...damn I need a fresh drink, Trevor can you get me one said Shayla.

Yeah replied Trevor getting up from the chair and walking across the yard.

Thank you said Shayla after him.

I'm going to break that nigga in and make him mine watch my word...he just playing hard to get right now but I always get what I want sooner or later said Shayla.

Shayla looked at another girl drinking and talking to one of the guys there.

Hey Holly, We havent really talked since you got here like you throwing mad shade or something said Shayla.

Oh girl it aint like that, we cool said Holly.

Girl please, you know you dont like me and I damn sure dont like you...you are such a bitch that it's unbelievable...fucking worthless is what you are to be frank said Shayla.

Why dont you like me, what have I ever done to you girlfriend? Holly asked her.

Shayla looked at her for a moment: You really don't know do you? She asked her.

That's why I'm asking said Holly.

Shayla sighed and got up and walked over standing infront of her and twisted her lip.

Well…said Holly.

Because you're a whore Holly and I'm one too and 2 whores cant get along simple as that said Shayla.

Dean's brother came over to the table near Dre and looked around rubbing his wrist.

What's wrong you lost something? I know it can't be your mind you lost that a long time ago fucking with that ex wife of yours Debbie…I told you that bitch was crazy and jealous and already ran a couple of her boyfriends in the past over with her truck but no you had to be another speed bump…glad you left her though…love Debbie but bitch got problems for real said Shayla.

I sat my watch down right here on this table, just a moment ago and now it's gone anybody seen it said Tony as the crowd shrugged.

Nope but I know you must be talking about that expensive Rolex you had for a long time, it was the only damn thing your ex wife left you with after the divorce and she took all your shit…bitch bad said Shayla.

Tony looked at Dre. Hey man you see the watch that was up here where you was sitting that cup that belonged to you? He asked.

I saw it but naw man I didn't touch it or nothing or know where it is said Dre.

Tony looked at Dre and saw his tatted up city boy disposition and wasn't buying it. I guess it must have walked off or something then… it was right here beside you man just saying he said.

Okay but I didn't take your watch man nor touch it…I don't know if you accusing me of jacking your bling but if I want one I can buy one said Dre.

I believe you man so you wouldn't mind emptying your pockets then? Tony asked him.

What? replied Dre getting up standing in front of him as Shayla got big eyed and turn her head away starching it. Oh shit…she mumbled.

Look I told you I didn't take it and I'm not stripping unless it's to fuck something so stop fucking crying to me about a damn watch because I don't even wear them said Dre.

Trevor came back over. Whats going on? He asked.

Yo check your boy Trevor he saying that I stole his shit and aint touch nothing said Dre.

My watch was right there beside him just a couple minutes ago and if he didn't take it than why is he getting so defensive about me just wanting him to prove it said Tony.

Yo man real talk, you better get out my face with that said Dre.

Why you jumping to conclusions so fast man, he said he didn't take it and I believe him said Trevor.

Yeah but he your friend from the big city and we know they like flashy stuff…he was telling me a little while ago how much he liked it said Tony.

It was a fucking compliment fool and I think I better go before I really flip the fuck off this dude pissing me off T said Dre.

You not leaving with my watch man said Tony.

Naw you right I'm not going to leave before I knock a few of your teeth out said Dre.

Yo Dre chill man said Trevor holding his arm back as Dean walked up.

Hey what's going on over here said Dean.

Somebody stealing shit and I'm trying to find out who said Tony.

Stealing what? Dean asked him.

My watch said Tony.

Trevor glanced over in the distance and saw Dean's daughters tossing the watch back and forth.

Eh you mean that watch said Trevor as Tony looked over.

Annie sweetie come over here said Dean as she ran over.

What daddy? She asked.

Did you take your Uncles watch? He asked.

We were just playing with it…sorry she said giving it to Tony who felt dumbfounded.

Face cracked said Shayla.

So I guess we solved that out said Trevor.

Damn, eh man I want to apologize for accusing you-said Tony.

Naw fuck you and your apology...you judging me and you accusing me of shit and you don't know anything about me...I may be a lot of things but I'm not a thief...yo Trevor I'm ready to bounce the fuck up out of here...nice party he said walking off.

Trevor I didn't know said Tony.

Still...that wasn't cool putting him on blast like that man if you didn't see him do it...enjoy the rest of the party though think were leaving for today...see you later Dean and have a good one said Trevor walking off.

Damn....that was fucked up Tony and you ran off the best dick up in here before I could get to it...I'm so pissed with you right now she said taking a sip of her drink.

Chapter 17

One weekend, Dre was in his room talking with his girlfriend Gia on the phone not really listening to her as he watched Trevor in the bathroom from his room with his door open shaving his face in the mirror with his athletic tone bare chest and looking at his jeans just below the nape of his ass and he could tell he wasn't wearing any underwear…just by glance anyway and somehow drifted off from the conversation with Gia who was talking about school and girls she didn't like or who was beefing and wanting to fight.

Hello-Dre…Dre! She yelled.

Ye I'm listening said Dre.

Know the fuck you won't, what did I just say then? Gia asked him.

I mean I wasn't following you word for word because you be talking fast sometimes but I'm listening said Dre.

Umhm…what are you doing? Are you jacking off right now? If you are you better be thinking about me said Gia.

I was when I did this morning said Dre.

Oh for real awe that was so sweet…just hold on baby and you'll be getting the real thing again 24/7…my poor boo bear over there stuck in the country getting blue balls…I know its selfish of me but I'm kind of glad you're in a place where you in the middle of nowhere and can't go fuck bitches behind my back…I trust you to be faithful but some females are straight hoes and be trying to throw they ass in a nigga face and don't care if he got a girl…ugh,I hate this long distance in fact I'm thinking about something because I can't wait another 2 months to see you/hit that said Gia.

What you thinking? Asked Dre as he watched Trevor wash his face in the sink then dry it with a towel and go back to his connected door in the bathroom to his room and close it back.

About coming down there to see you and bring the baby one of these weekends…plus your people can meet our undisputed love child and we can spend time together…I'm sure a bus goes out there in the desert or wherever it is they stay…I'll go anywhere on earth to be with you even if I have to come to that barnyard…do you want to see me and your son? Gia asked him.

Ye baby…of course I do, so do you think you really coming? Dre asked her.

Yep…I'll let you know when I get there and we can spend the weekend together…you don't think your people are going to trip do you? Gia asked him.

Naw of course not, I think they would love to see that visit and so would I said Dre.

Awe…I'm coming to see my baby…that mother of yours can't separate love as ours that easily…I love you Dre…you think we going to be able to sneak and do something when everybody sleep said Gia

Dre laughed a little.

After a bit, Dre went outside and saw Trevor washing his truck and cleaning it in silence not really speaking when he sat down nearby on a stool then wiped it dry with a towel but it was weird that he was acting more quiet and distant from everybody for the past couple days and he wondered why no one seemed to notice it but him but he figured as much time as he had spent with him thus far he'd be able to read him a lot more than them.

I see you giving her a spit shine said Dre.

Yeah man, keep her dirty going up and down those dirt trails to your uncle's farm…I want her to look nice for a little ride out in a while said Trevor.

Word, so where are you going? Dre asked him.

I got this place I have to go too but when I get back maybe we can go into town or wherever you want said Trevor.

Alright cool…said Dre.

Is everything good with you? Dre asked him.

Yeah…I'm good man said Trevor continuing to wipe down his truck and Dre left it alone.

Soon Dre walked back into the house after Trevor had drove off and went into the kitchen where Erika was just tightening a lid on a jar and looked up at him and smiled.

Oh I see Trevor left his little riding buddy home for once, he even took his dog Charlie with him this time who occupying the spot you stole from him lately said Erika.

Ye whatever…I don't be trying to follow him everywhere…everybody need their alone time said Dre.

But in seriousness though today is a very personal day for him… which is why he wants to be alone and he gets in that little mood every year around this time…guess the memories are still as painful now as they were then said Erika.

What do you mean? Dre asked him.

Today 7 years ago, is the day he lost his parents in the house fire… there was nothing left after that incident and the only thing he was able to recover was a smoldering family album that he keeps to this day…half burned and damaged pictures that they had but it's all he has to remember them by…every year this day he goes into town and buy some flowers than ride out in the far edges of the country and puts them on their grave…afterwards he goes out to a liquor house in town alone gets pissy drunk comes home sleeps it off and in a few days he's himself again…but there were a few times Trevor drinking got a little out of control and he couldn't work and would lock himself in his room or disappear altogether somewhere but my dad talked to him and he's been pretty good ever since said Erika.

Damn,I know it must be some shit to have to experience a tragedy like that…to be honest if that happened to my dad right now considering our relationship currently…I'm not sure if I would even shed a tear said Dre.

Don't say that said Erika.

It's the truth, I mean he's worthless and never done anything or been there for me...who is he to me if he hasn't been my dad really tell me? Dre asked Erika who was silent and unable to answer it.

Your dad,my Uncle,has been more of a father to me in this month alone than my real dad has been my whole life said Dre.

I'm not even trying to go there, I'm in a pretty good mood and don't feel like even thinking about him to ruin it he said walking outside to the back porch and across the backyard when he saw his uncle driving up with a load of stacked hay.

Glad your still here nephew, I want you to help me put this hay away in the barn said his uncle.

Yes sir said Dre.

You're doing a good job down at the farm working with Trevor but I want you too to focus more on work and stop talking so much and horse playing with all of that wrestling when I turn my back...you can be buddies but I prefer you be work buddies...time in a place for everything said his uncle.

Yes sir, I apologize I'll cut it out...Uncle my girlfriend Gia is thinking about coming down here to visit one weekend soon and bring the baby to see me and meet all of you...its cool if she comes right? Dre asked him.

Well of course it is nephew...I think that's a great idea...I'll let your Auntie know so she can have the guest room prepared for a visit...now I know it's been a while since you seen her and your little boy hormones jumping up and down but you going to have to control yourself while you living under my roof...don't be making another baby while she there understand? Uncle Richard told Dre.

Yes sir...no more babies for me for a while said Dre.

Good, birth control might not be a bad option either...do your business but protect yourself and wait to be fruitful and multiply later on in life when you're both in a better position to take care of kids and yourselves said his uncle.

Later that night after dinner,Dre had just got back up to his room and put on a wife beater and jogging pants when Trevor knocked on his door.

Ye come in said Dre.

Hey man…are you going to bed? Trevor asked him.

Naw not yet but probably just listen to music or something for a while…what's up though? Dre asked him.

I was about to go in town to a bar spot and get a couple drinks was wondering if you wanted to roll with me…you can't drink but they got pool tables there you can do that grinned Trevor.

Alright cool, let me throw something on and I'll be ready to go said Dre.

Okay said Trevor leaving out.

Soon they both put on their jackets and left out the house as Erika stood folding her arms.

Well how about that…on the saddest day of his life he invites the baddest one in the house to keep him company…smiled Erika and went upstairs.

They rode into town to the bar and while Dre played rounds of pool with a couple guys there Trevor sat at the bar getting countless shots in as Dre glanced over at him every time he said hit me and they slid another glass to him..Dre never seen anyone get them down like that and as the hours past Trevor was getting really fucked up because Dre could hear him at the bar singing, talking loud and laughing which was unusual for him to act this way like he was a whole new person then the bar closed and he heard Trevor trying to get another round.

Comon baby girl, just one more drink said Trevor.

No Trevor, the bar is closed and I think you had enough said the bar tender.

I'll know when I've had enough and I pay damn good money in

here so look out…one more…promise then I'm done please? Trevor asked in with puppy dog eyes.

No…sorry Trevor, go home and get some sleep she said.

Man fuck that…I'm not ready to go home and sleep it off you go home and go to sleep Jalisa said Trevor.

Yo homie said Dre walking over.

Eh what's up yo…look they shutting down here man so we about to head over to the liquor house for a bit where the service keeps going like a seven eleven let's roll partner said Trevor getting up and stumbled a little as Dre caught him.

Damn yo you fucked up…Naw I don't think you need anymore said Dre.

Yeah you right…I need more said Trevor.

Naw man I said you don't stop twisting my words laughed Dre a little.

Wait hold on-said Trevor.

What? Dre asked him.

Yo…When you get here? Trevor asked looking at Dre strangely.

Yo I rode with you…damn, you far gone man. Give me the keys I'm driving you home…think you might crash or something speed and alcohol don't mix said Dre.

You right…that's why I'm choosing one…alcohol, tell you what I give you the keys and you drive my truck home-wait you know how to drive right? Trevor asked him.

Ye man I do said Dre.

Oh alright…so you take the keys and drive the dog home and I'm going to walk over to the liquor house and then call you when I want you to pick me up said Trevor.

Charlie didn't come with us said Dre.

Oh…I love that dog like a son I swear man…love my Charlie… fucking best friend for like a hand full of years…stole his ass from those white people and never gave him back…he stay with me always and forever said Trevor.

Ye I know man you love Charlie and right now I bet he miss you and want to see you so I'm taking you home alright? Dre asked him.

Home? Fuck that Dre I want another drink first said Trevor.

Dre took his keys out his pocket.

Naw you going home now bring your ass on said Dre putting his arm around his shoulder and walked him out.

You a mean little fucker big city...thought we was cool...you tripping said Trevor.

Take care of him and have a safe drive home said the bartender as Dre nodded and waved.

Bye Jalisa! Trevor yelled back waving.

Soon Dre had them on the highway headed home.

Man...I hate doing the same shit over and over day in and out... work,home,work,home...wish I could just drive away...I don't have family beyond your relatives man...I love your people...don't get me wrong...just wish I had people of my own...family said Trevor.

I know homie...they care and love you man...me included said Dre.

Say wha? You love me? Trevor asked him.

I'm saying I care about you man laughed Dre a little.

Why? You don't even know me like that said Trevor.

I know enough and you good people that's why Dre told him.

Oh word...I care about you too big city now pull over for a sec said Trevor.

Why? Dre asked him.

Because I gotta fucking piss yo bad said Trevor.

Dre pulled over on the side of the road as Trevor got out and walked a little over unbuckling his pants and pulled them down past his ass and grabbed hold of his dick and pissed as he sanged to him self as Dre grinned shaking his head and turned away from his apple booty muscular cheeks in the dim moonlight.

Damn…now that felt good said Trevor pulling his pants back up and buckling them up then got in the car.

Are you straight now? Dre asked him.

Yep…I'm good said Trevor.

Soon they got back to the house and Dre made sure Trevor got inside.

We home peoples said Trevor a little loud.

Yo shut up man…comon said Dre helping him upstairs to his room and closed and locked his door then Trevor walked over to his bed and flopped down on it.

Damn homie I'm fucked up…said Trevor.

I know, now you can take your drunken ass to sleep said Dre going over and took Trevor's boots off.

Get up said Dre as he got him out of his jacket and wife beater.

Thanks man said Trevor.

You welcome said Dre.

Eh…can you stay and talk with me for a little bit? Trevor asked him.

Ye said Dre taking off his jacket then went over and sat on the bed beside him as Trevor relaxed his arms behind his head.

You want to know something big city? I'm glad you came down here…I like your company…know you paying off your debt and ready to bounce up out this boring ass country but glad you around for now….good to have some male company besides your Uncle you know…somebody to hang and chill with…talk too shit like that said Trevor.

Ye…said Dre.

Do you know how it feel man? To work from morning to evening and keep yourself focused and busy on work and how good it feel when the day end to just lay back and relax? Not me…even when I relax I have time to think about shit I don't want too…the past…my parents, best friend Brent…everything I love and care about I lose…

loved that guy hard…I've moved on because shit, that's the life we live…I'm good now though…I'm really good now said Trevor.

Dre was shocked. He loved dude…I knew something was up with them he thought to himself.

Fuck yo…that's why I hate getting too close to people I start to like because once I do…they always gotta leave me…stop fucking bitching and moaning to you yo…know you don't want to hear that shit said Trevor.

Yo, I'm not good with giving people advise and shit but…stop beating yourself up over things and people from the past…just let it go and go forward the best way you can…all you can do said Dre.

Trevor nodded as a tear fell down the side of his face he closed his eyes and tightened his jaw not wanting Dre to see him so vulnerable and emotional but he was a guy and despite what he was raised to believe that man are suppose to be strong and suppress feelings that make them weak…man still have feelings.

Focus on the now and enjoy the moment homie…live in it and be happy…let that shit go…let it go said Dre as he leaned in slowly and kissed his neck then glided his hand down his chest slowly as Trevor closed his eyes moaning to himself then Dre slid his hand down his pants groping Trevor's dick slowly stroking it then try to unbuckle his belt as Trevor took his hand and stopped it.

See you in the morning man said Trevor as Dre looked at him and nodded.

Ye…see you in the am said Dre getting up and clicked off his light then went through the bathroom connected to their rooms and closed the door.

Chapter 18

That Monday when Dre was helping his uncle work on the farm with Trevor, the day went by as a slow and quiet one…neither of them spoke about what happened that night and Dre started to wonder if what he did was the reason Trevor was acting standoffish to him a little…but Trevor was so drunk that night he wondered if he even remembered it…but left it alone…on the way home was just as quiet as Dre smoked a cigarette and looked off in the other direction.

That night at dinner, as they ate Dre kept making quick looks at Trevor as he ate who looked at him back and at one point took a deep sigh as if having some kind of pent up tension and Dre was starting to wonder if he had made a big mistake coming onto him like that.

Damn…why the fuck did I have to go and do that…now shit really awkward between us…I mean he got down with dudes before so why he so bent out of shape about it…maybe because he don't do that shit no more and I just out-ed myself…fuck…didn't think about that thought Dre to himself.

Later that night, Dre laid in his bed unable to sleep as he relaxed his arms behind his back just staring at the ceiling fan then saw the bathroom light turn on from beneath the door as Trevor moved about in there for a few minutes than left out turning off the light and heard him close the door from the other side…a minute later he heard his room door open in the hall and him walking downstairs…then closed his eyes and listened to dirt crunching outside his window as he got up and stood to the window and saw Trevor walking toward the back yard area of the house with a backpack in hand then he went inside of the shed turning on the light and closed the door.

Dre thought to himself for a moment then walked into the bathroom turning on the water and closed the door.

Trevor sat inside of the shed in a chair pouring him self a glass of liquor and drinking it than smoked the blunt he had fired up.

Yo he heard a voice from outside the shed as Dre peeped in then came inside.

Aint that some fucked up shit man, you out here smoking without me…I outta fuck you up said Dre walking over.

What are you still doing up man, we got work in the morning said Trevor not really looking at him as he swallowed down the drink.

I know that…but it seem to not be stopping you from getting a little buzz on in here…so I guess you getting in another night of the good stuff huh said Dre.

I'm nowhere near as fucked up now as I was that night and I don't plan too…I just felt like having a little bit that's all said Trevor.

I want some said Dre.

You want some what? Trevor asked him.

That said Dre pointing at the blunt and took it pulling it hard and gave it back to Trevor and some of this he said taking his liquor and pouring some more in the glass and drank it down.

Damn…that's good shit…I thought you told me that you wasn't going to do those things with me anymore…why didn't you stop me? Dre asked him.

Eh that's on you big city, you going to do what you want too anyway…just hope in the morning your performance is up to par and you're not sluggish out there on the work front or your Uncle is going to be yelling at your ears until they fall off said Trevor.

I'll be good…I'm not the one going to sit in here and drink a whole bottle of 5th…think you need to cut back on that a little bit bra said Dre.

You need to take yo ass back in the house and stop killing my buzz Trevor laughed a little.

Word…damn homie, I see you get a little mean when you start

sipping…what's really good…you mad at me? Dre asked him.

Naw man, you always asking if I'm mad at you…should I be said Trevor.

You a tough dude to figure out at times, you know that right… you send clear and unclear vibes, mixed signals, no signals, hell your overall connection is just as shitty as the phone reception in this area said Dre.

Word big city…thanks said Trevor reaching for the bottle as Dre put his hand on it.

You want to let go of my bottle? Trevor asked him.

Nope…because you don't need this and whatever you think it does to help whatever you be feeling said Dre taking it from him than walked and put it on a shelf.

So you want to talk about what's really going on up there? Dre asked tapping his head.

You want to get in my head now…I'm good man really…were good… so end of that said Trevor.

Naw…not the end of that because I'm not good and deep down neither are you…tired of walking around here on egg shells when were around each other…I don't like it…there's this tension between us now and has been there for a while correct? Dre asked him.

Trevor looked at him for a moment. I don't have any problem with you big city he said.

I'm talking about sexual tension homie…you been horny for me and I been horny for you let's keep the shit real…that's why you be avoiding me because you scared that you going to act on it…not saying you gay cause I don't believe you are and I know I'm not gay but I have this feeling toward you…maybe because of the time we spend together or the way we vibe…hell all I know is that you make me horny nigga and you know I do the same for you so what we going to do about it because I told you what I was into while I'm down here should it pop off…so tell me,the truth will set you free said Dre.

Trevor looked at him for a moment and nodded his head grinning to himself.

It's not right man, feeling this way about you…I could give you a hundred reasons why we should just create a line in the sand…but it's getting fucking harder to control myself around you…for a while now said Trevor.

So you saying you want me? Dre asked him.

What? Trevor relied.

Do you want me… as in do you want to break me in that's what Dre asked him.

You're too young for me to fuck with like that and it wouldn't feel right…for one your 16, 2…how could I be living up under your people who trust me to look after you and smash you behind their back and 3…statutory rape said Trevor.

It's only rape if I say no and you can't take what somebody trying to offer to you homie and your only 20 get a grip said Dre.

Well I'll say no…no said Trevor.

Your mouth say no but your eyes say yes homie, fuck you so scared of not like I'm going to say shit said Dre going up to the shed door and looking out than closed it back and turned around.

What's good said Dre.

This is fucking crazy man said Trevor.

Ye it is…tired of chasing your ass around this house…nowhere to run now said Dre walking toward him then mounted him in the chair and put his arms around his neck and looked him in the eyes.

You ever…do this with a dude before? Trevor asked him.

Naw…well haven't ever went this far…guess you can say I'm one of them curious cats…you act like I just proposed to you…I just want to fuck said Dre kissing his neck.

How you know you want to try it? Trevor asked him.

Shit…I mean I know it may hurt a little at first but I want to try it with you…only you…put this to rest once and for all said Dre.

Stand up said Dre as Trevor looked at him for a moment and stood up in front of him:

Dre took off his wife beater and threw it in the chair then took off Trevor's and threw it in the chair then unbuckled his pants a little then unbuckled Trevor's belt and unzipped his pants and slid them down just a little as he begin to grope his dick and feel his swollen fat nut sack.

Damn...you was the first time I touched a nigga piece besides my own...he pulled Trevor's pants all the way down then got down on his knees gripping the base of it then put his lips on it and begin sucking it slowly at first then begin stroking as it sucked it faster as Trevor closed his eyes and bit his lip as Dre licked his balls then sucked them while he stroked his dick in his hand as it made a slippery wet sound then begin to slowly deep throating it moaning as he did it as Dre took his hand and put it on the back of his head forcing him to make him take all his dick in his mouth then popped it out and stood up.

Fuck me said Dre as he unbuckled his pants and slid them down to his knees not even wearing underwear then stood against the wall putting his hands to it and propping his ass forward as Trevor walked up close to his back gliding his hands from his chest rubbing and squeezed his cheeks then slid his hand between them and felt that Dre had already lubed it up before he came outside.

Comon put it in said Dre.

You bring a condom out here? Trevor asked him.

Dre smacked his lips and grabbed his dick and pushed it forward into him slowly as both seem to gasp at the same time.

Go easy homie...ye just like that said Dre as Trevor slowly pushed his dick into his tight ass.

Fuck...comon give it to me said Dre.

As Trevor begin slowly thrusting forward then picking up speed as he held both sides of his hips pushing himself deeper and deeper into him then seemed to push forward almost taking him off his tippy toes smashing him harder as Dre bit his lip.

Ye…comon give me that nut said Dre as Trevor pumped his ass faster.

I'm about to cum…I'm about to- I'm pulling out said Trevor as Dre locked him in when he tried to pull out as Trevor yelled out busting all inside him panting hard as he fell against his neck.

Fuck man he said breathing hard.

Ye…Hope it was as good for you as it was for me said Dre turning around and pulling his pants up then grabbed his shirt and put it back on.

Yeah Trevor replied back still caught in the moment of ecstasy and very certain that he had just made the biggest mistake in his life.

Night man said Dre as he went to the shed door and peeped out then left out closing the door when he got back to the house and in bed he masturbated thinking of his girlfriend Gia and busted a huge load across his chest then cleaned himself up and went to sleep.

Chapter 19

The Next day work day was a pretty busy one at his uncle's farm, but that they got through fairly easy and there was no tension between Trevor and himself at all as if last night finally solved that issue and got it out the way…almost as if it was something that had to be done but they hadn't spoken anything about it since and there was nothing to be said after all it was what it was…toward late afternoon as they were headed into their last break:

I like the way you boys are moving along getting work done today at a quick pace, I told you what a good night's rest will do for you… keep up the good work said his uncle Richard.

Yes sir…those late nights can be hard on your back in the morning said Dre as Trevor cut a quick glance at him wondering why he just said that.

Take a 30 minute break and then we'll set out the fertilizer said his uncle walking off as they both walked to a small lounge area near his uncle's office inside.

Yo why did you say that just then? Trevor asked him.

Yo he doesn't know what I'm talking about, chill damn said Dre.

Still, be careful with that said Trevor.

Dre smirked to himself it was kind of funny how scary Trevor was acting a bit now every since they got down and for many obvious reasons but there was no need for him to be it was going to be quiet as kept.

They both stood near Trevor's truck on their break eating snacks and talking.

So…said Dre.

So what? Trevor replied back as if trying to pretend he didn't know what the question was going to be about as if nothing happened between them.

How many guys have you got down within the past between girls? asked Dre.

Well…my first was a girl name Jessica…I was 15 and around the time I started driving because she stayed on the deep ends of the country out here…I'd drive like a hour in a half to go see her and I can say she was my first love or at least what we think it to be at that age… messed around for a bit and she got pregnant…her parents were pissed about it and your Uncle took it fairly simple telling me that I was going to have to man up and prepare to take care of my responsibilities as a father after I told him and I was ready but she ended up miscarrying and months after went into this big depression and anger blaming me for all kinds of shit of not being there when I was working my hands to the bone trying to provide for the baby's arrival but she was convinced I was cheating on her too and truthfully I did…this girl Rachael but I was young and not ready to settle my whole life until what she wanted but I was trying…that took a big strain on the relationship and distant things between us and we just kind of moved on…wasn't a bad break up or anything but it just ended said Trevor.

Then I met this guy name Dennis who I use to just play pool with and shoot our guns together…real guns man…we both dated girls and talked about our latest scores but there was this curiosity in us both that were both too scared to act on or at least were suppressing…we both clearly wanted to experiment…with each other sort of speak…we didn't get too far into it…we jacked off together a few times and a couple times each other…did some oral but after that he kind of freaked out saying that it was all a mistake and he couldn't get down like that no more so I understood and respected that…crossing that line ruined our friendship I think because gradually we started to distant ourselves from each other and I went back to talking to another girl Patricia…we didn't date so much we were just drinking and smash buddies…then Brent and I started hanging together a lot… with us it was different we were friends but also a little more because we only got down with each other like that for about a year not messing with females at all…besides that 3some we did once in a while together with one said Trevor.

Then he and his family moved away and we did the long distant things for a bit but started drifting apart so it was what it was…I started dating girls again…that's when I dated Trixie for about a year… must admit though I fucked around on her with Brent a couple times during when he would come back down…I told him that I was in a relationship and we couldn't get down like that anymore but when I saw him and we spent time together it all just like…back on laughed Trevor.

Then I got down with Shayla and that's it said Trevor.

You forgot one, doing a boy still counts said Dre raising his hand.

Yeah…I guess I did Trevor grinned bashfully.

So what about you? He asked.

I lost my virginity to the baby sitter at 12 homie…I been with a handful of girls in my life about 5 or 6 give or take…only 2 of them I was in a relationship with…girl name Draya and then my current girl/baby momma Gia…Gia actually came along and stole me from Draya…Gia was a persistent, manipulative yet no bars hold type of chick doing whatever she had to do to get what she want…flirting and seducing me and trapped me into a pregnancy which is then when Draya found out and dumped my ass…I say she trapped me because she told me she was on the pill and yeah we used protection but there be times man where you just…slip up you know and now I gotta son trying to do what it do with that situation and I love her…not in-love but I love her a lot…our relationship just happened so fast…but I never got down with a dude not all the way…I was curious and met this one guy Coby…there was some touching and feeling on his part but I freaked out and couldn't go through with it…wasn't trying to be a fag or become gay by the experience I guess at the time said Dre.

So this guy....did the encounter happen during Gia or before? Trevor asked him.

Dre looked at him and grinned. It happened, almost happened or didn't happen period he said.

Trevor nodded and smiled wondering why he got a little defensive just then asking him that.

At the end of the day homie,I love my girl despite what other things I may be curious about or do...I let you pop my cherry so that mean something to me because that's not something I would do on a normal circumstance type basis you feel me...so respect me as a dude and I'll return it back...what I'm saying is don't treat or deal with me like a female that you would typically smash and go...I'm special remember that said Dre as Trevor beginned to panic confused if Dre was all of a sudden sprung out or catching feelings since he knocked him down and had to throw it back off his direction.

I feel you man but to be clear...you raped me last night grinned Trevor.

I didn't rape your grown ass and I didn't see you exactly trying to fight me off...you enjoyed it every minute of it so don't front... probably was the tightest thing you had in a while running around here fucking with all these loose ass females...I liked what we did....didn't you? Dre asked him.

Yeah it was cool man said Trevor.

Do you want to do it again? Dre asked him.

Considering if I wanted too?

I don't know man...I'm just thinking that for right now we just kind of play it cool until I can figure out some things said Trevor.

What? Figure out what things? Dre asked him.

Just right now...I prefer we just keep what we had going before we did that said Trevor.

Oh....alright...I'm good with that...we'll break about over....

see you inside I gotta talk to my uncle about something said Dre.

About what man? Trevor asked as if worried about something.

Nothing major said Dre poking out his lip and walked off.

Trevor begin to think out all the possibilities and get paranoid… fucking jail bait, why didn't I see it all before…I'd be stupid not to think that he wasnt scoping out this place and every situation going on since he arrived…what if he try to black mail me or extortion me for money to keep quiet about this…how far is he willing to go…he got a baby and its clear he'll do anything to take care of it…not to mention that slick comment he made to his uncle…trade dudes he talk about in the city do shit like this…how do I know he haven't been setting me all the while…he knows so much about me and what I got…he was so fucking bold and aggressive and the way he came at me…I didn't see it coming…how do I know he won't use this situation and the fact he underage to turn this on me…either way I look like a rapist or that I took advantage of him…not to mention the smoking and drinking I let him do…oh fuck Trevor thought to himself and lit a smoke and pulled it strong taking a deep breath.

Chapter 20

That Night, after dinner Dre sat in the living room talking to his girlfriend Gia on the phone as he drifted from their conversation and watched Trevor walked across the living room with his wife beater and ripped jeans on and went upstairs not even looking once in his direction and his new thing was just observing Trevor and trying to get in his head about how he was feeling or acting.

Dre…Dre did you hear me? Gia asked him.

Yeah I heard you babe…you said that you was coming down the week after next to visit me and I can't wait to see you in the baby… I'm really looking forward to it and I'll be right there at the bus station when you get off said Dre.

Umhm…are you okay? Gia asked him.

Ye…what you mean? Dre asked her.

I don't know but for the past couple days something been a little off with you…you been acting hella strange…you already know we got this bond and connection and I can pick up when something is going on so what is it said Gia.

It's nothing baby damn,I just be working hard and be a little tired at the end of the day that's all…sometimes we don't leave the farm till dark…I'm not acting weird…maybe you acting weird and trying to throw it on me because you feeling guilty about something said Dre.

No I'm not, I haven't done anything but take care of our child and be your emotional support while you all the way up there…I love you and I want to make sure you alright and keeping it 100 with me that's all said Gia.

I am…I swear on everything…I'm not down here cheating on you with any girls whatsoever that's my word said Dre.

Smh okay…you better not…but I trust you…I can't wait to see you said Gia.

I can't wait either said Dre.

Later that night, Dre laid in his bed with his hands relaxed behind his head just staring at the ceiling thinking to himself with his bathroom door open as Trevor came into the bathroom and brushed his teeth and gargled with his shirt off and boxers on as Dre stared in at him but Trevor didn't look into his room once and after he was done taking a piss he went back into his room and closed the door as Dre sighed to himself and closed his eyes for a while until he heard Trevor's door open part way but he never came out.

Hmm…is that an invitation? Dre thought to himself.

Dre got out of bed after a minute and walked across the room into the bathroom then stepped into Trevor's room which was dark and he was clearly in bed as Dre closed his door and went over to the other side of the bed and got inside of it with him then he wrapped his arms around him lying against his head for a moment then slide his hand beneath the cover and begin to stroke his already rock hard dick in his hand hearing low grunts from Trevor then took the cover off him and begin sucking his dick while stroking it as Trevor gently put his hand on the back of his head as Dre deep throated it but Dre wanted more aggression out of him as he once again took his hand and forced Trevor to make him sucker it deeper down his throat as Trevor's other hand begin to caress his back and groped his little plump cheeks in his hand then Dre popped it out his mouth and sat up some stroking it.

Comon said Dre as Trevor took some Vaseline off the dresser and lubed his ass up as he sat up and Dre laid down on his back as Trevor grabbed his legs and forced him up to him and slowly pushed his dick into him thrusting with ease as Dre stroked his dick but partially hard and precumming as Trevor pumped deep into him for a while and grabbed both his ankles fucking him harder as Dre begin to yell out a little but not loud enough for anyone to hear as Dre stopped him after a moment forcing him out of him then pushed Trevor down on the bed and crouched over him and gripped the base of his dick and slowly pushed it in as he sat down on it slowly at first than bouncing on it as he gripped both Trevor's arms.

Trevor begin to moan like a girl and caught himself the way he was throwing it on him.***damn…he spoke aloud in a manly voice to cover it up.

Dre easily took his dick out and mounted him playing with his nipples as Trevor grabbed his dick and started jacking off until he busted all across Dre's ass while Dre was still panting stroking his dick over him as Trevor tried to take it but Dre moved his hand stroking it faster busting all over his chest breathing hard but before they could relax in the moment there was a knock at Trevor's door.

Trevor saw Dre shoot him a quick glance in the dark then silently jump up and quickly go into the bathroom and silently closed the door as Trevor got up with a bewildered scared look on his face turning on the light and looked around and saw Dre's boxers that he left and wiped Dre's cum off his chest with them and throw them in his basket then put on his wife beater and jogging pants on and walk up to the door taking another few seconds to compose himself then opened the door slightly to hide his still hard dick and it was Erika.

Hey…what's up he said rubbing his eyes as if getting up and yawning from a good sleep.

Dre listened from the bathroom as Erika apologized for waking him so late but was telling him something about what his uncle wanted him to do in the morning before they leave and then heard Trevor close the door back as he went over to the bathroom and opened the door.

Dre walked into his room and looked around for his boxers as Trevor went over to the basket and held them up with cum he had wiped on them.

Sorry about that man…first things I grabbed Trevor whispered.

Nigga, you know when this shit dry it turn crusty and Auntie be doing laundry first thing in the morning, I don't want her seeing that said Dre.

It's yo shit man said Trevor as Dre snatched them and went into the bathroom and begin to wash them with some water to get it out then stuck them deep in the laundry basket as Trevor stood at the bathroom door as Dre turned and looked at him.

What? I took care of you...good night said Dre as Trevor looked at him smacking his lips and closed the bathroom door on his end.

Later on down the work week at the farm, Trevor got a special visit.

He and Trevor were out in the field when a truck drove up to the farm blasting Trina as the door opened as Trixie stepped out with her long dark curly hair...her real hair...a bloused tied up in a knot with her breast poking out exposing her stomach and her belly button pierce with short shorts with rips in the ass cheeks and looked like fashionable high cowboy boots she smoke a cigarette and blew from her pink luscious lips and rolled her eyes at nothing unparticular twisting her little ass walking toward his Uncle Richard who was outside near his office talking to a man.

Trevor and Dre looked up.

Damn dangerously sexy red bone at 4:00 he said.

Yeah I know...that's Trixie said Trevor.

Yo that's her? Damn said Dre.

Trixie took another pull of the cigarette and threw it on the ground and stepped it out then walked over to Dre's Uncle and smiled.

Hi Mr. Richard she said.

Trixie how are you doing? He smiled.

I'm doing great thank you...I stopped by to give you these papers my father wanted me to give you concerning all that business stuff you farmers do I'm sure she said handing him a brown envelope and swinging her hair behind her shoulder and smiling at him.

Thanks I really appreciate that Trixie, so are you still working at that produce market in town with your mother? Richard asked him.

Yes sir I'm still there earning my own, independent girl has to take care of herself…say I know that Trevor is hard at work for you right now and I hate to disturb him but can I steal him away from you for a few minutes and have a couple words with him…it's really important sir…promise I'll give him right back she said.

Sure go ahead said Richard.

Trixie smiled and walked past them as he and the man looked at her.

Damn…they don't makum like her no more…If I was 20 years younger…I'd give her all my paychecks said the man talking to Richard's father.

Trevor stopped the plow tractor and stood up on it and hopped off as Trixie stood at the edge of the field and waved at him as he walked across over to her as Dre watched.

Hey Trevor…long time no see stranger said Trixie.

What's up…so what are you doing out here? Trevor asked her acting as if he wasn't too happy seeing her.

Just making a run for my father and I also came to see you said Trixie.

Oh really? Trevor asked her.

Yep…I been thinking about you a lot lately and I feel so bad that things didn't work out between us…I want to apologize for hurting you the way I did…I don't know why I cheated on you…you were my everything and I blew it…just hate that we didn't fight harder to stay together and make it work said Trixie.

Naw don't feel bad…it is what it is and I already forgive you and it's all in the past…I've moved on and so have you no biggie said Trevor.

Umm no I haven't moved on…I'm still in love with you and you know that duh said Trixie.

Trevor rolled his eyes taking a deep breath. I gotta get back to work he said turning as Trixie grabbed his arm.

Trevor stop acting like that...I was hoping that we could talk... get up...I'm not saying we go back together because I know you don't want me but I miss you...talking to you...we were more than just beds and backwoods...you left me that day and I never saw you again because you broke up with me over the phone...do you know how mortifying that was to me...for the guy I love to not even give me a proper goodbye face to face?

Until we truly have decent closure we'll both be miserable and unable to move on and you know that said Trixie.

What do you want from me Trixie? Trevor asked her.

Not much...just a little more of your time...tonight Trevor...I'm leaving town in a few days and won't be back for another month... come to my place...we talk, have a drink...blow back one and give me a kiss goodbye that's all said Trixie.

Trevor looked at her. Where are you going? He asked.

Away to pursue some personal goals and my future and by the end of my journey I'll figure out if I'm coming back or staying there...the country limits opportunities...love this place but it's nothing to offer but hard work and calices...the city has more to offer and much more comfortable office type jobs instead of all this field and corn on the cob bullshit...so you coming to be with me or not said Trixie.

I'll think about it said Trevor.

I'll see you at nine she said kissing him on the cheek then walked off as Trevor looked at her and went back to the field.

Dre grinned. That sure is a sweet piece of pie he said.

Yeah...pretty on the outside....smells good...but she's straight rotten and cold on the inside said Trevor getting back on the tractor.

Damn....you really don't forgive easy said Dre.

Later that night, Trevor ended up going out to see her and when he got back to the house around one and was getting out his boots Dre opened his bathroom door and stood smiling and looking at him.

Welcome back home so how was your night with Trixie? Dre

asked him.

It was cool...said Dre.

You have that I smashed her good face still on...I don't blame you though even if she played me and broke my heart I'd still go back in smash it said Dre.

It meant nothing really said Trevor.

Word...so did you fuck her raw? Dre asked him.

What? Trevor asked him.

I hope that you used a condom considering how you told me how grimey she did you because I'm letting you fuck me raw and we having unprotected sex and I'm not trying to get caught up in whatever shit your other people might got lurking just saying...hope you wrapped it up...like I said respect me homie that's all I ask and don't be doing me and running in everything else too...I play but I don't play that way... said Dre.

You initiated sex without a condom both times we got down said Trevor.

So, you didn't object...yo whatever just let me know if you raw dogging like that so I can leave you alone said Dre.

Trevor looked at him for a moment then took an empty magnum condom wrapper out his pocket and threw it on the bed.

Yeah I used one said Trevor.

Alright cool...so how was that goodbye sex? Dre asked him.

That bitch lied, she aint moving nowhere she just wanted to get my dick and after we finished she told me how she made it up just to get back with me...I hope she enjoyed it because I never want to see her again said Trevor.

Who really got who though? I mean you said you didn't want her like that anyway and even if she did lie you just smashed it for old times' sake and left her ass when she thought it would keep you there with her and fall back in love from it...no biggie you the one that got yours so who cares right? said Dre.

Yeah…guess that's true said Trevor thinking to him self.

Yo you gotta stop putting too much thinking and emotions into shit…let the hoes play themselves…look, I want you to know that despite these treachery ass people you may deal with or run into that I have no side motives nor plan to use what we doing to get something more out of it…I'm getting what I put in and when I want it return and at some point I will…you'll do the same…simple as that…good night man see you in the morning said Dre.

Yeah…night said Trevor as Dre closed his door.

Chapter 21

The weekend of Gia's visit, Dre's Uncle and Aunt took him to the bus station in town as Dre eagerly waited in front of it with them for the buses to unload and finally he saw Gia getting off with his son Darius telling the old lady in front of her to hurry up and when she saw Dre her face lit up with a big smile.

Omg Dre! It's really you, my other baby…it's been too long…I told you I was coming, Darius its daddy she said meeting him with many kisses then handed his son Darius to him.

Hey little man, how you been doing…daddy misses you smiled Dre happily kissing him on the forehead.

I am so happy right now I don't know what to do, our little family is reunited back together…I was starting to forget how you look but I see that you still sexy as ever and all mine…I got my baby back in my arms after so long she said kissing him again.

Gia this is my Uncle Richard and Aunt Marylnn, Unc, Auntie this is my baby Gia said Dre.

Hi, Unc, hi Auntie I can call you that can I? Gia smiled hugging them both.

Awe smiled his Uncle Richard looking at his wife.

Yes of course you can, it's nice to finally meet you after all those calls you make on a daily basis laughed Dre's Aunt.

Yes I know I may have did it a little too much but I just love my Dre thing so much and calls were all I had to stay connected to him… this is our son Darius say hi to Dre's nice people…you want to hold him said Gia.

Yes said Dre's Aunt smiling as Dre handed him to her. Awe look at him and those fat little cheeks and got Dre's eyes and little button nose…so pretty she said as his uncle played with his little fingers.

I know, he get it from his momma and daddy aint that right Dre said Gia who smirked at her.

I want to thank you both so much for inviting me into your home and spending the weekend with the love of my life and taking him in and the trouble times in his life and provide him an opportunity to make money so he can do his daddy duty said Gia.

Your very welcome and we love having you here, we'll introduce you to the rest of the family back at the house said Dre's Uncle.

Sounds wonderful I can't wait said Gia as they walked toward the car as Gia held Dre's hand.

You happy to see me Dre said Gia.

You have no idea, I'm glad you're here both of you said Dre.

I love you Dre she said looking into his eyes then kissed and hugged him tight as he sun her around.

I love you too said Dre.

I told your mom that I was coming down to see you said Gia.

What she say? Dre asked her.

She wasn't exactly thrilled about it, she was talking about why you going all the way down there to try to spend time with him when he busy helping his uncle and working…just wait till he get home in another month it aint that long…he need time to get himself together… please later with all that she talking about…I said I was coming to see my boo and I'm here…who cares if she don't want us to be together because we know we belong together and that's all that matters…she might call you talking about I picked this weekend to leave on purpose because this was her weekend to keep the baby but don't even listen to her okay…hold up we gotta get my stuff from the bus…look at you so eager to get me to yourself so sweet said Gia.

On the drive back home, Gia and Dre were kissing and making out with the baby between them as Gia begin to moan.

Oh my said Dre's Aunt.

Young love…we remember those days don't we smiled his uncle to his aunt.

Yes we do indeed she said.

His Uncle glanced in the mirror and saw Dre rubbing her arm and kissing her neck.

You have that separate bedroom prepared? He said to her in a low voice.

All ready she said back to him.

The baby started crying.

Go back to sleep Darius mommy and daddy trying to have some free time said Gia as he begin to cry louder as she cradled him closer rocking him then smacked her lips rolling her eyes.

Shhh she said loudly as he cried louder.omg… I had to hear this on the bus almost all the way down… Dre can you please take him and quiet him down…he might be thirsty or need a diaper change…I just need a break for a bit…he just get like that sometimes and won't stop…its crazy she said laying her head back.

Its okay daddy got you said Dre holding him.

Dre don't hold him like that…support his head or he might get a cramp said Gia.

I know how to hold him said Dre.

Okay,Then do it said Gia as they looked at each other.

I got this alright said Dre taking the bottle and feeding him.

Good…he probably crying because he forgot who you were thanks to your mother said Gia.

Dre's aunt looked at his uncle and shook her head.

Soon they got back to the house and out of the van:

Here we are home sweet home said Dre's Uncle Richard.

Omg your house and land is so beautiful…Dre didn't tell me that it was all nice like that said Gia.

Yes I did Dre snapped back.

They all walked into the house as Trevor and Erika got up from the living room and came to greet them.

This is Trevor and our daughter Erika said his aunt to Gia.

Hi, nice to meet you Erika said Gia.

Hi,nice to finally meet you too and welcome to our home…is this Darius…awe let me hold him…awe…too cute she said taking him.

Girl you can hold him as long as you want cause I need to unwind and get my mind right for real…that was one long exhausting trip changing from station to station, bus to bus and I'm just about wiped out…hello your Trevor right said Gia.

Yeah nice to meet you said Trevor shaking her hand.

Dre talks a lot about you, good things…I'm so glad to know somebody looking out for my boo and keeping him out of trouble because if it's any to find any out here he bound to get into it…I love this hard headed boy so much said Gia.

Oh most definitely…I got his back all the time said Trevor looking at Dre who gave him a look with the slick remark and figured he was getting him back for the Uncle thing.

Well I'll give you a tour of the house and show you to your room where to put your things then you can rest up and we can have dinner…how does that sound said his Aunt.

Sounds lovely…you are so sweet Aunt Marylyn and Erika I can tell you got a good heart because I can pick that up from people right off the bat real talk…I wish Dre's mom was that nice to me but she been against our relationship from the start…but through hell and high water we still stand and were staying she said taking his hand.

Dre smiled at her then glanced in the kitchen at Trevor pouring a glass of milk and put it in the fridge then looked across at Dre smiling to himself closed the door and left to the other side.

A little later after dinner, Erika, Gia and her baby sat in the living room watching TV and talking when Darius started crying again.

Omg…not this again…I just put you to sleep please go back she said rocking him.

Here let me said Erika taking him in her arms and gently rocking him and singing him a song as the baby got quiet.

Oh wow…that's my baby, how did you get him to be quiet so fast? asked Gia.

Easy…I just snuggled him in my arms as if I was his security blanket and held him close to my heart said Erika.

Oh…you got kids said Gia.

No, not yet…unless you count all the baby animals we have that I take care of said Erika.

No girl that doesn't count laughed Gia.

But on the real I think you'll make a great mother said Gia.

Yeah one day…said Erika.

That's what's up…usually to get him to sleep I have to shake him until he hush up said Gia as Erika looked at her.

Girl it was a joke I was just playing, I don't do that to my baby said Gia.

Oh I hope not and I was about to say, I would have to call the police and put you away for life laughed Erika.

Naw never that, I love my baby and hate people that abuse their children…I want to be a social worker said Gia.

Oh okay…said Erika.

Well I'm going to let you and your little nephew get that bond thing going on while I find my Dre and get a few minutes of our time in smiled Gia getting up and going upstairs.

Alright…said Erika looking at her strangely then rolled her eyes and shook her head. City moms…she's a mess…god bless you she told the baby.

Dre was in Trevor's room playing cards on his bed when Gia came up to the door and knocked on it.

Hi,sorry to interrupt your game but I was hoping to pull Dre away for a few minutes…I just want to go outside and talk with you and stuff said Gia.

No prob said Trevor.

Dre got up and went downstairs with her then as soon as they had gotten out the house and closed the door Gia looked at him with a mean look and put her hands on her waist.

Okay for real…I need to talk to you because this is crazy and I'm about ready to bust outta my seams…what the fuck is going on here? Gia asked him.

Huh? What are you talking about now? Dre asked her.

I traveled 9 hours on a nasty hot stinky bus to this stinky place to spend time with you and so you can kick it with your son and you dumping me off on your cousin while you upstairs chilling with your boy and acting like I'm not here…you can hang with him any time… you need to get your mind right for real because I'm feeling neglected and its pissing me off already…like I'm here as one of your friends and I'm the mother of your child…where they do that at?! Gia snapped at him.

Okay you need to calm the fuck down, I'm not dumping you off on anybody and I just wanted you to get to know my people a little better and I only stepped off for 20 minutes damn said Dre.

Damn is right, like for real Dre where the love and kisses I should be getting non-stop…like this place is changing you and you-Ugh she said storming off the porch.

Yo where you going? Dre asked her.

I forgot…nowhere to go out here…I feel so hurt right and unwanted by you now said Gia standing folding her arms and begin to sniff as he came behind her and wrapped his arms around her.

Stop talking crazy, you know I love you with all my heart he said kissing her neck.

Yeah right…you probably want to be a farmer now and have chicken fights and sleep under the stars with cows… said Gia.

Comere said Dre turning her around and kissing her as she wrapped his arms around him.

I love you…I mean that and I'm sorry if I made you feel like you weren't here…promise I won't do it again…all about you from this moment on…I'm only here to make some money for us that's it…I don't care about anyone or thing but us said Dre.

Okay…said Gia kissing him.

Later that night, Dre snuck into Gia's room and with the baby fast asleep they got in a good fuck that ended all too soon.

Damn…that was good baby said Dre panting hard then kissed her and lay down beside her.

What? You came already? Gia asked him.

Ye,it was just so good and it's been so long since I had some…plus I got worried that Unc and Auntie were going to be making rounds and catch us…plus the baby like right there…it was a little weird you know said Dre.

Oh…well you going to have to get use to the baby being in the same room as us when you get back…my minute man…Ugh…it was good but wish you could have held on a bit longer…I almost got mine said Gia.

You still can Dre replied spreading her legs and eating her out as she moaned biting her lip.

Yes…I remember that…still good as ever…I'm so sorry that I was acting like a bitch earlier Dre…so sorry…damn… she said in a low voice and as soon as he got her off he got up and left the room and snuck back to his and closed and locked the door then went into the bathroom and took off the condom and flushed it taking a shower and brushing his teeth and gargling his mouth out then went to the other end of Trevor's bathroom door and opened it to his room and closed it then got into his bed beside him and put his arm across his chest.

I see you waited up for me said Dre.

No I didn't Trevor replied to him.

So I'm here now, waking yo ass up…I want some…do you he said stroking Trevor dick as he nodded.

Do you kiss? Dre asked him.

Yeah...why? Trevor asked him.

You never tried to kiss me said Dre.

I didn't think you liked that said Trevor.

Dre leaned in and kissed him as they got into a deep tongue session as Trevor got on top of him and started to kiss down his chest past his dick and started licking and eating his ass out.

Oh fuck...what you doing? Dre asked him.

Eating you...you don't like it asked Trevor.

Naw not that...it feels good that's all...keep doing it said Dre stroking his dick.

Trevor ate his ass getting it wet then bucked Dre's legs and pushed his dick into him fucking him down.

When you about to come,pull out man and nut on my chest said Dre.

When Trevor felt himself reaching that climax he pulled out and busted all over Dre's chest who almost busted at the same time.

Ye man....that was a great fuck said Dre getting up and going to the bathroom to wash off as Trevor came in behind him and kissed his neck.

Yo...you good man grinned Dre backing up.

Trevor took a cloth and hit him in the head with it then went to his room closing the bathroom door at that end.

Chapter 22

Another work week was passing by and after loading a large quantity, Dre's Uncle sent him and Trevor to deliver a truck shipment with crates of fresh crops to a purchaser that sells them on his independent produce ban in town and as they both walked to out his office to the truck an associate of Dre's Uncle saw them both talking then Dre playfully pushed Trevor to the side who playfully pushed him back as Trevor got him in a lock from behind holding him in it whispering in his ear then let him go as he held out hand as Dre took it then he hugged him in a intimate type way for a moment one might conceive and patted his shoulder a little as they both got into the truck as the man put out his cigarette and walked into the office.

Hey Richard, I see you've taken some crops off stock to make a quick and hefty hustle to market man George and sent the boys to make the delivery… say them boys of yours seem to be mighty close he said.

Yeah, Trevor seems to have taken my nephew under his wing… despite all the trouble he has gotten into back in the city I think all he needed was a positive male role model to kind of guide him…his father has never really been involved in his life and his older brother is in jail…I think that if either one had been available more in his life to show him the way or stay on the right path then he wouldn't be in some of these situations but he's learning and growing…progressing while he's here…hopefully he'll take something valuable about honest hard work and integrity before he goes back home to the big city and stick with it said his Uncle Richard.

Trevor seems to bond well with a lot of your help over the years, must be a very impressionable young man replied the man.

Yeah…He's been with my family since he was a little younger than my nephew now and I think of him as a son…I love him and trust him to get work done and watch my nephew…he's a hard worker…have some big plans for him in the near future…always envisioned that my son Antoine would help carry on the family business but he seems to have his heart set on staying in the city so I'm going to give Trevor a portion of my business and farm to run…his own unit…he disserves it for his all his loyalty over the years said Richard.

I agree…work wise he is loyal and I believe that he is taking care of that nephew of yours just fine said the man.

Richard stopped writing and looked up at him: What…are you implying something Frank? He asked.

Not at all…I just observe the way they interact with each other and they get along very well…just like that Armstrong boy and Kenneth…long time ago…they can't keep their hands off each other like women out there just now and I seen this behavior in them on quite a few occasions said Frank.

Their boys what do you expect…to be clear we both know that comparing their relationship and that one you just referred to is a little offensive and I don't take too kindly of that…Kenneth got caught screwing that boy and it was found out that he had been in a sexual type dealing with him for years while he was working with him…my nephew isn't like that…nor Trevor…those boys have already had more tail than you and I both combined in our lives to date…the problem with your way of thinking is that 2 man can't be affectionate to each other without something being strange about them and I don't live in that world of thinking…you ever thought of the fact that both may not have had that love from a strong male role model in their lives and finding some kind of validation and confiding in each other to fill that empty void…doesn't make them that way because they like each other…what would even possess you to judge the nature of their friendship like that? Richard asked him.

We both know that it's out there, that little secret between man… we grew up when men were men…making love to pretty ladies then engaging in this unspoken activity behind closed doors…plenty of hiding spots to play in this deep vast country beneath noticing eyes… but nobody talks about it…just turns a blind eye to it…hell, found out years later that friends of ours were like that and we never had a clue…what I saw out there just now…wont 2 boys playing but 2 boys that's been playing around…I'm not saying they are gay because I don't believe it but boys experiment…maybe you should just pay closer attention…you know make sure things are or aren't what they seem said Frank.

I think it's refreshing that this generation of men can show love to each other while being as tough as bricks…I have a lot of work to do here so get out my office with that nonsense…I'll see you later Frank said Richard going through papers shaking his head.

That weekend, Dre's Aunt sent Trevor and himself to the grocery to do a little shopping for her as they hit the road with Trevor's dog Charlie with them.

Trevor glanced over at Dre smoking a cigarette and looking out the window as if in deep thought.

You alright big city…seem to have a lot on your mind said Trevor.

I'm good said Dre.

This not about your girlfriend Gia having a guilty conscience when she was down last weekend and telling you before she left that she had lied about that being her cousin and really her ex boyfriend when you called…think it was a coincidence that he dropped into town when you were leaving out…she planned that shit man before you even left… confiding to him about you going away and missing you and old boy ending up giving her a spanking because she got all vulnerable and her girlie parts got all hot and bothered said Trevor.

It's called tapping ass where I'm from man and on some level I already knew what was up at the time but it's not even about us…I'm going to do what I have to do and take care of my son and when I get back...well see what happens with us...ye we love each other but we still young man...so I'll respect her for her honesty and leave it at that...she got her a little dick...I got me a little dick...we even said Dre.

Well said big city replied Trevor continuing to drive.

Soon they both arrived to the grocery store in town and did some shopping for his aunt.

Yo Trevor said Dre from nearby as he looked up from ale and saw Dre holding a cucumber and pretending to fuck an old lady standing in front of him looking at produce as Trevor smirked shaking his head and went down the ale.

You better watch it before I stick that thing all up in you pretty city said Shayla coming up with a grocery cart.

Yeah right, sup with you said Dre turning around.

Doing some shopping for this get together at my house later on, where my Trevor at? Shayla asked him.

Around said Dre.

Ye I know...you his 5 o'clock shadow now, I was watching you a minute ago back there and you seem to have a little swivel in that step now...guess that sugar coming out said Shayla.

Yo what's up with you in all the gay jokes, you think I'm flaming huh...bet if I am my pussy is better than yours said Dre.

Hell yeah I can smell that cake,cake,cake,cake...boy I'm playing... I just like fucking with you...when you get back to the city are you going to tell your hood boys a bitch had you kissing another nigga...I still want to taste that dick...hell you and Trevor owe me that good mouth fuck when you stormed off that day probably better you did after dude accused you of jacking his bling when all the while that ugly ass little niece of his came up and took it...thought for a sec you was going to start capping...I know how you city boys get down and shit...yall fucking crazy yo and stalkers said Shayla.

Ye you wish a nigga like me would stalk you said Dre.

Naw I just want to fuck you said Shayla.

Trevor walked over from ale.

Hey Trevor boo, get your friend he talking about how he going to have his way with me without my consent and make you watch said Shayla.

Really…well you can't rape the willing said Trevor.

Whatever…I see you shopping but you in the wrong place, you need to be shopping for me in the ring and bridal stores said Shayla.

Yeah keep dreaming on that said Trevor.

Bitter ass nigga, Trixie played you like a fiddle and you hate all women now…anyway I'm having a party at my spot this evening and you both invited to come…plenty of hoes and cold drinks going to be there and of course that herb so stop by and I get first dibs on the dick if you do…I gotta go, too many people I know in here and I need to get out before they want to talk and shit…later said Shayla walking off.

A party with an abundance of pussy pals in attendance…I think that could be fun, what do you think about it homie? Dre asked him.

Ye said Trevor.

So you want to check it out? Dre asked him.

I don't know maybe I guess if I feel like going out later said Trevor.

What do you mean if you feel like it?

Man it's the fucking weekend and I know were not going to sit around doing nothing said Dre.

I don't party every weekend man, sometimes I just want to be to myself and play cards and shit but if you want to go I'll drop you off said Trevor.

Naw forget it man…If you aint there I don't even want to go… nobody to split the pussy 2 ways and I'm not getting raped by a bunch of horny high chicks…besides I'm sure most of them there will be goat and duck looking…yall gotta a lot of country bitches looking like that down here said Dre.

Well do something big city…I'll entertain you said Trevor.

Cool said Dre.

A little later that afternoon, Trevor and Dre went to the barn on the other end of the house to the top floor of it and smoked a blunt; they didn't have to worry about their Uncle catching them because he was away fishing with friends for the afternoon.

You know when you're not down here too busy being a farmer and raising hogs you should come to the city one of these days and visit…I'd be your tour guide and take you to some pretty happening spots…I'll show yo country ass how we get down in the city said Dre pulling the blunt.

Trevor smoked a cigarette and nodded. I think I just might he said.

Cool…I hope you do, hate to think that our little summer friendship ends here said Dre passing him the blunt.

How about this man, when you go back I give you time to handle all your business and schooling…then I come to visit you and if you can get away then I kidnap you for a weekend said Trevor.

Sounds like a plan said Dre drinking down a bottle of water.

Trevor looked out across the yard and looked down to Dre unbuckling his belt and unzipping his pants then took his dick out and started sucking it as he closed his eyes then pulled the blunt and exhaled.

In the house, Erika walked into the kitchen were her mom was cutting vegetables up.

So Trevor and Dre still working on that wagon wheel project out in the barn said Erika.

Yeah, they been working on it for the past few weekends…must be some fun project because they go in there and stay for hours on end…I'm glad they find something productive to do with their time and I think it's very nice that Dre is finding a interest in Trevor's hobby…they must be starving by now…I'll make them a little snack and you can take it out there to them…just drop it off…I'm sure they don't want to be disturbed while their working too much you know how boys can be said her aunt.

Okay said Erika.

In the barn, Trevor stood against the wall on the top deck as Dre gave him head as he fucked his mouth hard.

Erika finished making the lunch and walked outside across the yard with it.

Dre stood up and unbuckled his pants and pulled them down and stood against the wall as Trevor stood behind him and spit on his hand lubing his ass then pushed his dick into him and begin thrusting it pumping him fast in hard knocking him into the wall with both their pants to their ankles.

Erika walked up to the barn door and slowly opened the door smiling ready to surprise them with the lunch and didn't see them on the floor where the wagon they were working on at but heard noises…sex noises as she listened and looked around strangely then crept inside looking around in above the top deck where the wooden ladder was up to it and was in absolute shock seeing Trevor pounding Dre out doggy style as her mouth gapped open unable to move for a moment and they didn't even notice her being too into it as she backed up and quickly left back out and silently closed the door back then walked across the yard thinking to herself shocked by what she saw and went over to the pig pen and fed them the food then went back into the house.

Hey, I bet they were hard at work weren't they but happy to see some lunch…those boys can eat smiled her aunt rinsing off more vegetables.

Yes mam…it's coming along nicely…I can't wait to they finish it she said putting the tray on the table and went upstairs.

Chapter 23

Dre's Uncle didn't feed into the allegations that was told to him from an associate about Trevor and Dre possibly and secretly getting down on the low but decided to separate them at work and had them performing different jobs in distant spaces on the farm just to see how they operate on their own. It was mid-morning during the work week that Dre's Uncle came to him while he was feeding the livestock.

Hey nephew, I talked to your mother about all the progress you were making here and some very fine stacks of money you saved up while working here and she thinks it's time for you to head home soon and get ready to get back in school with it starting back soon so next week you finally get your ticket back to home sweet home like I'm sure you been wanting…I'm proud of you nephew and I hope you keep up the good work down there like you did here said his Uncle.

Dre nodded. Thanks…I thought that she agreed that I'd come back in a few weeks…don't think it would hurt for me to earn just a little bit more before I head back he said.

I see the country life has really had a great affect on you, glad to know nephew but you've done your share already and have more than enough in harvest…no more stalling…time for you to get back to the city to begin your life anew there and take on your responsibilities and obligations as a young man…your son needs his father…its time to go said his uncle leaving out as Dre thought to himself and sighed then went back to feeding the live stock.

When he and Trevor got home they saw his aunt and cousin Erika standing outside on the porch as if waiting for them with a unreadable expression on their face looking at each other than at them.

What's going on here…said Dre to Trevor.

I have no idea said Trevor.

They both got out of the car and walked toward the house.

Hey…everything alright? What's going on? Trevor asked unsure what they were about to say or if they knew anything.

Trevor…I'm sorry to have to tell you this but…Charlie died late this morning said Dre's Aunt.

What? Trevor replied as if not wanting to believe it.

Yeah…I thought he was just asleep this morning when we both left but we found him on the back porch still the same lying the same way and when I went to wake him up that's when I discovered it…he was an old dog Trevor but you gave him the best years of his life here and a home said Erika as if particularly sad about it.

Dre looked at Trevor who had a sharp pain of sadness across his face and swore that dude looked as if he was about to cry as he balled his mouth as if holding it all in then without a word walked past them into the house and out to the back porch deck and looked in the corner to where they had put a white sheet over him as he slowly walked over and knelt down and took the sheet and looked at him rubbing him for a moment and took his collar off him that he had bought and put it in his pocket then picked him up and carried him across the yard.

Trevor buried him somewhere on the acres and made a stone indentation marking it, Dre knew how much he loved his dog and decided to give him some distance and some time alone but as the days passed and he was getting closer to having to leave Trevor still seemed to be caught in his pity funk of adding another lost love to his list and Dre tried to cheer him up but it wasn't working and he was getting frustrated wishing that he would just move on from it but he didn't suffer lost easily as he figured out although to Dre it was just a dog.

The weekend came and Dre sat out on the porch listening to music and Trevor came outside and stood to the front of the porch looking out across and didn't look his way or say anything as he lit a cigarette as Dre took out his ear plugs and looked at him.

What up man Dre asked him.

Trevor glanced over at him and nodded as the silence continued between them as Dre decided to spark up a conversation.

I had a pit-bull I loved once, his name was King and I was sad when he died...actually he got molly whopped in a fight with another pit-bull that I had betted him to fight...that was fucked up...lost a bet, money and my dog all in one day...damn...I remember shaking him telling him to wake up, keep fighting and if he died I was going to kill him said Dre trying to make Trevor smile but it didn't crack a smile on his face.

Hmph he replied.

Trevor took another pull of his cigarette and left the porch and went to his truck and got in it as Dre stood up and walked over.

Hey man, where you going? Dre asked him.

Just riding out...to the lake said Trevor.

Cool, can I roll with you? Dre asked him.

Trevor unlocked the passenger door as Dre got in then they both left.

At the lake, Dre stood on the bank tossing rocks making them skip across as Trevor sat on his hood drinking a bottle of liquor and not saying much as the radio played in his truck and when they played that old classic song Brandy about a man missing his best friend that was a dog it really depressed Trevor.

Dre was getting bored throwing rocks as he turned around and walked over to Trevor.

I want you to cheer up man real talk and get out this fucking depression, its bringing me down too...we all die man...its apart of life accept it...I get it, you lost your best friend...not the end of the world said Dre.

Trevor took a drink and looked at him starting to get pissed.

What the fuck would you know about that, you take your dogs and hype them up for money to be slaughtered in fights...you have no respect for animals...he's not just a fucking dog...he was with me during the worst parts of my life and I always kept him by my side… you don't understand so don't fucking speak on it said Trevor.

Word…well at least he didn't go the way of old yellow and it was a peaceful natural death…take him out to the field and lay him to pasture shot gun style said Dre.

Are you trying to be funny right now? Trevor asked him getting extremely angry.

Naw I'm just saying, like your cousin said he was an old dog…old things die after awhile said Dre.

Just shut up and stop talking to me…matter fact get the fuck out of my face said Trevor taking another swallow.

Oh wow…guess it's back to the bottle taking it to the head huh… keep that up and you'll have a alcoholics grossed out stomach…why the fuck you taking it so personal…what, were you fucking the dog or something? Dre asked him.

Get the fuck out of my face! Trevor yelled at him as mad as Dre had ever seen him as he looked at Trevor and shook his head.

You tripping dog….no pun intended said Dre walking off and sat on the back of the truck as a few minutes past of silence then he looked down in his truck and found some rope and picked it up and begin playing with it.

Look at me, I'm a cowboy about to lasso up a philly heehaw! Dre shouted swinging it around then jumped down off the truck and walked back over near Trevor looking at him as Trevor tried to not look at him and Dre stepped in every direction his face went.

You irritating as fuck big city said Trevor.

You country as fuck homie said Dre swinging the rope around.

Imma loosen you up like you did me, he threw the rope wrapping it around him.

Get this shit off me said Trevor.

Eh look, you ever hear of that game Mortal Kombat imma do what Scorpion do when he locks someone comere!!! Dre yelled pulling forward hard as Trevor flew off the hood and slammed to the ground spilling his bottle.

Damn my bad…guess I don't know my own strength said Dre.

Trevor looked at him. You stupid little dick head he said getting up rushing forward and pushed him with such force he flew and slammed back to the ground then Trevor violently choked him down.

I told you to stop fucking playing! Trevor yelled at him.

Get the fuck off me man! Dre yelled.

Trevor begin jacking him by his shirt and slamming his head to the ground repeatedly as Dre punched him in his face as hard as he could and head butted him as Trevor stumbled back grabbing the side of his face as Dre rushed him Trevor slamming him to the ground punching him as they traded blows back to back and choked each other out hard.

You give up mother fucker huh…I can do this all day…tap out mother fucker said Dre.

As they both passed out on each other finally in exhaustion then silently got into the truck and drove home looking beat the hell up.

They both walked into the house as his Aunt glanced at them and almost went crazy covering her mouth.

Omg!what in the world happen to you too she said as his Uncle came over as they looked at each other still pissed.

We ran into some rednecks in town calling us out our name and we got into this big fight….we kicked butt despite what it may look like said Dre.

His Uncle looked at Trevor who he could read and had a mixed expression of what he had just told them like feeling guilty.

Trevor is that what happened? He asked.

Trevor just looked at him and didn't reply.

Let me talk to you said his uncle as Trevor left out the kitchen with him outside.

His aunt touched his bruised face. You young boys I swear, let me get you some ice she said.

Dre's Uncle stood with Trevor outside.

Tell me what really happened? He asked.

We had words and we got into a fight...said Trevor.

I expected better of you Trevor, your older and had no business hitting on that boy no matter what the argument was about...I'm sure your rough housing is over and you've both calmed down and will be fine in no time but don't put your hands on him again understand? Richard told him.

Yes sir...I apologize said Trevor.

Now go apologize to him...I'm taking you both on a camping trip next weekend to honor his last week here...is there anything else going on between you too that I don't know about? Richard asked him.

Trevor looked at him for a moment. No sir...nothing else he replied as Dre's Uncle looked at him for a moment then nodded and patted his shoulder then went back into the house.

After a little while,Dre walked out across the yard over to the stable where Erika was washing one of the horses and looked up at him as he came up to the fence.

Hey Dre...yikes...what in the world happened to you...look like you just got hit by Tyson said Erika looking at his cut lip.

It's nothing....me and Trevor got into a little scuffle...things got heated and maybe I shouldn't have made those remarks about dogs trying to cheer him up said Dre.

You ass hole...said Erika.

I know...not intentionally one...just happens when I open my mouth at times said Dre.

So you 2 over this beat down, made up and cool again? We girls aren't like that if we fight we beat the crap out of each other and hate each other forever but you guys can fight and blow it off and be friends like its nothing said Erika.

I guess...think we'll get over this...I'm not mad really said Dre.

Good said Erika putting the brush in the bucket and walked over to the fence looking at his face.

Damn he got you good said Erika.

I got him better said Dre.

Water under the bridge now right…now go kiss and make up or something or at least when no one's watching and do me a favor… lock the barn the next time you're in there busy working…quiet as kept…I won't tell a soul said Erika smiling at him and going back to the horse as Dre looked shocked that she knew and had walked in on it but didn't say anything up to now and could do nothing but grin in embarrassment as he walked off.

Later that night, Dre lied down in his bed with his arms relaxed behind his head touching his cut lip and thinking to himself and got a knock on his bathroom door as Trevor opened it and stood as Dre looked at him for a moment then away as he walked over and sat down on the bed beside him.

I'm sorry he said.

Cool… said Dre.

Trevor turned and touched his face gently as Dre sighed to himself closing his eyes than touched his hand rubbing it as Trevor leaned in and kissed him and Dre reciprocated in a long passionate kiss.

Alright slugger…time for you to return the favor said Dre taking out his rock hard dick stroking it as Trevor grinned at him then took it stroking it in his hand and sucked it down deep throating it as Dre moaned as he put his hand on Trevor's head and this was in fact the best head he had gotten ever.

***damn,if I knew you could blow one like this…I would have initiated these services a long time ago said Dre panting as Trevor continued sucking and stroking his dick then licked his balls as Dre jacked his dick fast and hard and nutted all across his chest panting as Trevor kissed his forehead and went and got him a cloth and wet it wiping his chest off then got in the bed with him as Dre laid on his chest and closed his eyes while Trevor rubbed his head like a sweet lullaby.

Chapter 24

That weekend, Dre, Trevor and his uncle went on a camping trip with it being his last weekend there...Dre never thought that he would miss this place as much as he did...he expected to be happy and relieved when this time was approaching to go back home to the city but he knew he had too and would enjoy the last few days here the best he could.

His Uncle rode on his truck with the boat trailer attached to it while Trevor and Dre followed behind him in his truck with the camping supplies and equipment...It wasn't a long drive to the lake but it was a rather quiet drive between them like trying to avoid the in evitable that they would soon part ways and go on with their lives though keeping in contact from so far away.

Well looks like this is almost it big city, guess it's time for you to head back home...bet you can't wait to get back...know you must miss it after all the time here said Trevor.

Ye I miss it...but it was fun here while it lasted said Dre.

So being worked the shit out of for the most part was fun to you? Trevor grinned.

Not at first...it hurt me like fuck but I took that shit like a man...I had to prove to you and my Uncle that I could take it...but like you told me I had to get my back broken into it and you were right...I got use to it and have a fine appreciation for it now said Dre.

The city/country boy alliance we had went very well all and all besides beating the shit out of each other near the end anyway laughed Trevor a little.

Ye I figured I might would have to tag you before my stay was over...when I first met you and you had that smart mouth I knew we were going to have problems…but we got along for the most part… that's how we consecrate friendships in the city…we beat the shit out of each other and shake hands said Dre.

How cordial…well I hope you keep in touch and stay in contact though I'm sure after while your life will get too busy and I'll understand…you got a lot of responsibilities on your plate and just a little more growing up to do but I think after it's all said and done…we'll be just like this again said Trevor as Dre nodded and looked back out the window.

When they got to the lake, they unloaded the boat to do some fishing first in the lake together as his Uncle lit up a cigar.

Dre glanced over at him. Hey Unc, I didn't know you smoke cigars or anything period he said trying to see if he smoked weed too.

No nephew, cigars is all I smoke but your Aunt hates the smell of them so I usually take my fine box of cigars when I'm fishing or playing cards with the buddies said his Uncle.

That's what's up…I wish I had a cigarette right about now said Dre looking at his Uncle corner eye.

Go ahead…I know you been smoking all the time anyway…I won't give you grief about it since it's your last days here he said.

Dre smiled at Trevor.

Yo Trevor hit me up with one he said taking it.

I'm not one to get in your personal business concerning the relationship of you and your girlfriend Gia but keep that one in control… she won't fooling us with that innocent sweetie pie act we know she a hell raiser…don't let her drive you crazy and keep her in check… believe it or not your aunt was the same way when she was young… took a man like me to break her in and calm her down…you gotta let them know their place and who wear the pants…she get a handle on your balls now at this age and she'll never let go said his Uncle.

Yes sir laughed Dre a little.

Hey look what else shark is in the water said Trevor nodding his head.

As Shayla with her sugar daddy and some of her girlfriends were speeding in the distance on their boat as she stood up shouting.

What up yall I gots me a boat too! Check this view out mother fuckers! She screamed lifting her shirt flashing her big tidies as her girlfriends cheered with cans of beer in hand.

Oh man, I'm blinded said Dre covering his eyes.

Lord have mercy said his Uncle turning away.

She better sit her big ass down before she tip that damn boat over said Trevor.

After fishing, they went to a remote part of the woods to set up camp pitching up 2 tents and after a little while of finishing took a break.

Be right back gotta bleed the lizard said Trevor walking off.

The what now? Dre asked him.

He gotta take a piss son…it's a country term said his Uncle.

Oh…said Dre.

After a little while, Trevor had vanish from sight and Dre went to go look for him and found him carving something into a tree with his hunting knife as he walked over to him.

Hey man what are you doing? Dre asked him as Trevor turned and smiled in bashfulness like not wanting to get caught.

Dre read what he carved in the tree Dre and Trevor 4 ever:

Aw for me homie…were you going to tell me? Dre asked him.

Naw…but I wanted to make sure the memory of this summer lasted…most trees live far longer than people so we carve initials in its skin to keep us there after were gone sort of speak said Trevor.

Damn…now I feel all mushy and shit like a female right about now, hate you for that said Dre as Trevor smirked.

Later that evening to night, they created a camp fire and had a fire cooked dinner as they sat around it talking.

Camping has always been a great bonding experience for males roughing it in the outdoors and getting away from the women folk for a little while because we need our personal time just like they do… camping out is tradition in the deep country, I did it with my father and although I'm not your blood father I think of you both as my own sons…so let's drink to that he said pouring 3 glasses of liquor and handed one to Trevor then Dre.

Um Unc…is this what I think it is said Dre sniffing it.

Yep 100 percent certify liquor, stop acting like you haven't snuck in my cabinet while you were here…I know Trevor wasn't the only one getting it down and I took my first drink with my father when I was 16 now toast to good times and life in the country he said as they raised cups.

I'll drink to that said Trevor.

Ye I bet alchie said Dre as his Uncle laughed.

Shut up said Trevor.

Trevor I want to offer you a business proposition…ready to hear it? Dre's Uncle asked him.

Yes sir said Trevor.

I want to give you a portion of my farm to run and manage…giving you an office and a unit…you're a hard worker and for years helped me maintain the family business even in those hard times and trials we faced…the farmer's life isn't an easy one and not every year promises to deliver good results but you always were by my side through it all and I want to sign you over as my supervisor…time to let someone else do the hard work and you sit back and watch progress so what about it? Dre's Uncle asked him.

Sir…I don't know what to say…wow…this is an honor said Trevor.

You say yes said Dre.

I'm your man for the job said Trevor.

Dre's Uncle smiled and shook his hand.

You disserve it Trevor, Dre I want you to sleep in my tent tonight I have a lot I want to talk to you about one on one concerning home and all your plans when you get back said his Uncle.

Yes sir said Dre.

Damn…he messing up tonight's goodbye fuck…but he has to go to sleep at some time Dre thought to himself.

Later that night, Dre and his Uncle talked for a while then settled in to sleep but Dre was fake sleeping waiting for his Uncle to nod off and soon he heard him snoring and made his move he crept up and out of the tent and walked over to Trevor's who was sitting up waiting for him and saw his shadow outside it as he unzipped the tent from the outside and came in then zipped it back up and got on top of him kissing him.

I thought he would never go to sleep, what a chatter box…he sure talks a lot when he drinks said Dre.

I know but I would have waited all night if I had too…no way you leaving here without straightening me out said Trevor.

Ye I always wanted to do something freaky like fuck outdoors said Dre.

Dre kissed Trevor as he stroked his dick then sucked it down deep throating it as Trevor closed his eyes and bit his lip.

Fuck he said forcing Dre down to suck it deeper and harder.

Dre got up and pulled his pants down and laid on his stomach as Trevor got up stroking his hard dick and put some Vaseline on it then in Dre's ass and pushed it into him slowly at first than thrusting it deep into him as he growled gripping the covers as Trevor smashed him down fucking him like he had never fucked him before than busting all in him in a sexual growl and laid down on top of him then moments later kissed his neck and rolled them over to their sides fucking him again gripping his hips as Dre moaned stroking his dick.

Ye…that's what I'm talking about…fuck this ass…fuck it …co-mon…do it like you mean it…do it like you going to miss it said Dre as he started busting his load and Trevor busted another.

Trevor took a few moments closing his eyes and panting.

Stay in here with me a little longer, we can just lay here beside each other and cuddle or something if you want? Trevor asked him.

Aw you are such a gentlemen homie and I don't feel like just a piece of hit it, I don't care much about cuddling but I will lie across your chest and close my eyes for a little while said Dre.

Alright Trevor replied back.

A short while after Dre snuck back into the tent looking at his uncle sleep on his side and got under his blanket and settled to sleep as his Uncle woke up listening the whole time but just laid there thinking to himself unable to say or do anything.

The Next Morning, they put out the fire and loaded their equipment and headed home and he observed them acting a little strange together and for the first time saw what he had never notice before but still didn't know how to deal with it or what he heard that night.

How you boys sleep? Dre's Uncle asked them.

Pretty good said Trevor as Dre's Uncle looked at him for a moment nodded.

Good to hear…alright lets head home he said going to his truck.

Chapter 25

The day arrived for Dre to leave and instead of taking the bus home, Trevor offered to drive him there himself as he prepared to say his goodbyes to his relatives.

Dre hugged his Uncle: Take care nephew and I expect the best of you when you get back home and stop giving your mother a hard time…the only reason she stays on you is because she loves you and wants the best for you and always be there to take care of your son and raise him above all things…break the cycle he said.

Yes sir…I will Dre told him.

His Aunt hugged him: I'm going to miss you so much Andre and it was wonderful having you here staying with us…you'll always have a home here and a family…I want you to take care of yourself and I'm going to pray for your girlfriend Gia…you got a lot on your hands to deal with and I'm not kidding she said.

Thanks, pray for me too while you're at it laughed Dre.

Of course I will she said.

Erika sighed and hugged him. Goodbye cousin…I want you to be good and stay out of trouble from here on out or I'll make a trip to the big city and jack you up…don't think I won't she smiled.

I'll try grinned Dre.

Goodbye fam, until we meet again said Dre.

You ready to hit the road big city? Trevor asked him.

Ye…I'm ready said Dre as he picked up his bags and headed for the door.

Trevor…can you come in here for a moment said his Uncle as he turn and walked over to him in the kitchen.

I want to talk to you when you get back he said in a serious low voice.

Trevor nodded and picked up the rest of Dre's bags and left out the door with him.

Dre saluted to them as they all stood out waving as Trevor headed to the highway.

Looks like you moving on up homie, Uncle just offered you a high power position on the farm…you going to making more paper and get to sit in an office with ac on those hot summers after all said Dre.

Yeah I'm really happy about that but I didn't mind getting my hands dirty…like working out in the field said Trevor.

Ye I get it, it's all you've ever known but now it's time for you to sit back and let somebody work they ass off and even better for you… enjoy it man said Dre as Trevor grinned.

Halfway through their trip to Dre's house, Trevor made a detour and got a hotel for the rest of the evening and night leaving out first thing in the morning. They had some drinks and lit up a couple of blunts and got into another hot steamy fuck session.

Dre was on top of Trevor kissing his neck and looked at him.

I want to do you he said.

As in you want to fuck me? Trevor asked him.

Ye…wait…are you like the top dude when it comes to getting it on with guys? Dre asked him.

Yeah I've always been that and never been popped but I always figured that if I met a dude who I truly vibe with on that level after some time…I'd bend the rules…so if you want to than we can do that said Trevor.

Dre nodded that's what's up he said.

You could have been got it but I figured that you were…I don't know…didn't think you did that or like it said Trevor.

Naw it won't that, I just liked having you in complete power for a bit but now it's time to share it…so can I be your first like you were mine? Dre asked him.

Take it said Trevor.

Dre stretched both Trevor's arms across and held them down interlocking his fingers then kissed down his chest and licked his nipples and working his way down his chest past his stomach and gripped his rock hard dick in his hands and gave him a wet deep throat blow job before licking and sucking his sack and got to his ass spreading both his thighs apart with his hands and licking his ass out as Trevor jacked his dick and gasping in a manly moan as if introduced to a new orgasm experience.

Hold on to your manhood throughout this and don't go bitch on me no matter how much you come to like it…that will turn me on more said Dre as Trevor nodded.

Dre took a big spit on in his ass then one his fingers gliding it inside his ass.

Yo…we got lube over there said Trevor.

You'll be alright now brace yourself said Dre stroking his dick and slowly pushed it inside him as both let out a surprising growl at the same moment then Dre took easy thrust at first then gradually picked up speed pushing his way into him as Trevor jacked his dick grunted low and pinching Dre's nipple then Dre lifted both his legs to his waist pumping him deeper and closed his eyes biting his lip then after a few more thrust pulled out and stood over him stroking his meat as he busted all over Trevor's chest who starting busting his load during the same time.

Damn homie…best porn star sex scene ever said Dre.

I'll second that grinned Trevor.

Good job kiddo you took it like a pro said Dre lightly smacking his head and getting up going to the bathroom and stood to the door.

Eh comon lets take a shower so we can do it again in a bit said Dre as Trevor got up and went into the bathroom with him.

The next Morning they were back on the road and early afternoon finally got back into his city, Trevor was looking around like he was seeing another world with all the traffic, buildings and people as Dre told him things about the city.

Damn so you never been to the city once? Dre asked him.

Nope…told you I'm from the country born and raised said Trevor.

Well now you have a reason to come back said Dre as he nodded.

Finally they got to his house:

Looks like my mom is already gone to work…good… but I got a house key and I can give you a tour of my crib before I unpack we gotta unload one last time…for right now anyway said Dre as Trevor nodded.

They were just getting out the car when Gia hit Dre up as he looked at it and smacked his lips then answered it hello he said.

Hey baby! Welcome back Dre! love you! love you! Welcome back to good cell phone signals and life for miles around…so are you home yet, wtf is taking so long said Gia.

Ye I'm back…just got in said Dre.

Good and about damn time too…I thought you were suppose to get home late last night said Gia.

Was…but made a slight detour said Dre.

Oh…why? Gia asked him.

Felt like it said Dre.

Excuse me? Look don't come home with that fucked up attitude and shit,trying to be brand new like you been somewhere important…nigga please you back and yo ass belong to me said Gia.

Oh…said Dre.

Yep…I don't care about the mistakes we made or what I did… shit, everybody slip up at some point in time aint no bitch perfect… we going to be together for the baby…he needs us to be his solid foundation…fuck that broken home shit me being on welfare and government aid while you run around making more kids…this is the final destination Dre…destination Gia she said.

Oh okay…Dre yawned.

Um excuse me he said.

Hurry up and come over here said Gia.

In a little while, I got something to do said Dre.

Like what? Gia asked him.

Like I said, I'll be there in a little while so stop fucking asking me questions said Dre.

Okay so I know you lost it thinking you can talk to me like that; don't think you going to treat me like garbage because I made a mistake said Gia.

Please I'm not even thinking about that…talk to you in a bit bye… said Dre.

Dre! said Gia.

Bye said Dre.

Dre! You better not hang up said Gia.

Bye said Dre.

Dre said Gia as he ended call.

Dre shook his head looking at Trevor then opened the door as they both went outside.

Hope I dont seem to have too much drama going on in my life man said Dre.

I'm good…that aint got nothing to do with me said Trevor.

He gave Trevor a tour around his house.

Now I'm going to give you a tour to the best place in the house my room said Dre as they both went upstairs and went into it.

Just the way I left it…looks like mom prepared my bed for my arrival…too bad it's already time to mess up the sheets he said taking off his clothes as Trevor took off his.

Stay a few more hours said Dre.

Alright, gotta say I am so loving the see you later sex said Trevor.

Ye,I know right said Dre.

After 2 more steamy fuck sessions, Dre put his bags in the house and stood at Trevor's truck.

What do you say when your sharing your last moments with someone…not knowing if you'll ever see each other again even though you say you will…when they live a world away seemingly…if you feeling a lot more than they know or you realize you would…me…I keep it gangster thought Dre to himself.

Have a safe trip back man, take care and call me along the way and when you get in said Dre.

You got it, later big city said Trevor with an expression of not wanting to go but not wanting Dre to know how hard it felt as he drove off and Dre stood watching him vanish in the distance then took a sigh and looked around his neighborhood.

Home sweet home…but it's not over…not by a long shot…this is just the beginning he said walking into the house.

Late that evening, Trevor arrived back to the house where Dre's Uncle Richard was sitting out on the porch in his favorite rocking chair smoking a cigar.

Trevor got out his car and closed the door and walked over to the porch smoking a cigarette.

Welcome back, how was the travel down to the big city? Richard asked him.

I finally got to see it up close and personal, big place, really busy,really crowded, really noisy, everything I thought it would be like but all and all a great experience said Trevor.

Dre's mom called and let me know that Dre never got home that night around the time you were both due to arrive back in the city and that he got there sometime late the afternoon or atleast after she got to work said Richard.

Ye,I got a little tired half way through so we parked to a rest stop and chilled until day break said Trevor standing against the porch ledge not making eye contact with his Uncle who was staring at him sharply.

I see, still baffles me though said Richard pulling his cigar and looking out into the far distance of the yard.

What's that? Trevor asked him discarding the finished cigarette in a can on the ledge.

I can't believe that it was happening right under my eyes and I'm more than certain under my roof said Richard still looking away as if he couldn't stand to look at Trevor.

Trevor was silent unsure but very sure what he was talking about and his heart felt like it had plummeted from his chest.

He knows he thought to himself.

Richard finally looked Trevor directly in the eyes.

You were in here messing around with my under age nephew, I always had a high opinion and respect for you Trevor but seems that I was mistaken replied Richard finally getting up and walking to the door.

You and I are going to talk about what happens from here replied Richard going into the house and closing the door leaving Trevor outside.

Chapter 26

The months passed along and he kept long distance communication with Trevor in their seemingly city to deep country complicated relationship but were about to have their first conversation on Skype that Dre had introduced to Trevor so they could have a much more personal conversation, Trevor didn't keep up with the latest software, technology and devises like the he did although he was very aware of it. he was indeed a down in the deep country boy who was comfortable in the old ways which made them both truly different people but the one thing they had in common was each other in the summer that created their friendship.

Dre sat in front of his laptop in his room with his head set on as Trevor's image popped up on the screen in front of him as he grinned.

What up partner, looks like we face to face again now…or at least something close to it said Dre.

Yeah man, so this is how Skype works…pretty cool…I really like this said Trevor.

Ye man, I had to introduce you to some modern day software because you truly an old fashion country dude real talk…you do know that technology has far exceeded past the inventions of the home phone and satellite TV right? I just turned you to texting too Grinned Dre.

I know but I don't keep up with everything, they constantly throwing new stuff on the market every time you turn around and I'm too busy most of the time to pay any attention to that…but I'm glad you told me about this…feels like I'm right there in front of you…look good man said Trevor.

Thanks you too said Dre.

So how is school coming along up there? Trevor asked him.

Doing good man, back in it and getting broke back in to homework and studying and the whole nine after a hard summer of the farmer's life…gotta say that I'm missing the money I made there… trying to get a part time job after school even cut out my smoking habit for a good while now if you know what I mean, just to get me in the door anyway…still waiting for these people from footlocker to call me back…I want it too so I can be a employee discount on all the latest shoes and my funds are running low now a day's laughed Dre a little.

I hear you man, but you know I got your back…I'll send you a little something in the mean time to get you by said Trevor.

Naw you don't have to do that man…I'm good for right now said Dre.

I want too so take it or I'll be offended said Trevor.

Dre smiled. Thanks man he said.

So how is the relationship with the girlfriend and baby going? asked Trevor.

Pretty good man, we just trying to make it work being young and full time parents already which has its big issues but I focus on being there for my kid for the most part…so what about you, dating anybody yet or still playing the field with all that country girl ass running around in it? asked Dre.

I actually met this real cool girl at karaoke one weekend in town and we hit off, I been seeing for a minute and I can say that it's on developing into a dating type basis said Trevor.

Cool…that's what's up…guess you found somebody to occupy your time with…I guess that doesn't leave too much time for me considering you nearly 900 miles away said Dre.

No, I will always find a way to make time for us big city…like I told you I don't care about the distance because I don't mind traveling said Trevor.

Ye, I hear you but still haven't seen you since you bought me back down here that day…I understand you got a lot of work in farming type business you in charge of though…figure we'll get up at some point in time when it's good for both of us said Dre.

Yep replied Trevor.

So I see you finally moved out of my Uncle's house and got your own spot on a nice piece of land that he bought for you…that's what's up said Dre.

Yeah man, I loved living with the family but thought it was time to have my own personal space said Trevor.

I feel you on that…sure that part of the reason you left wasn't because Uncle found out about us and he had some issues and feelings of disrespect toward you? Dre asked him as Trevor looked surprised that he knew about it.

How you know about that? Trevor asked him.

My cousin Erika gave me the inside scoop when I called to see how she was doing…why didn't you tell me about that? Dre asked him.

I don't know…I guess after it all went down I just left it alone, when I got back home after dropping you back to the city, your Uncle confronted about it and knew we were messing around…the camping trip man…he heard us that night…he felt that I had disrespected his home and him doing that and he was right…felt so fucking bad man…he didn't take away the supervisor job he promoted me with but told me that it would be best if I found my own place to stay and when I say there was tension between us…it was so thick I could cut it with a knife…work wise and dealing with each other on a daily basis was tolerable and he treats me the same…but in the back of his mind I know I betrayed him on a level that was unforgivable said Trevor.

Damn, I didn't know that he knew….shit…I'm sorry for all that man…I never wanted to risk you losing your job with him or your close relationship…feel so fucking bad about that said Dre.

Hey it all happened and we can't go back in change it, so nothing to do but move on from it…I think our relationship is improving…

went out to town together to play cards last weekend and had a good time…I think that I can regain his respect in time and deeply apologized to him for it said Trevor.

So do you regret us going as far as we did…because of the fact that I'm his family and 16? Dre asked him.

I always knew that it was a possibility that it would be complicated if I went there with you but I was prepared for this outcome on some level…but honestly…no I don't regret it…just wish the circumstances could have been different and you were a wee bit older so it wouldn't feel a little weird said Trevor.

Yo, you only 20…stop acting like you molested me where not that far apart age wise said Dre.

Trevor nodded.

Oh…I think I see what's going on now…is that why you not making real effort to come see me and get up because of my age? Dre asked him.

No man…that's not the real issue or reason said Trevor.

But it is a issue…I wish you would get over that…I'll be 17 in a few weeks…that close enough for comfort said Dre.

So you got a b day coming up big city…that's what's up said Trevor.

Yep…I know it's not possible but I think it would be nice if you were able to come down that weekend and celebrate it with me…I'm going to have a party that night…you could come down and get a room at a hotel and attend than at the end of the night we get up one on one…trust me you wouldn't be wasting your time or gas I will guarantee you that we going to fuck and all that said Dre.

I will make it a priority to be a part of your special day, I'm coming down there and booking reservations and I'll break you off with a little birthday gift said Trevor.

That's what's up…I look forward to that man real talk…you promise? Dre asked him.

Yeah big city, I promise grinned Trevor.

Cool…I'm mad tight so getting up in it again will be brand new like when we first started said Dre.

Damn the torrent memories you bring back…said Trevor shaking his head.

Ye I know…good times said Dre.

Indeed…It was nice talking to you big city and seeing your face on scope after all this time said Trevor.

Its Skype yo laughed Dre.

Ye…Skype, I got a busy work day in the morning and I know you got school…I tell you that office work is as straining as field work at times said Trevor.

I bet…before you go let me see that piece said Dre.

Aw so you want a little goodnight show said Trevor.

Yes sir, now strip said Dre.

Trevor got up from his chair and unbuckled his pants and pulled them down flashing his semi soft but still long thick piece.

Stroke it for me said Dre as Trevor begin groping his piece getting it stiff rock hard.

Ye that's hot…now play with those fat balls said Dre as Trevor rubbed and squeezed them in his hand and Dre felt his own dick getting hard.

Damn yo…I see the cows aren't the only things that need milking down there…whip it back and forth said Dre as Trevor let go of it and swung his dick back in forth hitting each side of his leg.

You happy now? Trevor asked him.

Yep…very happy…I don't want you doing anything with it off screen tonight…put a ice bag or whatever on it to keep it down and save that bust…we going to have a little masturbation session right up here tomorrow said Dre.

You got it…I'll hold it for you said Trevor.

That's what's up…night man said Dre.

Night big city said Trevor as they cut off their connection.

Damn...we gotta do the real thing soon though...finding it hard as hell to keep waiting said Dre to himself when there was a knock at his door.

Dre got up and opened his door to Jay standing in nothing but his jogging pants, he was the son of his mom's friend who was staying with them while his new place was getting remodeled, he was a dj at the club and constantly traveling around to paying gigs and making a little hustle on the side...he was 24, 6ft caramel complexion with a slightly stocky build but carried it well with a very cute face and dimples commenting his side burns and goat tee but the living arrangement was very good and they got along.

Hey sorry to bother you man but I was hoping that I could use your laptop for a minute, my shit keep freezing up and I'm trying to post a on line flyer at this club I dj at this weekend said Jay.

Ye, your shit keep freezing up because you need that damn virus protection after all those porn sites you be up there looking at...I checked out some of the shit you got up there man...you're a fucking porn fanatic said Dre.

Ye a little bit, I didn't catch you at a bad time did I...you won't up in here jacking off or nothing were you? Jay asked him.

If I was I wouldn't have answered the door said Dre.

So can I use your laptop? Jay asked him.

Ye...you can use it and for my generosity you toss a pack of smokes my way said Dre.

You got it man but you know you too young to be smoking, hell can't even buy your own pack of cigarettes because you aint old enough said Jay sitting down at his chair.

I'm too young to be in a serious relationship with a baby but I have both so this is just another thing I'm too young to do but I'll do anyway said Dre sitting on his bed picking up his cell phone.

I hear you but just don't let your mom find out you getting it from me nor that weed I hit you off with time to time said Jay.

Why would I do that homie,your little stay is working for my benefit as well as hers…you paying her a little rent and I'm getting the complimentary gifts it's a win win said Dre.

I bet it is with your spoil ass said Jay typing.

Yo why you say that? Dre laughed.

Your mom be giving you whatever you ask for, you only children grow up stingy and don't like to share because you never had too said Jay.

Naw man I'm not the only child I have a brother, I'm just the only one living in this house with her said Dre glancing over at Jay's big shoulders and backside in the seat.

Damn…he got a fat ass for a dude he thought to himself.

You ready for your birthday in a few weeks homie? Jay asked him.

Ye man, looking forward to a big party and a good time said Dre.

So you'll be 17 right? Still a young buck said Jay.

Ye but I'm getting there said Dre.

Yep and I got you little partner, I'll be your dj that night free of charge and I rented out a location for you too said Jay.

Don't act like you doing me a favor yo; my mom's told me that she already paid you in advance said Dre.

I still would have done it though…what you want me to give you for your birthday said Jay.

Huh? Dre replied.

Trying to give you something, so tell me what you want homie no matter what it is…well except a car I'm not balling like that right now said Jay.

I'll think about it…I'm going to be getting a lot of shit that I want already…guess I gotta figure out what I want from you said Dre looking at him from behind as Jay looked back and grinned at him then went back to typing on the laptop.

Chapter 27

Dre was spending another weekend with his girlfriend Gia at her mom's place as he usually did helping her take care of their son.

Dre talked to his son Darius as he was taking off his dirty diaper in the living room on the couch while Gia fussed in the bathroom finishing her shower.

Damn Dre, I mean really would it kill you to lift the sit when you piss and you even got a little on the floor, why do you guys have to be so fucking nasty like that and you just threw your overnight bag and all your clothes everywhere in my room...that's why I know when we get our own place together that you going to have to get your act together and be a little more coordinated and organized because I'm not going to have a nasty house...I'm a clean bitch, so clean I'm Mr. Cleans' daughter said Gia.

Mommy need to shut the hell up don't she...with her complaining, nagging ass...you coming to stay with me next weekend at my house where my mom hates her and she won't dare set foot in...you being here is the only thing that make it bearable the weekend long... swear if it wasn't for you...I'd had left her ass a long time ago...I'm going to be the best daddy I can be...way better than my father ever was said Dre in a low voice putting on a fresh pamper and picking him up and kissing his forehead.

Dre we need to go shopping tomorrow the baby is almost out of everything, don't worry it's not coming out of your pockets this time since you seem to be lacking lately...my mom got it and I hope that job come through for you soon because we need the cash...not like we can put the babies wants and needs on hold now can we? Hell, I can go without...but he can't Gia told him.

I fucking know that and I'm still taking care of him so be patient something will come through and until then he still won't go without rather I have a job or not…damn for once in your life have a little patience in faith…fuck…money don't fall out of the sky every time you open your hands said Dre shaking his head.

Oh I got plenty of patience and faith-fullness anyway…Especially with all those ballers and high rollers trying to holler at me all the time…offering me rides in their caddies and low riders…offering shopping sprees and trips to the beach… but what do I do…I stay blocking them…As much as I hated having you all the way out there in the country, that money you was making was outstanding but now it's all gone if you aint got something stashed away…really hope you not holding out on me and your son…that would be so selfish said Gia.

Females son, beware…when you first meet them they all nice and sweet doing whatever it takes to make you happy and then after you have a baby by them they feel like they got you trapped and start bringing out all that crazy shit and then threatening to keep your child from you…I love you but please beware of that trap alright? Dre told him as his son smiled.

Ye you know what I'm talking about grinned Dre then took his cell phone off the table checking it for messages and missed calls mainly hoping Trevor would get back at him.

Gia walked into the living room: You're here with me so why do you keep checking that phone and keeping it close to you like that… something I need to know? She asked.

Nope, I have friends and associates just like you do…never said I was going to cut off my social life because I'm in a relationship said Dre.

That's just fine with me as long as none of them got kitties, I'm the only pussy cat you need in your life…bad enough I'm fighting off all those tramps at school throwing themselves at you constantly knowing you got a boo and a baby but you don't be paying them any attention…I trust you, its them I don't trust which is why I don't have girlfriends so they can be trying to get at you behind my back and I know with your birthday coming up they going to try to give you birthday sex but that's not happening I'm keeping you on lock the whole day and night with me said Gia.

If you trust me like you say you do than why do you feel the need to have to do all that bird watching shit? Dre asked him.

I do trust you to a certain degree, but I'm not stupid either Dre… I got both these eyes open…just so you know said Gia.

You do realize that all that isn't necessary because you and I aren't together together right now, we both agreed that we were more so together now for the baby than each other…that's what you wanted if we couldn't work things out and truth be told because I keep it gutter…I'm not really feeling us together like that right now so stop going around here acting like we in a fairy tale and raising hell in the back ground…its not a good look said Dre.

No you just ready to be a hoe again and fuck other females, we been arguing and had our drama and issues all this long and now all of a sudden you just want to cut us up like that…I swear that if you got another bitch in the picture you need to let me know said Gia.

No I don't, there is no other girl in the picture I can promise you that…just on some new shit now and don't want to deal with all this on and on…I'm here because I got a lot of reasons to be here…I still love you, my son too of course and doing what I got it do to take care of him and that's what's really important right now said Dre.

Yeah you been on new shit every since you got back from the damn country trails, I think we need to restore our relationship and get us back to where we were said Gia.

Not really interested in that right now…you did some foul shit… cheating on me with your ex before I'm even out of town good yo wtf is that…think I was going to forgive you that easy like that's okay… you got me fucked up if you do said Dre.

No you just don't want to work things out and on some trip type shit because of me making a mistake and stepping out on you a while back when you left town....but its cool I am so good with that... we can chill, hang, operate or whatever the fuck we are now but even still when I'm with you than we together and nobody better not forget or disrespect me in my face or I'm going to end up fucking up some bitches and that's word said Gia.

Dre sighed rolling his eyes as his cell ranged as he looked at it.

Who that one of your sleazes, tell her that you with your baby momma and your son said Gia.

This is my boy Trevor said Dre.

Oh your little country buddy and summer field partner...I imagine that you too must have bonded very well because you talk to each other all the time and are awfully close...any broke back mountain activity that went on there that I need to know about? I mean your rooms were connected together and maybe you moved those beds together at some point and made it a California king said Gia.

Yep, we hit it off all summer long and banged back to back...he's a gentle yet aggressive and incredible lover...I love him and we getting married said Dre.

Ha ha whatever...I was just playing with you, I know for certain you aint like that...just the hoes I gotta worry about said Gia

Dre looked at a text message Trevor sent him and had a short back and forth:

Trevor: was sup big city, what you up too this weekend:

Dre: With the baby and girl, chilling back...what about you?

Trevor: Doing the same, I'm with my girl Jessy...we still at the bar having some shots

Dre: That's what's up, wish I was there kicking back some with you.

Trevor. Me too big city.

Dre: So you still coming down the weekend of my birthday right?

Trevor: Yeah man no doubt, I'll be there.

Dre. Cool, I'm going to let you get back to your night…talk to you soon I'm out.

Trevor. Alright man, have a good one…missing you-delete this last message I know your girl a snooper lol.

Dre. Lmao.

Dre are you done chatting it up because I need a back massage, all those after school fights are so hard on my back said Gia putting the baby in the crib and walking over and sitting beside him leaning on him rubbing her neck.

Am I still allowed to get those since were not together together? Gia asked him.

Comere said Dre turning sideways and massaging her shoulders as she closed her eyes.

Damn Dre, your hands are so soft and sturdy now…guess all the hard work the summer gave you a pair of man hands…I'm still going to have access to that dick too…once mine always mine remember that she said.

Later that night, Dre was asleep on Gia's bed when she crawled up on the bed over him naked touching his chest and kissing his neck and whispered in his ear.

Dre…wake up…the baby's asleep…time for us to get it in…I want you to make love to me Dre she said unbuckling his pants as he looked at her with sleepy eyes and closed them as she took his dick and gave him a blow job as she stroked it as he moaned all the while thinking about Trevor was doing it then grabbed her head to force her deeper down on it.

Easy Dre, I just got my hair did…she said taking his hand off and continued sucking it as he rolled his eyes then looked over at the dresser.

Hold up he said reaching over and taking a condom out of it and biting off the seal.

I'm on the pill Dre, we good we don't have to use that said Gia.

So…I'm still using it, don't want any unexpected pop ups in your ovary area he said getting undressed as she rolled her eyes and laid on her back as he put the condom on and lifted her legs and pushed his dick in her banging her out as she screamed grabbing his arms as he looked at her he saw Trevor in that same position but he had to remember it wasn't him…it was her he was looking at and hard to forget that with her screaming like a real bitch so he flipped her over and fucked her doggy style thinking that it was Trevor beating her back out and ending in a orgasm yell panting then smacked her ass.

Omg Dre…that was so fucking good said Gia.

Ye…it was for me too, now get up and make me a sandwich or something and be quick about it said Dre.

Chapter 28

It was the day before Dre's birthday and school was out, he was home cleaning up the house while his mother was at work which was her strict requirement that she expected of him besides school.

Dre slept in his bed when the covers were snatched off him.

Wake up boy! yelled his mom.

Dang mom, what's up? Dre asked rubbing his eyes.

What's up? What's up is there is still a kitchen full of dirty dishes left from yesterday and last night, get your dirty ass up and go in there and clean them, you aint got school today and if you want to have a good birthday I suggest you get to it on the double she said.

I didn't mess up all those dishes, Jay was in there messing up the kitchen cooking shit before he left out of town yesterday evening... he always doing that and leaving and I'm not cleaning up after a grown man so when he get home in a little while from his hotel stay he can bust some suds said Dre.

How about I bust your ass, I don't care who did it...all I know is I want them cleaned right now so get in there...I gotta go to work again soon after leaving a damn shift the least I can do is come home to a clean house...I'm going to make sure you do it too because I'm going to sit right in the living room watching you than take my power nap then I want you to vacuum and mop the kitchen floor, take out the trash, clean the bathroom and do our laundry she said.

Man said Dre jumping up and walking toward the door.

Call me a man one more damn time and I'm going to knock you 2 ways into Sunday, you are not too grown up for an ass whooping she said.

Wow, you cussing a lot now and you a Christian...you backsliding said Dre.

You are going to back slide when I back slap you she said.

The only reason you making me clean up after him is because you like all that extra money coming in here and don't want to make him upset in leave said Dre.

Go! She said.

Dre started walking real slow like turtle.

Boy she said jumping at him with her arm raised as he took off running down the stairs laughing.

Silly ass self she said.

Early that afternoon, Dre was mopping the kitchen floor when Jay got in from one of his traveling gigs with his bags and his tot suitcase and came into the kitchen.

What up soon to be birthday boy said Jay.

Ye what up and I just mopped there man stop making tracks and freeze frame said Dre.

My bad dude…damn this place looking spotless and the ac air is so fresh good job bra said Jay.

Ye, I know one thing you better start cleaning your own shit before you go to do your club gigs…think I like cleaning up after you?

Who the fuck do I look like your wife? Dre asked him.

Naw because I hoped that she'd be a bit prettier, Yo I didn't mean to leave you with all the clean up, I had to pack up and leave to handle some other things before I left town but I think this will make up for it he said putting a quarter bag of weed, 2 packs of cigarettes and a bundle of cash on the counter as Dre looked up at it than him.

I think that just about covers it…good looking out said Dre.

You got it smiled Jay going upstairs.

Dre bobbed his head happily as he mopped the floor than his cell ranged it was Trevor which was a surprise because he never really called him around this time but he answered it.

Hey what's good man said Dre.

What up big city, what you up too? Trevor asked him.

Not much man, out of school today and cleaning the house...ready for you to get down here so we can chill for old times' sake so what's up said Dre.

Damn big city, I really hate to tell you this...really man... but I have to pros pone my visit this weekend some things came up and it's not a good time for me to travel down that way said Trevor.

What you mean you can't come down here and what came up? It's the fucking weekend and I know you don't got work and you pulling out on me man when I was looking forward to seeing you...what kind of shit is that man said Dre.

Eh man, I wanted to come...really bad and I hate to not be able to see you on your birthday after I promised you but I have other things I have to deal with that came up and need my attention and yeah I'm off on the weekend but doesn't mean I don't have to go into office at the farm to oversee developments and reports...beyond that I have other situations so please don't be mad at me...we can reschedule said Trevor.

Dre paused for a moment on the phone.

So are you telling me whatever you got going on that it's so important that it can't wait? I haven't seen you since you dropped me back home he said.

I'm telling you that I can't make it down and I'm sorry, I'm still sending your gift though...I'm wiring you some money and where to pick it up said Trevor.

Whatever, I don't even want it forget it said Dre.

So you telling me that you can't understand my situation? You claim to be so mature and shit and you acting like a fucking spoiled kid right now said Trevor.

I'm good man...so I hope you work out whatever you got going on and I'll just get at you when I can I guess said Dre.

Comon big city stop tripping said Trevor.

I'm not...not anymore believe it said Dre as if indicating something.

I'm sending you the money said Trevor.

Later Dre said as if not caring.

You better pick it up said Trevor.

Later homie said Dre ending call.

Shit...I'm about tired of waiting on you he said in a low voice when there was a rang at the doorbell.

Dre went to the door and looked out than opened it to an old homeboy of his Darrell.

Yo what up homie, what it is birthday boy! He said slapping five with him coming inside and got him in a bear hug and spun him around.

Yo put me down nigga said Dre.

Man, long time no see real talk, with school and being wrapped up under your baby momma I rarely see you anymore...shit you know I dropped outta school a while back and don't fuck with that place they won't let me on the grounds but I'd never forget your birthday homie so happy birthday said Darrell.

My birthday tomorrow man and you know my mom don't want you anywhere near here no offense bruh said Dre.

Ye I know man and I don't appreciate her chasing me out the yard on her car the last time I was here...well at least I was close to remembering your birthday...bought you a little gift he said rubbing his hands and going back outside and coming back in with a shoebox wrapped up in newspaper.

Damn homie, appreciate the thought but this gift wrap is ghetto as hell said Dre.

Keeping it gangster cuz, shit open it said Darrell.

Dre tore the paper and opened the shoe box to a glock.

Boom surprise said Darrell.

Yo...you got me a gun? Dre asked him.

Hell ye nigga and its clean, got a friend of mine to buy it out the shop because he got a license for a gun so now you can carry around and rock that legal style said Darrell.

It aint legal for me if I'm not the one with the license said Dre.

Smh, you and your details…telling me you don't like it or something…now my feelings hurt said Darrell.

My mom told me if she finds a gun in her house she kicking me out no questions asked said Dre.

Then make sure you put it up good duh, you need a cuddy buddy like that holding your hand when you up on these streets…the bible offers the peace of all understanding but this right here yo is the peace maker…plus it's a no return policy so it's yours to do with as you please happy birthday said Darrell hugging him.

I'm not keeping this said Dre.

Yo you use to love guns, man wherever you were the summer and fucked your mind up has took away your gangster lean and made you straight soft said Darrell.

Chapter 29

For Dre's birthday night, Jay hosted it at a complex he rented out for the night and was the dj for the night and he really appreciated him shelling out major money bringing it all together and still offering to give him a birthday gift and rather enjoyed having him stay with them for the time he was there and had a few weeks left before he went back to his place being remodeled.

Dre had a birthday dance with Gia in a circle as the crowds watched and cheered them on and even though their relationship was hellish most times they could freak like no other couple when it came to the dance floor.

A girl from the crowd Megan looked at Gia dancing with jealous eyes and spoke to her girl friend beside her.

I don't know why the fuck he still with her, she is a straight gold digging hoe and think she can beat everybody…she got hands but my girl Nina rocked that ass a month ago…look at her, acting like she aint got no baby at home…that's where she need to be… fucking club mom said Megan in her girls ear as she laughed.

After a while, Gia stood with her cousin Anita on the other side of the club having drinks.

I don't know why Dre invited half these hood rats to this party, they act like its their damn birthday, damn bag back some and let my fucking baby shine…where he at, oh okay there he go over there,telling you right now these hoes better stay the fuck away from my man or I'm pulling teeth said Gia.

Somebody said that he told them that he wasn't with you like that nowadays said her cousin Anita.

What the fuck they know, people always in our business like they right there in our relationship,I hope the roof really do catch on fire and wet up all these mother fuckers in here,I'm ready for this party to be over so I can take him home…boring now said Gia.

Dre look like he is having fun and not ready to leave any time soon, do you want me to take you home? Anita asked her.

Hell naw, I'm staying here with my man,we came together and we living together, not to be funny but you came here with all your little girlfriends and I'm not trying to be packed in that little ass car…so Mexican your ass right on with your squad because I'm good, I'm el Gucci baby said Gia.

Okay I was just offering,You sound ignorant said Anita.

You look ignorant said Gia.

Bitch, I will be ignorant all over your mother fucking ass, now try me said Anita.

Ugh, what ever, I'm going where my baby out later my bitch said Gia chucking up the deuces and walking off.

Anita took a sip of her drink shaking her head at Gia.

Dre was talking to some of his boys having a birthday drink when Megan squeezed through the small gang of guys touching them sensually as they checked her out and came up beside Dre.

Hey birthday boy, I wanted to personally wish you a great one and many more she said hugging him.

Ye thanks…you smell good he grinned.

Thank you, So what's good, where your little girlfriend at she been at your side all night and now she vanished all of a sudden leaving you unattended…did she have to go home to get the baby you 2 have or something? Megan asked him.

Naw, I think she chatting it up with some friends she know said Dre looking around.

Oh…you look good tonight and you fresh to death said Megan touching his chain and playing with it.

Thanks said Dre.

So what you getting into after the night, you got an after party going on or something...run her home and I can keep you company...I been trying to just get to know you for the longest but you always seemed to be under,around,beaneath and above her...can we talk? Megan smiled at him.

Um...Not right now said Dre looking over Megan's shoulder seeing Gia power walking through the crowd.

Um excuse me but can you back the hell up off him please thank you said Gia budging past her and standing beside Dre.

Megan looked at her then back at Dre.

Enjoy your birthday Dre she said walking off twisting and swung her hair behind her back and went over to her girl talking and both looked at Gia and laughed rolling their eyes.

Fucking stupid bitches,Why the fuck you staring after her like that for Dre...do you want her or something...I saw you watching her all night and if you want to hit that be my guest but make sure you make an appointment to a clinic because she burns like nobody's business said Gia.

Yo can you get out my ear with all that please thank you...this my birthday so don't kill the vibe with all this bullshit go somewhere with that said Dre.

I'm ready to go before I have to hurt somebody Dre said Gia.

Dre looked at her. Okay later he said.

So you're not coming? asked Gia.

Wtf?This is my birthday what I look like leaving my own birthday party are you that dense? Dre asked her.

It's about over anyway and the crowds breaking up, why you want to stay so bad so you can get you some extra birthday sex from twiddle Dee and twiddle dumb bitch over there and if she keep looking this direction my pony tail is coming off said Gia.

Yo really?You want to start drama on my fucking birthday?yo wait for your birthday to roll around and act crazy don't ruin mine....fuck you so fucking simple at times I swear said Dre taking a sip as his boys got big eyed as Gia looked at him with her mouth open.

Simple? Oh really?You trying to be hard in front of your boys right now? She took a drink and dashed it in his face.

Sip on that said Gia walking off fast.

Oh snap! Yelled his boys laughing.

Dre wiped his face and went after her and grabbed her arm: What the fuck is wrong with you comere he said.

Get off me Dre! I'm leaving said Gia.

How you going to get home, you don't have a car and you came with me said Dre.

You don't have a car either but I will find a way now let go of me said Gia.

Yo Gia you alright? said her ex Jerell.

Oh Jerell...yeah I'm fine said Gia.

Nigga don't worry about how the fuck she doing and move your ass on said Dre.

You want a ride home? Jerell asked her.

Yeah I mean I do need a ride but...I don't want to disrespect my baby's father like that said Gia.

Yo did you hear me man, move the fuck on before you carried away last time said Dre.

Dre you need to stop acting a fool, he does whip and you not ready to go so I'm outty said Gia.

Trick carry yo ass on then, you aint fucking worth me putting him in the emergency room tonight said Dre.

Eh dog, don't disrespect her like that, not cool said Jerell.

Shut up bitch said Dre pushing him back as their boys held them back.

Yo chill birthday boy we got this, dip off before we send you off... who the fuck invited you here anyway said one of his boys Monty.

This is crazy, Jerell go! You know you already on your third strike please said Gia walking out as he looked at Dre and walked off.

Oh so you going with him bitch, cool I'm done with your ratchet ass anyway but I'm coming by there to get my son said Dre turning to his boys balling his fist.

She want to ruin my birthday and who the fuck let that nigga in my party, bitch ass pussy...I'm about to bring out the old Dre and she just got him fucked up... yo lets roll out I'm going to get my son and while we there we busting that nigga ass and beating the blood out him said Dre.

She is such a drama queen, Dre why are you chasing after her when I'm right here for the taking said Megan.

Dre looked at her. I'll holla, lets bounce he told his boys as they left out.

You're lost said Megan turning around and going back to her where friend was.

After Dre and his boys served him up Gia's ex with an ass whooping he took his son and his stuff and took him back to his house and fed him and laid him on his bed beside him into he fell asleep with a bib in his mouth and kissed his forehead then went to the bathroom to clean his skinned knuckles and saw Jay in the bathroom with the door open and a towel around his waist just getting out the shower and turned and looked at him.

What up champ, I saw your crew start to get heated up during your birthday party and you dipped off...what's good? Jay asked him.

Had to handle some business that's all Dre told him.

Damn shame, I swear black people feed on drama, your one night to celebrate it and have a good time and you push it to the side to chase after some negro and yo baby momma...not worth it man, just let it go and focus on your son...fuck all that extra stuff said Jay.

It wasn't about her, it was the principal and no mother fucking showing up uninvited to my birthday party and disrespecting me like that said Dre.

Alright Mr. bad ass, so what you doing now? Jay asked him.

I just put my son to sleep…I'm about to wash this nigga beat down off me and call it a night…all and all I had a good night…gotta take a piss too…mom keeps her room locked up so I can't use her bathroom said Dre.

Go ahead man said Jay continuing to brush his teeth in the mirror as if wanting Dre to go in while he was in there and take a piss while he was in there.

Naw I can wait man…just give my door a tap when you done said Dre.

Okay cool…so you figured out what you want me to give you for your birthday said Jay looking at him in that way.

You good man, you did enough and I appreciate it said Dre.

You sure….what's good? Jay asked him.

Dre knew that he had been hitting on him ever since he moved in and clearly had dl tendencies despite having tons of females and pretended not to be aware of his advances…he was attractive but Dre just won't trying to go there with him…too close to home and everybody had already find out about him and Trevor in the country almost and was not trying to drag that into the city.

I'm straight man; let me know when you done said Dre walking back to his room as Jay nodded.

Chapter 30

Dre woke up late the next morning and immediately looked down beside him and his son Darius was gone as he looked around in a panic.

Eh where my son at?! Dre yelled aloud.

He jumped up quick and ran out into the hall as his mom stood holding his son and feeding him with a bottle.

Boy slow down I got him, I got home this morning and he was in here wet, crying and just like a true daddy you was knocked out sleep so I took him…aw look at my beautiful baby, I love me my Darius and I swear he is the only good thing that came out of you and Gia's relationship, she been calling the home phone this morning asking about you and the baby and I know she been blowing up your cell too so when you up give that crazy thing a call…how was your birthday bash last night? Dre's mother asked him.

It was cool…said Dre touching his son's hand.

Good, well I'm off work today so I'm going to spend some time with my Darius before you take him back to that little strumpet girlfriend of yours she said.

She not my girlfriend no more, she just the mother of my child now and that's it said Dre.

Thank god, you both were too young and trying to grow up too fast and not ready for a serious relationship like that anyway…just take care of your son and you don't need to be with her to do it…you both are still kids and need some space and honestly you can do a whole lot better than that but I don't want no more grandkids any time soon said his mom.

Me either said Dre.

The phone ranged downstairs.

That's probably her again, I just want to take that phone and throw it out the damn window…She calling here talking about where Dre at, where my baby at, I'll be over to get him when my mom get home and I told her that you was sleep and I got the baby and she can come get him later on and he is in good hands…you going to spend some time with grandma aren't you huh? Ye look at you smiling with those dimples awe…I'm about to go feed him…get the phone she said walking downstairs with him as Dre sighed and went behind her and answered the phone.

Yeah Dre replied.

So I see you finally up, like for real Dre was that really necessary attacking him last night like that with your people, snatching my baby out my arms and riding off with a car load of hoods do you know how fucking scared and I was and you best believe that if I didn't trust you with my son like I do I would have called the police and got you locked up but I'm not a bitch like that said Gia.

Darius is with me and he fine and your little ex should have kept his damn mouth closed and what the fuck was he doing at my party…. yo did you invite that nigga?asked Dre.

Of course I didn't, why the fuck would I do that like really? I saw him at the store a while back and might have mentioned it making conversation and trying to get away from him said Gia.

It was none of his fucking business what I was having period; yo I gotta get off this phone…got things to do Dre told her.

Oh you do huh Gia asked him.

Fuck, I just woke up and haven't even wiped the crust out of my eyes or brush my teeth yet and you blowing up the phone all morning chill out said Dre.

Smh bye said Gia ending call.

Fucking ignorant ass said Dre.

Dre picked up his cell and saw the countless calls left by Gia but none by Trevor.

Fucking dude a trip for real...Didn't even call me back after that happy birthday yesterday morning to ask me how my party was or nothing...whatever though he said laying back down in bed and made a couple calls to him as the morning passed and noon but got the answering machine both times.

Yo home, what's good...calling you to let you know that I had a great birthday party last night and wanted to get at you for a few... thanks for that gift...I picked it up...get back at me man yeah I'm out:

What up man, I see you can't get back...cool...guess you busy or whatever right now still... but I'll just let you get at you...later man he ended second call that afternoon.

Dre got on his laptop pissed at Trevor for ignoring him and horny, he found a bi/gay chat site looking at it for a bit than created a picture less profile and scrolled down the list of guys in his city just reading information on them and found one guy's profile that he particularly liked who had a picture less profile as well...discreet bi dude currently in a relationship with his girlfriend but looking for cool masculine dudes to get at, chill and smoke with strictly no relationships, masculine bottom,...nsa encounter, no gay dudes, strictly bi-dudes only, not showing pictures on line but If we vibe then we can exchange via phone,5'10, 170,20,brown skin, low cut mustache and goat tee.

Dre saw that he was on line and sparked up a conversation as they got a feel on each other's status and background although Dre did lie about his age and say he was 19...after about an half an hour of chatting on the phone they exchanged numbers and sent each other pictures...Dre sent a picture of him with fittie over face naked and he sent one with a hoodie on with his face blurred out but his body was sexy....dude was liking what he saw and wanted to get up and asap at his spot giving him address which was in a location he didn't know too many people which was perfect... being that his girl was away until the night and although it seemed too soon to be getting up with a guy like that he knew that bi-dudes had limited time and he was ready to just fuck today and relive some stress and both go their separate ways which is what he wanted…although the guy wanted a ongoing get up with a masculine dude Dre went in knowing that he was going to fuck him and not call him back.

Dre got dressed, took his own condoms because dudes had a tendency to be treacherous out there on the low or not and walked downstairs heading out.

Where you going? Dre's mom asked him.

I'm going to my cousin Dennis house to get a late birthday present he want to give me, I'll be back after awhile said Dre.

Okay make sure you do, I need to get the day started in a bit and you need to watch your son until Miss Thang get over here said his mom.

Jay came out of the kitchen eating a sandwich: Yo, you need a ride homie to where you going? He asked.

I'm good man but thanks though said Dre leaving out.

Dre caught the bus to that part of town where he lived and went up to his apartment where both met face to face and liked what they saw mutually and sat down talking although Dre told him that he couldn't smoke weed because he had to work the afternoon but he didn't want to come back home with the scent deep on him since his mother didn't know about him smoking it, from keen observation he could tell that dude had fixed his place and all pictures to conceal who he knew or who his girl was but he was cool and respected that because he would have done the same.

So you got a girl and a kid huh, that's what's up…do anybody know about you? asked the guy who introduced himself as Rhode.

Naw man nobody down here, what about you? Dre asked him.

No one, I keep a extremely discreet profile on and off the streets, got a fiancé…trying to get it in before I get married and cut it all out in a month for good and settle down in a relationship with her…I'm telling you it's going to be hard dedicating myself to one female like that but its time man…gotta do my grown man…shut it down with other males and females altogether you feel me he said as Dre nodded looking at a ring on his finger that could possibly be an engagement band.

You mad cute man, you know that right smiled Rhode and had a pretty smile with gold in his mouth.

Thanks man you good too said Dre.

Rhode nodded glancing at the clock as if he was rationing out time putting out his cigarette then moved from the recliner to the couch beside him rubbing his leg and moving his hand to his crotch groping it.

So do I get to taste what you saw me in the pictures? He said.

Dre nodded.

That's what's up…I'm going to handle this…he leaned in to kiss Dre neck then try to kiss him in the mouth.

Yo sorry man but I don't kiss said Dre.

Cool…keeping it gangster huh…I'm feeling that he said getting on his knees in front of him and unbuckling his belt and pulled his pants down taking his dick out stroking it looking at it for a moment.

This mad pretty he said as he went down on him and sucked his rock hard dick deep throating it on the spot and he could give some good head as he stroked and sucked the fuck out of it.

So can I get it? Put it in me? Rhode asked him.

Dre nodded.

They both took off all their clothes as Rhode went and laid a towel across the sofa as Dre put a condom on and sat down as Rhode mounted him stroking his dick and pushed it down into his ass which was fairly tight as he moaned and started riding Dre who held his waist then bounced on it like a pro as Dre closed his eyes and bit his lip.

Damn dude bad he thought to himself.

Rhode turned around and sat on his dick bouncing on it fast and hard as Dre felt himself reaching his climax he moved him and took off the condom jacking off and busted all over dude face who had his mouth open to catch it but seemed to not be interested in getting off himself.

Damn that was hot man, we gotta get up one more time though… you got some good dick said Rhode.

Ye definitely man said Dre getting dressed washing hands and leaving.

It was strange though…all at once he was feeling and relieved and at the pit of his soul some sense of guilt that he had cheated on Trevor as if they were in a relationship because he had fucked another dude for the first time after so many months of waiting on Trevor and it wasn't a big deal when it was a girl but this had him feeling some kind of way and he shook it off deleted Rhode's number realizing for the first time how much he must have really cared about Trevor to feel so bad and headed back home.

When Dre got back to the house he got a phone call a short while later from the Manager called him and told him that he got the job and start that week.

Mom, I got that job at the footlocker in the mall and start the coming week after school said Dre.

That's what's up, I'm happy for you now you can make your own money and stop spending all of mine up for a change she said.

Shit…I'm not spending it I'm stacking it thought Dre to himself.

Here take Darius, I gotta take get up take me a bath and cook dinner…you never bought back a gift you said your cousin had for you she said.

He gave me a peace of mind said Dre taking his son as a car horn beeped outside as he went to window and looked out to Gia outside with her mom getting out the car.

Who that? asked his mom.

Gia said Dre.

I didn't know she was coming already, did she call you? asked his mom.

Naw said Dre.

Aint that a blip, she been blowing up the phone all morning and then want to show up not even telling us…she is working my last nerves please get Darius stuff ready so she can be in and out at the same time said his mom.

Dre opened the door as Gia came in glaring at Dre and then glanced over at his mom.

Hey she told her waving slightly than taking Darius from Dre into her arms.

Umhm said his mom.

Dre gathered the baby bag and walked out the house with her to car.

It's alright now baby, mommy here you okay? He looks like he been crying a lot his face all red she told Dre kissing the baby head.

Is he alright? What is she trying to say…that little Um she said going upstairs.

That Night, Dre finally got a call from Trevor and was happy to hear from him but hid it as he answered the phone.

What up replied Dre.

Hey big city, I'm sorry I didn't get back at you today or earlier rather…I went to church with your Uncle and my girl came along and we had dinner together and chilled at his house for a bit…so I listen to the voice mails and I'm glad that you had a good birthday…I was hoping you did said Trevor.

Thanks man, just got a call back about that job and I'm starting it this week said Dre.

That's what's up, congratulations man, find out your schedule so I can decide when to come and see you said Trevor.

See me when? Dre asked him.

Soon man, like this weekend soon, can I? Trevor asked him.

Ye that's cool, let me find out what's going on and either way if you serious this time I want you to come down…I won't be crossing my fingers homie…with you I'm sure you'll come up with some excuse to back out last minute said Dre.

Nope not this time man, I'm coming down Friday and getting a room for the weekend so be ready said Trevor.

Alright cool then so things work out work wise this weekend? Dre replied back.

It was a task getting things together but I did it…I'm going to take a shower and call you back later tonight and we can chat on Skype want to see your face again said Trevor.

Okay get at me said Dre.

Alright later man said Dre ending call then sighed and laid on his bed thinking to himself.

Fuck, if only I knew I would have waited for you…

Chapter 31

That Friday noon, Trevor arrived into town just like he said he would and Dre was packing up some bags in his room with Jay walked by and stood to his door.

I see you going on a little get away homie said Jay.

Ye man just for the weekend, getting up with an old friend from a while back to chill with said Dre.

That's what's up…shit I'm heading out for the weekend myself too, got a gig at a couple clubs out of town…well be safe and I'll see you back later on then…you need anything…you good? Jay asked him.

Ye I'm straight man said Dre.

My place will be ready in another week or so and I'll be moving back in there…bet you'll be glad to have your space back to yourself huh Jay asked him.

You were cool man, kind of going to miss the perks of free smokes and bud when you were here said Dre.

Well just let me know if you need anything, still got your back… know you just starting your job and got school and the baby and a little extra never hurts here or there said Jay.

Appreciate that man said Dre.

I'll let you get back to packing then said Jay walking off.

Dre cell ranged, it was Trevor as he quickly answered it.

Ye what's good said Dre.

I'm just pulling up outside your place big city said Trevor.

Word, you didn't have any trouble finding it after all this time? Dre asked him.

Nope, the wonders of the navigator and the fact that I keep mental blue prints of my surroundings…what a drive…I'm tired and need to take a shower…I called and the room ready…you still packing? Trevor asked him.

Ye almost done but I'm coming out now to see you homie said Dre ending call then ran down the stairs and opened the door and saw Trevor outside in front of his house with a new truck this time as he hid his big smile but it still came out as a grin as he walked up to it.

Damn, long time no see homie said Dre slapping his hand in a shake and holding it as he leaned into the passenger side window.

You telling me said Trevor.

I see you got a new whip said Dre.

Ye, still got the other truck but I upgraded a bit…your uncle helped me to get it…you like? asked Trevor.

Ye this is hot, you know you stay with your big ass trucks smiled Dre.

Just keeping it country said Trevor.

Damn man, you really came this time…still can't believe it… starting to think you would never come back after having time to think about screwing the kid said Dre in a low voice.

O ye of little faith, I was always coming back…so get the rest of your stuff packed and let's get to this room, got a nice one on the top stairs floor in the nice part of town for the weekend so let's go man said Trevor.

Yep, be right back said Dre quickly going back into the house.

Is that your boy? Jay asked him.

Ye, Trevor the one I worked with in the country when I was staying with my Uncle said Dre going upstairs and grabbed his bags then came back down.

See you later homie said Dre.

Alright cool said Jay trying to get a closer look outside as he left.

Soon they were headed to the room talking along the way.

I have to be to work at 4,but I'm off tomorrow so you can drop me off there and come pick me up when I get off tonight and while you at the room if you get bored you can just ride around and get a better look at the surroundings just don't venture too far off or unknown areas without me as your guide then tonight I can take you to this spot to play some pool…sorry I can't take you to the major spots but I'm still not legally aged enough to get in according to the stupid laws you know said Dre.

Sounds cool man said Trevor looking at him and nodded as Dre went back to a short pause just looking out the window.

You alright man? Trevor asked him.

Ye I'm good…happy to see you that's all said Dre as Trevor nodded.

As soon as they got into the room and put their bags down Dre went over and hugged Trevor for a long while as Trevor laughed to himself.

Wow…glad I still have that effect on you he said.

My bad man just didn't realize how much I missed you until I actually saw you said Dre.

Don't apologize, its cool and the feeling is mutual said Trevor taking his hand and leaning in and kissed him.

Sorry…didn't mean to get all gay there for a moment said Trevor.

Its fine, the feelings mutual said Dre leaning in and kissed him again.

Man at what point did we get this flaky? Dre smiled.

I can't tell you, guess it just snuck up on us…I'm about to get in the shower but I do have something I want to give you…I actually made it for you some time ago and planned on giving it to you when I came down…you do know I'm a crafts man right? Trevor asked him.

Oh yeah I remember, you build boats and wagons from scratch,in the barn,we both remember the barn said Dre.

We'll I couldn't fit all those in my bag but I was able to fit this he said opening one of his bags and taking out something that looked like a colorful wild flower and gave it to him.

For me...wow...it's a flower...said Dre.

Hey, it took me a few days to make that from plastic, paper mashe,paint and thread...it's actually the artificial replicate of a rare wild flower that grows out in the country and I want you to keep it so you'll always have a piece of the country with you and well- the memories said Trevor.

Wow, this is really touching man, really...thanks said Dre.

Yep replied Trevor.

So you go ahead and jump in the shower and clean those musty balls up a bit and I'll be waiting for you in the bed butt naked...fuck my mouth and my ass like I'm your girlfriend said Dre groping his crotch.

Oh really...damn when you put it like that, Let me run in and come back out then said Trevor grabbing his back pack and going in the bathroom.

Dre took off all his clothes then went over and opened his back-pack and took out a bag of rose petals and put them on the bed.

Damn too bad I couldn't do romantic shit with Gia like this with her evil ass thought Dre as he sat on the bed and relaxed his arms behind his head and closed his eyes.

Been waiting forever for this shit he said to himself as his cell phone ranged as he sighed and reached over on the dresser and looked at it and saw that his mom was calling he had packed up and dipped out before she got home as he thought of a lie to make moving his lips and answered it.

Hello said Dre.

Boy where you at and you didn't say nothing about going away for the weekend, Jay told me you left minutes before I got in and don't you have work today? She asked.

Yes mam and I'm going but um yeah I forgot to tell you that I went to go stay with some friends of mine this weekend to work on this big science project and we have a lot of work to do...I just want to do my best work so I'm giving it my full undivided attention said Dre.

Oh…well you could have told me that you were leaving and next time you check in before you check out…at least I got the house to myself for the weekend and can do what I want she said.

Like what, you Christian and single you either going to have bible study or a book club meeting said Dre.

Boy you don't know what I do, don't get it twisted I'm a momma but I'm a women too she said.

Ew bye now said Dre.

Umhm, I'll see you later she said ending call in time to hear Trevor talking on the phone with his girlfriend in the bathroom getting his lies right too.

Yeah, I just arrived into town and settled down in my room, I have this business proposition to look over concerning the agriculture developments and progression of farmer crops and exhausting stuff about that to up and coming people interested in the future of farming but I'm about to get a little shut eye, talk to them about when this meeting takes place and talk to you later…alright you too…bye he said ending call.

Trevor opened the door butt naked and saw Dre lying on the bed with the rose petals and smiled.

Sexy said Trevor.

I saw it in a movie once, so let's do this…I want to get a really good fuck in before I have to go to work in a little while said Dre.

Trevor walked over to the bed and got on top of him as Dre touched his chest and glided his hands down it groping his dick as Trevor kissed down his neck and chest licking his nipples then glided his tongue down his stomach then kissed his pelvis as Dre moaned biting his lip and bought his head in front of his face as if about to kiss him then bought his body forward until Trevor's dick was in front of his face and gripped the base of it and wrapped his lips around it just tasting the tip of it then begin swallowing down his dick as Trevor moaned fucking his mouth then grabbed Dre's head forcing him to do it faster and he was thinking how excited how aggressive Trevor seemed to be now while stroking his dick.

Trevor laid Dre flat across to the side of the bed then fucked his mouth down making him take all his dick down his throat as Dre held the pounding pistol with one hand while gripping his waist type with the other then Trevor stood up bringing him up to his knees and put both his hands on Dre's head and continued pumping his mouth full of his rock hard dick and as they got deeper into it they both grabbed condoms at the same time.

I know we kind of did the commando thing a while back but you know-said Dre.

Yeah I know said Trevor biting the seal off and putting it on his dick while Dre laid on his back he positioned his legs.

Be easy at first…been like almost 10 months said Dre.

Trevor nodded then slowly pushed it forward into his tight ass and both let out an orgasm gasp as if waiting and wanting to this very feeling for so long and after a few good strokes into Dre's ass the condom popped and for a moment Trevor didn't know if he wanted to pull out or keep going he was so use to this original feeling at that moment and Dre had the same expression but slowly pushed Trevor out of him and put another condom on his dick and continued forward and before long they were doing every freaky position…doggy style, had Dre riding it frontwards and backwards and even standing up on the bed pounding him out then both ended up almost off the bed ending it with both busting incredible loads of nut on each other's stomachs and both laid in bed panting for a moment smoking a cigarette.

That's the birthday sex I should have got from you said Dre.

Better late than ever said Trevor.

After a little while Dre laid in bed thinking to himself then looked over at Trevor.

Eh homie he said.

What's up? Trevor asked turning to him.

After me and since we part ways have you got down with another dude, don't care or nothing just want to know and be real said Dre.

If you want to know than obviously you do care on some level yes? Trevor smiled.

Whatever, have you or haven't you said Dre.

Naw man, I haven't...went back to familiar territory if you know what I mean and stayed there well up until now grinned Trevor.

Oh cool said Dre.

And you? Trevor asked him.

I did...one guy, one time said Dre.

Word...oh wow said Trevor as if a little bothered about it.

It didn't mean anything, just at the time I was horny and wanted to do it...because I couldn't have you to get down with it and it got hard waiting said Dre.

I got it man, you don't have to explain...you had the urge to re-experience the experience again...did you at least wait a while before you cheated on me laughed Trevor a little.

A while, It was a really long ass while Dre grinned.

Good, think you can be faithful to me now and vow as long as we both get down to not fuck with another dude but me? Trevor asked him.

Ye, I can do that...just don't have me waiting forever again said Dre.

I won't...so...when you and he did the business who did who... curious said Trevor.

All you need to know is that I saved the best parts for you, gotta get ready for work now...taking you out on the town when I get off than we got all night to reconnect said Dre getting up and going to the bathroom.

Can't wait said Trevor.

Chapter 32

Trevor took Dre to work than picked him up afterwards he went back to the room got dressed for the night life scene and both went to a pool hall in town he occasionally hanged out at and got a few games in while Trevor had an alcoholic beverage.

So did you enjoy sightseeing out and about around the city while I was at work? Dre asked him.

Yeah it was pretty cool, I went to the mall here or what we call in the country a super store…we don't have one of those in my town so all I can go by is people from my way who traveled up and down the big cities…coincidental thing is when I was walking around in there I saw your girlfriend Gia with a girl friend of hers on a colossal shopping spree and when she saw me she looked back twice like she recognized me from the past but I don't think she really remember me though and I kept it moving said Trevor.

Oh word…guess she doing what she best at most besides running her fucking mouth, she fucking ruined my birthday bash and I winded up mixing it up with her ex…I never knew this chick would bring so much drama in my life and it wasn't like that at all when we first got together but after the baby it's like she started acting out thinking that she own me and holding my son over my head…right now he the only reason I even deal with her…I'm more than certain if I don't feed into what she wants she'll try to keep him from me but she definitely don't want to play that game he said making a shot with the pool stick.

So you and the girl aren't on good terms right now huh big city said Trevor.

At this point homie,the only thing we have between us is our son and why I'm staying…whatever love or feelings I had for her are slowly dying…she showed me her true colors and I've dealt with all her dramatic bull shit long enough…figure when I'm 18 I'm going to get joint custody of my son and wash my hands with her once and for all or take him away altogether because she don't exactly provide a stable living environment but until then…do what I gotta do to be in his life and provide for him said Dre.

Very commendable said Trevor.

Yo Dre! Yelled a voice from across the room.

Dre turned to his homeboy Darell walking over and slapping five with him.

What's good with you man said Darrell.

Not much man, just chilling with my homeboy playing some pool…Trevor this Darrell, Darrell this my boy Trevor said Dre.

Hey what's good man said Darrell slapping five with him.

Hey what's up man said Trevor.

Not much man just out and about so you from here? asked Darell.

Naw, I'm from the Deep South…just down here kicking it for the weekend said Trevor.

Word, wow you come along way then homie…I picked it up in your accent…you from like the country huh said Darrell.

Yep, born and raised said Trevor.

That's what's up…well welcome to the big city man…lots to get into down here and I know all the crowds and places where it really jumps off…shit if you whipping then we can hit up one of the major spots now…know you blaze and drink yo…I know this party going on tonight on Denver avenue…so yall trying to hang? Darrell asked him.

Naw man I think I'll pass tonight got some other things going on and that part of town aint exactly the best place to be at after hours either they end up getting crazy into big fights or shooting said Dre.

Never stopped you from going there before in the past yo, we use to hit that area every weekend and get into all sorts of crazy shit…you forget how to have fun now or something…where your mom send you at last summer boot camp or something dog I feel like you losing your edge said Darrell.

Not at all but I got company and not feeling like trekking there tonight that's all, but you have fun man said Dre.

You changed big time man, I don't think I even know who you are anymore…ever since you got back the summer you been on that tired fronting ass bullshit said Darrell.

I'm still the same old Dre homie don't get it twisted I'm just on that new shit so respect my wishes and leave it alone said Dre.

Yo you getting soft real talk, what happened to my partner in the past ripping the streets and taking no prisoners? Darrell asked him.

He still here but he just grew up and left all that extra shit behind said Dre.

Ye I see you…got back in school, got your little job at the mall selling kicks, on your hands and knees kissing your girl pussy and think you better than me said Darrell.

Yo you where you at in your life because you chose to be so don't come at me like that…I got my hustle and I'm just fine with my situation… now go find yours homie said Dre.

You fake as fuck now that's what it is…cool, I'll step off and let you do you I'm out peace…artificial ass nigga said Darrell walking out.

Ye keep it moving before I shove this pool stick up yo ass said Dre going back to his pool game.

Big city said Trevor in a cheering voice.

No sweat, friends like that come a dime a dozen on these streets and that aint saying much…besides my life was much more trouble than he was worth when he was in it said Dre.

After a while Dre went to go to the bathroom and Trevor went outside to wait for him at the car as he left out smoking a cigarette he was stopped by 2 guys hanging in the parking lot.

Eh man you got another one of those on you? asked one.

Ye he said taking out his pack and handing him one.

Thanks appreciate that homie…you got a light? He asked.

Trevor reached in his jacket and gave him the lighter as he lit it up and handed it back.

Appreciate that man real talk…so you just leaving the pool hall? He asked.

Yeah just leaving said Trevor eying him and his shady hood looking friend.

Cool, think you can give us a lift a few blocks from here…we'll throw you a couple dollars said the guy smoking a cigarette and looking around.

Think I been generous enough already sorry got somewhere else to go said Trevor and suddenly the guy from the side punched him in the side of his face knocking him off balance as the other attacked him with punches and kicks as 3 more came out of nowhere pounding on him as he fought against them trying to rob him and take his keys as he threw wild punches knocking a couple back trying to reach his car and get his shot gun when Dre ran up to the parking lot and grabbed his glock from his waist and busted shots in the air in their direction as they took off running.

Ye scatter you fucking roaches! He yelled firing at them then ran over to Trevor.

Yo you alright homie? Dre asked him.

Trevor jumped up and opened his truck door and grabbed a shot gun from the back seat and loaded it and advanced forward in their direction.

Mother fuckers pick the wrong one to try to take from said Trevor.

Yo easy man, they gone let it go said Dre.

I kill bears and niggas with this shit said Trevor.

Comon man, let's just bounce you good they didn't take nothing did they? Dre asked him.

Naw…fucking crumb snatchers said Trevor pissed off and breathing hard as Dre put his gun in his waist.

Let's go man said Dre as Trevor looked forward for a while longer then finally went back to his truck.

They got back to their room shortly as Trevor sat at the table rolling a blunt.

They still got me steamy…I wanted to put a couple caps and they asses and blow out some knees said Trevor.

I'm sorry you had to deal with those scum yo but you can't be kind to people down here like you are up your way…they treacherous… fucking robbers and thieves come a dime a dozen too here…that's why I stay strap you never know when mother fuckers jump out the shadows for some attack shit…had your back man…hope a few of those shots landed in some of their legs and asses said Dre.

Damn,I come all the way to the city to see my boy and I get attempted robbery…you probably saved them because I didn't come this way empty handed…got a couple shotguns and rifles and I'm licensed to shoot in and out of deer season said Trevor.

Let it go homie, you good now so let's get back to our night said Dre walking out the bathroom butt naked with his fittie cap and timberland boots on.

Trevor looked up at him and grinned. Yeah, I definitely want to get back to our night he said.

Light the blunt up said Dre as Trevor fired it up and took a pull and blew it.

How you feel now? asked Dre.

A little better said Trevor.

I can make you feel a whole lot better homie said Dre walking over and mounting him in the chair he was sitting in and took the blunt and took a pull of it and turn head and blew it.

Let me give you my favorite gun he said taking another pull then Trevor opened his mouth and clipped it on the blunt as Dre blew it in his mouth as he blew it out as he gave it back to Trevor who continued to smoke it as Dre rubbed his arms and shoulders then got down to his knees and unbuckled his belt and unzipped his pants and stroked his rock hard dick for a moment then looked up at him.

I want you to fuck me gangster style he told Trevor then begin sucking down his dick while stroking it and deep throating it while licking his balls then looked at it moving wildly in his grip getting it all wet then stood up spitting on his hand as Trevor picked up a condom off the table and gave it to him as Dre tore off the wrapper with a seal and un rolled it on his dick while stroking it then pushed Trevor's dick deep inside him going slowly at first than riding him and grabbing hold off his wife beater as if straddling a horse faster and harder as Trevor put the blunt in the tray he was smoking and gripped his hips as Dre pushed back and forward on him then stopped and lifted it up from him with his ass muscles squeezing his dick tight and pulled off the condom at the same time as he threw it on the floor.

Trevor looked at him. Damn he said in amazement.

Stroke that dick and bust that nut on my face said Dre kneeling down in front of Trevor stroking his dick as Trevor stroked his dick faster closing his eyes then felt his climax and busted across on Dre's chest and face as Dre still stroking reached his climax stood up busting back across his chest and face.

Ye…eye for an eye nigga…that was hot said Dre.

Through the course of the night to day break they had 5 more sessions as Dre laid across his chest from the side smoking a cigarette looking at a countless condom wrappers across the bed and floor.

Damn…looks like we didn't bring enough it seems he said.

They slept in the morning and a little after noon then went out into town to various shops, the movies and went back to the room ordering food in, watching television, talking and getting in more sex then came the next day where they had to say their goodbyes and Dre found himself looking into the passenger side window once again.

Damn, I had mad fun with you homie…at least the weekend felt like it lasted forever…hate to see it end said Dre.

Yeah me too big city, It was good getting up and able to kick it with you…got me wanting to stay down a few more days but I know I gotta head back and take care of work in business at home…the one thing I hate about the city is the speed limits but you can best believe once I get on those deep country roads headed home I'll be burning the asphalt said Trevor.

I feel you man, gotta get back to our lives and our priorities… just glad we could be each other's for a little while homie…try not to make next visit too long alright?asked Dre.

I'm always going to make time for you big city said Trevor.

That's what's up said Dre reaching out hand as Trevor took it and looked at him.

Take care man said Trevor.

You too said Dre feeling like he wanted to say more but couldn't bring it to his heart too at that moment and the feeling of saying goodbye the second time around felt more pressing then the last time…like he was feeling more for him now than ever before but kept it cool.

I'll be back said Trevor.

Dre nodded.

Trevor drove off and once again Dre watch him ride off into the distance and vanish.

Chapter 33

At Gia's house she was chilling with her cousin Anita as they blasted music in the living room of her house while she was waiting for Dre to come over and bring things over that his son needed.

Yo cous, I don't care what the fuck nobody say Tupac is still alive said Anita.

I know right said Gia.

So what's up with you and your baby daddy girl, yall still going through it huh? I can't believe you 2 broke up I thought you would last forever you were like the perfect couple once upon a time asked Anita.

Hell yeah, he been thinking he can just treat me any kind of way but it aint happening and right now the only thing he can do for me is take care of his son and as far as a relationship goes I don't want him anymore…I tell you what he better get it together and stop handling me like I'm one of his hoes out there because I'm not the one and I keep telling him that…I think what it is for real is that he can't handle a chick like me but yeah we definitely going to get into it…then his mom miss suppose to be save and holy be trying it with me all the time…omg I can't stand that women and I'm tired of her said Gia.

Damn sound like you got problems said Anita.

No more than the next bitch with a shady ass baby daddy/mommas boy, I'm starting to regret ever fucking with him and having his baby…I'm glad he got that little job after school now so he can at least do something…but I'm about to put him on child support after awhile and just be done with it so I don't have to deal with him and his mother said Gia as the door bell ranged.

Gia got up and looked out than rolled her eyes sighing and opened the door to Dre holding 2 bags.

About time you get here with this stuff, how did you get here anyway…oh that's right your mom bought you…when you going to get your own whip so your mom doesn't have to carry you all over the place every time our baby needs something or has to go somewhere asked Gia.

Don't even worry about it, when I do get a whip, you won't be in it said Dre.

Anita giggled a little. Hey Dre she said as he nodded to her.

So you got everything I told you that-began Gia but Dre cut her off before she could finish her sentence.

Ye it's all here, I got it said Dre.

Don't be cutting me off she said taking the bags.

Where Darius? Dre asked her.

He is the room sleep, I just put him down for a nap because he was up for a while now so don't go in there bothering him and waking him up said Gia.

Shut up, I'm not going to wake him up…I just want to see him said Dre.

I got the door closed and he's resting comfortably so why can't you just come back to see him when he's awake said Gia.

So you want to start acting silly with that bull shit again, keeping him from me cause you mad at me…told you not to involve him in anything that has to do with us…this isn't a game and you not using him as a weapon… I'm coming in to see him said Dre.

For the record I broke up with you…Ugh go ahead but if you wake him up your not leaving until he falls back asleep and your mom will just have to wait outside for you until you do said Gia.

Dre walked into the room and quietly opened the door and went over to the crib and his son was wide awake smiling when he saw him.

Yo he in here wide awake in the dark, thought you said he was fast asleep said Dre.

Well he must have just woken up said Gia.

So why do you have the door closed and him in here by himself? How do you know he wasn't crying a Dre asked her.

Look, he was sleep and I closed the door because we playing music in there and I didn't want to disturb him…as you can see he fine so pick him up hug kiss so I can try to get him back to sleep said Gia.

Dre picked him up holding him and smiled.

Hi little buddy, how you doing? Yeah you happy to see me huh, daddy love you he said kissing him on the lips then holding him close to him as Gia watched and decided to use this moment to prey on his emotions and tell him some news she had recently found out.

Darius is always happy to see you, that's why he cries more when you're not here…I think you and I need to talk said Gia.

About what? Dre asked her.

What do you think? About us…we can't go on hating each other and having all this friction between us…we need to work it out for the sake of our son despite what issues we have…what happened to us Dre?asked Gia.

I don't know but for a long time we been doing this back and forth, I'm just tired of it and want to take care of my son…not about us anymore or rather we in a relationship he comes first said Dre.

Yes of course he does but I love you Dre and you know that, I don't think we should give up on us so easily we can work this out said Gia as Dre shook his head.

Naw, right now we good just like we are and I'm good where I am said Dre.

I know we both been going hard but I think I have some good news to tell you that will bring us closer together as a little family said Gia.

Dre looked at her. What's that? He said.

Dre…I'm pregnant said Gia.

Dre looked at her for a moment. You're joking right? He said.

No I'm not, I just found out not too long ago when I peed on a stick and started having symptoms lately of being pregnant…looks like we have another member to add to the team in 9 months said Gia.

Dre put his son back down in the crib. You a liar I don't believe you said Dre.

Oh really, I don't have to lie I can prove it she said going to the bathroom and bringing back the pregnancy test and showed it to him than the box.

See...this color means I'm pregnant, looks like another bun is cooking in the oven thanks to you said Gia.

You said you was on the pill said Dre.

I guess I been forgetting to take my daily dosage, I get so busy said Gia.

Yo how the fuck did this happen? Dre asked her.

Uh you use your imagination said Gia.

You know what I mean no way you can be popped up we were safe said Dre.

Yeah all but a few times remember and condoms are only 99 percent effective, what about the 1 percent...so you're not happy about this? Gia asked him.

Hell no I'm not happy, I didn't want any more kids right now and I never fucked you without a condom since I got back unless you tampered and poked holes in them...bet you would do some shit like that said Dre.

Already taking the high road and denying what's yours, typical dead beat in training said Gia.

Say what you want but I know there's no way I did this, you better be go find your ex or whoever else you might have been creeping with...cause I seriously doubt that its mine said Dre.

It is yours and I never cheated on you, so pony up and get ready to take care of responsibility number 2 said Gia.

You better call Tyrone or something said Dre.

Whatever, you better go out there and tell your mom you going to be a daddy again said Gia.

Your pathetic, you'll do anything to keep me with you but I don't want your conniving ass and I never will Dre told her looking her in the face then turn back to his son sitting up watching them.

Gia pushed him hard as he almost fell over in the crib and almost on his son catching himself.

Yo wtf is wrong with you bitch, you could have hurt our son said Dre as Gia slapped him across the face.

Comon hit me Dre so I can put you in jail! She screamed as she starting punching him as he shielded backing up as he grabbed her arms she slammed him into the wall as the baby started crying and Anita listened.

I do not get involved in domestic squabbles she said to her self turning the TV with remote.

Dre pushed her onto the bed as she jumped back up he grabbed her arms and twist one behind her back and pinned her down to the bed on top of her.

Let go of me Dre! Get off me! She screamed.

Calm your ass down now! Said Dre as the baby cried looking at them as Dre forced her face to look at him.

Look at him; look at what the fuck you're causing! You doing this! You the reason we are where we are! Dre yelled in her ear.

Let go of me Dre now! She screamed as he let go of her as she got up looking at him with tears in her eyes and picked her son up from the crib.

Shh, it's okay Darius; I'm fine, don't cry I got you she said.

Dre looked at her breathing hard.

You make it hard to be with you, for me to even be around you... I wonder if you even really want him or just using him to hold on to me because our relationship been dead for a while now...either way you're a fucked person and no matter what you do you can't keep me from my child...you know my dad was never there for me and I told you that I would never let that happen with him...you using that to try to control me…its what you always did said Dre.

He's my child…I had him, not you…you were just a sperm donor…get out…get out Dre!she yelled as the baby cried again as he shook his head and stormed out the house slamming the door.

Anita came into Gia's bedroom: Is everything okay? She asked.

Damn cous, you could have at least helped me when Dre was attacking me in front of the baby just now said Gia.

Then why is he the one with red marks across his neck and you seem to be fine without a scratch said Anita.

Smh, whatever said Gia walking past her with her son in hand.

Dre decided not to tell his mom about what happened or what Gia told him because one thing she and he have always done was keep their relationship business to their safe but her telling him about being pregnant was something he didn't need right now and his mom couldn't find this out but he had a strong feeling that this baby couldn't possibly be his but there were those couple of times and was she capable of poking holes in the condom just to do this to keep him?

When Dre got to his house he sat in his bed thinking for hours how he was going to deal with this situation and after a while he got up and walked down the hall and stood to Jay's door which was open and he was playing his x-box as he glanced up and smiled at Dre.

Sup partner said Jay.

Mot much man…can't sleep, so what you in here playing? Dre asked.

Ghost recon, want to join me? Jay asked him.

Ye…anything to take my mind off all the bullshit I been dealing with lately said Dre.

Dre and Jay played the game as Dre asked him a question.

Yo Jay, you got any kids? Dre asked him.

Not to my knowledge…long way away from wanting to be a parent…I run too much not to mention my job keep me constantly traveling said Jay.

Lucky you man, tell me something why do females gotta be so complicated and difficult? Dre asked him.

Well…guess that depends on the female, no reasoning with some of them said Jay.

I agree…I'm about to be 17 with a full head of grey hair real talk laughed Dre.

Eh, I know it can be stressful sometime dealing with the honey… I'm leaving in a couple days to move back in my place and any time you want feel free to stop by, chill and spend a weekend if you ever want to get away…just a thought said Jay.

Thanks, I'll keep that in mind man said Dre.

Chapter 34

The next week at school, Dre met Gia outside the cafeteria to talk to her about the growing situation inside her.

I got your text Dre,what is so important that you want to talk about after you said you didn't want me…just glad we in a open place so you can't attack me again like you did that night at our house in front of our son she said folding her arms.

Were we in the same place because I remember you jumping on me like you were a fucking wild cat but I'm not here to talk about that…I been thinking about the situation you informed me of said Dre.

Situation? I think this is more of a blessing, when our relationship was dying destiny sent us a sign that was meant to reconnect our bond…Dre…I'm having your baby again…of course I'm a little scared of this unexpected delivery but I know you and I together can handle this and were going to be okay…though we probably shouldn't tell your mom…not just yet anyway and I have to cut out the fights at school..Can't risk injuring the new one she smiled rubbing her stomach.

Naw see you don't get it, we don't need this in our lives right now Gia and I'm thinking hard that we should do something about it while there's still time…were not ready to have another baby and we struggling to take care of this one…I'm thinking you should get an abortion said Dre.

A what now?! In abortion! Gia yelled.

Keep your voice down…ye, I would pay for it and everything…I think it's the best thing for us right now said Dre.

Certainly not, I'm not killing this baby…I'm keeping it…I can't believe you would even suggest that…my friends are already noticing my glow said Gia.

Look, let's not be hasty and make any decisions yet…we should talk more and see what may ultimately be the best move…for now I just want us to call a truce on this hate war we got going on and be there for our son said Dre.

Wow, I never seen you so shaky and scared like this Dre, those expecting father gitters huh…I hope you're not worried about your mom whooping you…don't worry…what don't break us can only bring us closer said Gia.

I gotta go….talk to you after school said Dre walking off as Gia looked at him rubbing her stomach looking at it thinking to herself then smiled and walked off.

It was a month after telling Dre about the pregnancy that the guilt started to come over and she told him the truth.

Dre was over her house playing with his son Darius in the couch when Gia came into the living room after locking herself in the bathroom for a while and thinking over it and stood looking at them both as he looked over at her and could tell by her face that she had something to tell him.

Dre…I'm not pregnant she said.

He looked at her for a moment taking it in: What do you mean; I saw the pregnancy test he said.

It wasn't mine…it was my cousin Anita, she came over and told me about a possibility of her being pregnant and took the test over my house to find out because she didn't want her mother to know and it came out positive…I just used that situation to make you think it was mine…we were just in a place at the time where we hated each other and I just wanted…I don't know what I was thinking she said.

So how long did you plan to fucking keep this from me,you had to know sooner or later I would figure it out when your stomach wasn't growing…what were you going to do put a fucking pillow under your shirt?asked Dre.

No that would just be silly…I'm so sorry Dre said Gia.

Dre looked at her a moment longer but didn't say anything after that but went back to playing with his son then after he had fallen asleep left without saying another word to her.

After another couple months had past of not seeing Trevor who once again made up excuses or always had a reason for not coming down he begin to think that he was avoiding him again and proposed to be the aggressor once again to make it happen in a conversation they were having.

How about I come down there and see you for the weekend homie, I could take the bus down there…this would be a good time to get away…I can take off work Friday and don't have to be go back to Sunday evening…trying to see you because it's been a while again… less you don't want me to come or have too much going on said Dre.

Naw, I think that will be fine big city…just don't contact your relatives and tell them that you're down there…you know for the obvious reasons said Trevor.

Ye, I know said Dre.

Cool, I got you covered I'm going to pay for your way there and back and be at the station to pick you up said Trevor.

Cool said Dre.

That Friday, Dre took the long bus trip down there and when he finally arrived to the station, Trevor was waiting outside his truck smoking a cigarette and when Dre saw him and walking over to him he had a big smile on his face finishing the cigarette and putting it out with his boot.

Welcome back to the deep country big city he said slapping five in a hand shake and hugged him patting his back.

Ye man, figure the only way I was going to see you again was if I came all the way down here to you said Dre.

Not like that big city, we both have a lot going on…doesn't matter now anyway you here now right…know you must be hungry after that long bus trip comon I'm going to take you to a place that you liked when you were down here for a little lunch he said tapping his stomach as they both got in his truck and drove off.

After a bite to eat in town they headed back to his house on the long country roads as Dre glanced out across the vast fields.

Wow…been a long time since I saw the lonely roads and fields like this…all the memories of the summer start to pour in homie said Dre.

Yeah I know, you traveled all the way back down just to see little ol me…glad to see you big city he said taking one hand rubbing the top of his head.

Ye, somebody had to make the first move…seems like I always am said Dre.

That's how this all started right? Trevor grinned.

Doesn't really matter now, it happened and here we are currently…not afraid to admit I missed you a lot as the months passed on by said Dre.

I think about you a lot too big city; guess there's just that undeniable connection between us even from the distance said Trevor pulling the cigarette.

Dre reached his hand across and begin to grope his crotch.

Keep your eyes on the road I'm going to lay down for a few said Dre unbuckling his belt and unzipped his pants whipping Trevor's dick out then put his lips down on it and gave him a good sucking.

Damn…reliving more good memories said Trevor who after a moment pulled over on the side of the road as Dre sucked him off laying back in the seat and closing his eyes smoking a cigarette.

After a bit, they were approaching Trevor's house on the far back up a hill.

Damn homie, this house and all this land yours? Dre asked him.

Yep…welcome to my little home said Trevor.

When they got inside Trevor introduced Dre to his girlfriend Jessy.

Jessy this is my friend Dre, Dre this is my fiancé Jessy all the way from the big city, haven't seen him in a long time and told him to come visit for the weekend so we can catch up for old times' sake...he use to stay down here in the past with some relatives working on the farm to make some money and when he left back to go home to his girlfriend and baby we lost touch and just recently got back in contact said Trevor.

Nice to meet you Dre and welcome to our home said Jessy smiling shaking his hand.

Nice to meet you too said Dre.

Our home? Trevor didn't mention she was his live in girlfriend... he made it seem like she came and left...then he introduces her as her fiancé when I get here and she's rocking a engagement ring...wow dude been really closed mouth with his personal life he thought to himself.

Trevor told me about your arrival so I prepared a guest room, let me show you to it so you can unpacked and catch up with Trevor, he told me he was going to take you into town to hang out and catch up on old times with pool and drinking and all that...he told me that you turned 22 last week happy late birthday said Jessy.

Thanks smiled Dre looking at Trevor who didn't prepare him for the overall lie but went along with it.

This way she said walking down the hall as Dre looked back at Trevor surprised at all he just learned.

After a while they went into town to a bar spot they went to back in the day and played some pool.

Wow homie...you been really shut mouth on what's been going on in your busy life besides work...you didn't tell me about her being your fiancé and being engaged...you getting married man and you didn't bother to tell me...I thought I would at least get an invitation as your best man grinned Dre who was really hurt and surprised on the news but hiding his true emotions.

Yeah I was going to tell you homie but lately I been unsure if we were going to go through with it because we've had so much fights and issues lately…I was really drunk one night a while back and popped the question to her…next morning she told me about it and was so happy that I just went with it…just because I put a ring on her finger doesn't mean we're getting married tomorrow or anytime soon…I gotta leave that liquor alone sometimes homie because I do crazy stuff he grinned shaking his head.

Word…wow…you 2 seem pretty happy from what I seen so far said Dre.

Ye…looks can be deceiving said Trevor going back to the pool game.

After their time in town they went to Trevor's uncle place in the far out country and had some drinks and blew back some smoke and played cards with his Uncle who after awhile passed out on the couch snoring as Dre sat back on his sofa smoking a cigarette high out of his mind watching an old movie on his vcr and glanced down his hallway and saw Trevor standing at his bathroom door with his belt buckle unloosened and signaled to him to come back there as Dre got up and went in the bathroom with him and closed the door then Trevor unbuckled Dre's belt and pulled down his pants than positioned him over the toilet and bent him over.

This mines? Trevor asked him.

It's yours man Dre replied.

Then arch that back some more and take this dick Trevor told him.

Chapter 35

Later that night back at Trevor's house, he and Dre sat to the table talking over a dinner his fiancé Jessy made for them.

Trevor saids you want to keep a low profile while your down here visiting, slip in and back out without a lot of people knowing...he told me that you had some rough tension with Richard back when you was working with him and your still not on good terms after he fired you said Jessy.

Ye...think that would be best said Dre.

I was telling my friend Dre here about the multi-complex bird house project I was working on in my shed out back and after dinner I was going to show it to him said Trevor.

Yeah you gotta see it Dre,its like a little miniature condo for birds...this guy is so good with his hands I swear he can build just about anything from scratch...he's almost finished with it and he's going to set it up outside in the backyard...I think it's so cute said Jessy.

Word...I'd love to see it said Dre looking at Trevor.

Comon man I'll show it to you said Trevor getting up.

I'll just wash up the dishes and have dessert ready when you get back in said Jessy.

Sounds good said Trevor kissing her.

Comon partner lets go he said as they both left outside to his backyard lighting up smokes as they headed toward the shed.

You enjoying your time here so far? Trevor asked him.

Yep I am...good to be back in your company again...hope that we can see each other a little more often and not have to wait so long homie...when I get a car I'll be riding up here to visit a lot more or when I can...probably the only way I can see you since your locked down said Dre.

I wouldn't say that man, I actually been thinking of a way to tell her that it's not going to work out…more so because of a lot of things going on between us and I want to end the relationship before we get too deep into this…I feel like she rushed me into all of this way too soon…moving in,proposing,wanting kids…I want those things eventually but not right now…you know how females can get some time so forceful and talking you into things you're not ready for said Trevor.

Ye, I understand that man said Dre.

Trevor opened the shed and flicked on the light inside as Dre went inside as Trevor glanced back at the house and saw Jessy doing the dishes in the kitchen as he went inside and closed it back.

Wow…nice bird house man, I see you stay building some shit said Dre looking at it.

Yeah man, I guy gotta have his hobbies when he bored and don't his old playmate to have fun with said Trevor coming up behind him and massaged his shoulders then kissed his neck and glided his hands down his chest wrapping his arms around him for a moment and leaned his head against the back of his.

This right here…feels so right and so wrong…always have said Trevor.

Dre touched his hands then turned around and looked at Trevor and kissed him then unbuckled his belt and pulled them down as he went down on his knees and grabbed his dick as Trevor took the back of his head and motioned it back and forth closing his eyes and biting his lip then after a while stood Dre back up then pressed him against the wall rubbing his ass then knelt down and kissed his cheeks then stood up and took a condom out and tore off the seal and put it on then lubed his ass up with Vaseline on his work table then pushed himself deep into him as Dre gasped as he begin thrusting hard forward into him.

Meanwhile in the house, Jessy did the dishes when the home phone ranged it was Dre's Aunt calling to see how she and Trevor were doing.

Hi Marylyn, were doing just fine, Trevor and I just had dinner with a friend of his visiting in town and staying with us for the weekend... Trevor's showing him the birdhouse he's been building in the shed for a couple weeks now...yes were going to the festival tomorrow afternoon can't wait said Jessy.

Trevor continued pumping Dre's ass hard until he heard a pop from the condom breaking in his ass and stopped withdrawing from him.

What's wrong? Dre asked him.

Damn...the condom broke said Trevor.

Did you bring another out here? Dre asked him.

Naw...I just grabbed one from your backpack where I put mine said Trevor.

Dre thought for a moment. Comon keep on going...just pull out before you cum he said.

Trevor looked at him.

Comon said Dre grabbing his dick and forced it back into him as Trevor let out an orgasmic gasp and pressed Dre's head into the wall smashing him out as Dre lightly moaned out as Trevor felt his orgasm coming and pulled out standing to the side busting all over the floor as Dre still stroking against the wall busted his load onto the wall panting hard as Trevor panted for a moment.

Wow...damn said Trevor.

Dre turned around as Trevor touched his face and kissed him then they begin pulling their pants up and straighten clothes up as Dre opened the door and stepped out lighting a cigarette as Trevor switched off the light inside and left out closing the door.

Later that night, Trevor, Jessy and Dre sat in the living room watching a movie while smoking and having some drinks.

Jessy yawned and got up. That's it for me, I'm about to get some sleep baby she said kissing him.

Night baby, be back there after while said Trevor taking a drink then after a moment Dre got up from the recliner across from him and sat down beside him as Trevor held his hand massaging it continuing to watch tv and pulled his cigarette.

Later that night,Dre woke up to the slightly loud sound of sex coming from Trevor's room.

Damn, he had sex with me tonight and now he's plowing her…all in the same night, really? He thought to himself but knew perfect well the situation and one he could do nothing about as he rolled over and put the pillow on his head.

The Next Morning, Trevor told Dre to stay at his house while he went to his Uncle's farm for a little while to help him with some work there to wrap up the week's end and while he was away Dre had some time to talk to his fiancé and get to know her better:

I helped Trevor on the farm with Richard last summer and put in some work to make some money for my girlfriend and son back home…after my short stay here I had a true respect and appreciation for hard work here in the country…I get the country blues once in a while and miss it though at first I gotta say I never been this deep down and thought I would hate it here…its way different from the city that's always loud, bustling and crowded…like the peace down here said Dre.

You're more than welcome to come and stay whenever you like… being one of Trevor's good friends I'm sure he would like that smiled Jessy.

Dre nodded. So you 2 tied the knot huh…congratulations he said.

Awe thank you…it was so romantic in a corny country way one might say…we were at the karaoke one weekend in town and after he got up there and singed a silly song for me he got off the stage…got down on one knee and asked me to marry him and I said yes…smiled Jessy looking at her sparkling ring.

So that's the real story….why do he keep lying about his shit thought Dre to himself.

That afternoon when Trevor got back in, Dre was sitting in the couch watching television when he saw Jessy come into the living room dressed up in a pretty dress putting earrings on her ear.

Hey, I'm sorry you can't join us at the country side festival today; it's going to be a lot of fun and Trevor's family Richard and Marylyn are going to be there said Jessy.

Yeah Dre said he wasn't feeling well and just wanted to stay here so I told him to make himself at home…well be back late this evening so I can take you to the bus station alright said Trevor.

Alright cool…have fun said Dre as they both left out and after Trevor started the car and she was inside he went back into the house.

I'm sorry man, wish I could take you with us…I didn't want to go but I promised her that I would take her because she loves the festival but I know your people are going to be there because they already told us and I didn't want to explain to them why you're here, especially since they don't even know you down here…wouldn't be a good idea anyway considering your Uncle knows about us and I just barely repaired our relationship back said Trevor.

Eh I get it man, I'll be cool here just enjoy your time out and I'll see you later said Dre looking away a little pissed.

You sure you going to be alright man? Trevor asked him.

Ye just go I'm good said Dre picking up the remote as Trevor looked at him for a moment then left out and closed the door.

Dre thought to himself shaking his head.

Later that evening, when Dre had gathered his bags and sat outside in Trevor's truck he glanced up and saw Trevor talking to Jessy then smiled and kissed her as she went back in the house and he got into the truck closing the door.

You set to go partner? asked Trevor.

Ye I sure am liar said Dre as Trevor looked at him.

Inside the house Jessy smiled looking at her ring them just glanced out the window to see them leave but saw Trevor and Dre talking in the truck and by their body language it appeared they were having some kind of argument and wondered what it was about because they both had been fine his whole stay there and grew curious.

Why the fuck are you tripping big city, you knew the stipulations before you even got here said Trevor.

Yeah I did or at least I thought I did homie, I came down here not knowing that your girlfriend stayed with you nor that you were engaged to her and I been hiding here like a mole underground for the most part while you 2 went about, we spent what a handful of hours here when I arrived that day and the rest I just sat posted up until you wanted to sneak away in fuck…I came down here for more than that…you should have told me all this before I even got on the bus back home that you had so much going on said Dre.

I didn't think it would be as big a deal as you making it right now and I wanted to see you said Trevor.

We'll you saw me at least I can say that, I'm telling you, all these lies and stories to keep up with just to keep this visit confidential has been a job on its own said Dre.

What other choice did I have man! We both know what the deal is so stop bitching about it, damn it man…I went through all of this because I love you said Trevor and that caught Dre by surprise and he didn't know what else to say as Trevor started the car and left the house as his fiancé Jessy watched them ride off into the distance of the highway and wonder what argument had them both so heated.

The drive to the bus station was a quiet one, until Dre finally broke the silence by speaking to Trevor.

I love you too man, just this whole situation is complicated, not going to dwell on it because it is what it is and we have our lives to live said Dre smoking a cigarette.

Trevor held his hand in the car then pulled over on the side of the road for a moment and sat back thinking to himself.

Get out with me said Trevor opening the door as Dre got out and walked around to the front of the truck.

Trevor looked at him for a moment just staring into his eyes in the darkness which seemed pointless among the dark lonely highway and the moon light above, then Trevor embraced him with a long tight hug not saying anything and Dre returned it back.

They held hands until they drove up to the station then they both let go.

Dre held his bag in his hand in another on his shoulder as he prepared to say goodbye to Trevor again.

Until next time homie said Dre.

Until next time big city, next visit I'm coming to you man so look for me soon to head your way said Trevor.

Dre nodded. He wanted to believe Trevor but didn't know exactly if he was just lying to him again or was this the last time after their intense argument a little while ago.

He boarded the bus and sat down to the window and Trevor stayed there smoking a cigarette until the bus left out of sight.

Chapter 36

After Dre returned home he got back to his life just as he did before, he and Trevor's secret relationship had changed because even though they still communicated it wasn't that often or as meaningful as it once seemed and he blamed himself for letting his emotions get the best of him that time he was there just before he left.

His estranged relationship with Gia was no different, he only came around her to spend time with his son or take him back to his house for the weekend but he was about to get a urgent call from her one weekend concerning their son after he had gotten in from work and was about to take a shower.

Ye what's up? Dre asked her.

Dre, it's about Darius said Gia sniffing.

What about him? What happened? Dre asked her.

I was in the kitchen washing dishes a little while ago and had him in his play pen in there and I just turned my back for a few minutes just to get them done and I must have forgotten to secure the safety lock and he must have crawled out of it and across the floor and pulled a towel I had sitting on top some kitchen rare and it fell on his head... he's not hurt but he has a little bruised and cried but he's okay...I just wanted to let you know said Gia in a tearful voice.

Dre felt his heart pounding out of his chest and he was relived it wasn't serious.

Damn, you gotta make sure you secure areas you keep him in and keep an eye on him, who knows what could have happen he could have stuck his hand in the socket crawled in the bathroom and got a hold of something dangerous said Dre.

I know Dre, I'm sorry I feel as bad enough as it is, you don't have to yell at me…baby's have accidents all the time…it's normal said Gia.

This not the first time, he keep getting hurt all the time with some incident or another, wtf you be doing when these things happen said Dre.

I'm doing the best I can to take care of him Dre, I'm here by myself most of the time with him trying to watch him and keep this house clean because my mom be bitching all the time about the mess that be in it…he's okay Dre just calm down…Darius is okay said Gia.

I'm coming over tonight said Dre.

For what, to stay? Gia asked him.

Ye, if you don't have company over already or coming by later, cancel it because I'm headed that way now said Dre.

Who you bringing you over, your mom? Gia asked him.

Naw, she at work and don't get off for another few hours…I'm taking the bus.

I'm about to pack my bags and I'll be over said Dre.

Alright, see you then said Gia ending call then smiled to herself sneakily.

A little while later, Dre sat in the couch holding his son and feeding him with the bottle and kissed his forehead as Gia sat in the couch looking at him.

Dre…I can't tell you how shaken up I was when I heard that crash and turned around and he was lying there…thank god it's just a scar on his head said Gia.

Shouldn't have happened period said Dre still looking at his son.

I know…I just always felt more secure when both of us were there to watch him…I know our relationship didn't work out but I want you to know I still think that you're a wonderful daddy to him despite what I said in the past and he needs you in his life said Gia.

I'm here and I'll always be here for him said Dre.

I know, you and I both have always had daddy issues growing up and know what it's like to grow up without our fathers to be in our lives…I never wanted that for my child which is why I always told myself that when I did have a baby it was going to be with a guy knew was going to be there for the long haul said Gia.

I still wonder to this day even when you're here and leave out the door after one of our big fights or arguments…that one day you'll just never come back or abandon him…leaving me to be mommy and daddy said Gia.

A tear fell from Dre's eye: That will never happen, I'm going to be a better father then my dad ever was…I swear on my life I'll never leave him…not even after my last breath he said.

Gia smiled and touched his hand: Were both lucky to have you in our lives she said.

Later on the next week Dre would get a call but one he did not expect and one that would change their dealings forever.

Dre was lying on his bed after work before taking a shower and answered Trevor's call.

Yo, what's up homie said Dre.

It's over big city said Trevor.

What do you mean? Dre asked him.

Us, Everything…your people found out that we were still seeing each other and you came down here to stay at my house after I swore to your Uncle that I would never contact you again or see you after he found out what was going on between us…he took everything from me…everything said Trevor.

What are you talking about man, how did he find out? Dre asked him.

Me and Jessy were over there for Sunday dinner, lately I have been distant to her and told her that I wanted to cancel the engagement… when I wouldn't tell her why she must have figured it had something to do with you somehow…I don't know when or how but she must have suspected something about us and the whole secret visit down here because that's when she called your Aunt and asked her if she knew what kind of dealings you had with my Richard in the past, your Aunt told her that you were their nephew said Trevor.

Damn said Dre.

Your Aunt was confused when Jessy told her the story I made up about you and found out that you were down here visiting my place and didn't want them to know which she found strange and told your Uncle who hadn't told her about us and he connected the dots and knew why I told her the lies I did said Trevor.

He called me over to his house, I swore to him after messing with his underage nephew who he believes I manipulated and took advantage of that I would never see or contact you again…I betrayed him again even after all he had done for me in the past and present…he fired me, took away the truck he got for me, even kicked me out the house and land that was in his ownership…I told Jessy the truth…about us…she looked at me like I was some sick monster and left said Trevor.

Why do you think I wouldn't see you over long periods of time? said Trevor.

I thought that if I distance myself from you long enough that you would just forget about me and go on with your life…but you didn't and I couldn't let you go either said Trevor.

Dre didn't know what to say as he remained in silence.

He finally told your Aunt and now they're on shaky ground with each other because he knew this had happened long ago and didn't tell her…I saw her tears, she cried telling me how could I do that with you…that I'm a child molester and while they trusted me to watch over you, I lived under their roof and disrespected their home all the while engaging in this activity.

She said that I raped you and if she knew that at the time she would have pressed charges against me for sex with a minor and still might…Erika stood up and told her that what she saw a friendship develop between us that was becoming more and she believed that it was perfectly natural rather than unnatural to her.

That love like this exists between 2 people of the same sex rather we ignore, deny, hide or frown down on it and even she could see that we had deep feelings for each other throughout your stay here and finally came out to both of her parents that she was gay and I guess that overwhelmed them altogether said Trevor.

She told me that rather you willingly wanted to do it or not… that it was a shameful and abominable act better left unsaid and to just let you go on with your life since you seem to be carrying on this secret romance with me to this day said Trevor.

Damn man, I'm so sorry…I never meant for any of this shit to happen like this said Dre.

But it did, what happened between us should have never happened…I knew that you were growing feelings for me but I resisted you and kept my distance yet you continued coming after me, forcing yourself onto me and it's my fault for allowing it to happen and carrying it on…you were still a fucking kid and somewhere along the line I forgot that said Trevor.

It's still not your fault, its mine said Trevor.

I was the older one, I should have known better and never let it happened or go as far as it did.

Now I have to live with the fact that I betrayed the only family I ever had after my own died and gave me a home and everything I worked for is gone…everything! yelled Trevor.

A tear rolled down Dre's face.

Let me talk to them man, tell them that it was me who forced myself onto you said Dre.

It doesn't matter now, in their eyes you were still a kid and I'm the one that should have known better said Trevor.

So I say it's over…everything…lesson learned and I want you to take care of yourself big city…take care of your son and live your life…I just can't be a part of it anymore said Trevor.

So were done homie, just like that? Dre asked him.

Yeah…Just like that said Trevor.

I fucking love you man, please don't fucking do this to me…please man said Dre with his voice trembling.

Dre couldn't see but on the other end Trevor tightened his jaw and closed his eyes tight as a tear rolled down his face then after a moment he ended the call.

At that moment Dre felt like his heart was truly broken as he sat on his bed for another hour feeling crushed that he was the cause of Trevor losing everything.

It's my fault…I destroyed his life…I did it he kept telling himself.

He finally got up and undressed to take a shower and as he ran the water he sat down on the toilet and covered his face and began to cry, really cry for the first time in his life.

Chapter 37

Dre went on with his life focusing on school, work and taking care of his son but he was about to be hit with even harder at home with his mother.

He had just gotten off work and Jay gave him a ride home.

Thanks man I appreciate the ride home…mom doesn't get off until eleven tonight and the bus never runs on time so I'd probably would have gotten here late said Dre.

No problem man, I told you to call me if you ever needed anything, I got your back…I see you really doing your grown man now junior, gave up the bud, the underage drinking…good to see you staying on the straight and narrow said Jay.

Ye, guess you can say I'm on that new shit now and staying that way, got a son whose counting on me and that's my main focus said Jay.

That's what's up said Jay.

They pulled up in front of his house and he saw that his mom was there.

Hey, my mom's home…thought she'd be at work said Dre.

Maybe she got off early said Jay.

I guess…thanks again and see you later man said Dre as Jay nodded with a smile and drove off.

Dre walked into the house and closed the door looking around.

Hey mom, I'm home from work said Dre.

Come in the kitchen Dre his mom told him in a serious tone.

What's up said Dre walking around the living room corner and saw her folding her arms with his black shoebox holding his glock in it on the counter in front of her.

I see you keep the same toys your older brother use to stash in my house without my knowing his mom told him.

Dre looked at her speechless. How did you find it? He asked.

I was on my way to work this afternoon and your old stomping buddy Darrell came by and asked me to tell you he wants the gun back he gave you so after I chased him off with my broom, I took the day off to search this house top to bottom and I found it said his mom.

I told you that if you ever bring a gun in my house for any reason whatsoever that I would put you out of my house no questions asked…so don't talk Dre just gather all of your things immediately, I want you out of here by the end of the night so make your calls and see who will take you in because I won't tolerate this now go upstairs and start packing she told him.

Where am I supposed to go mom? Dre asked her.

The moment you bought that weapon in my house you should have already thought that plan out she told him.

Dre looked at her for a moment then went upstairs.

Dre called Jay for a place to stay for a few days until he figure out his next move, but he gave him a place to stay free of charge as long as he needed it.

It was one evening at work that Dre would get an unexpected visit that would tell him some startling news that would almost send him over the edge.

Gia's cousin Anita walked into the shoe store.

Hi Dre she waved going over to shoe shelves.

Hey said Dre.

Anita searched around trying on a few shoes then finally picked 2 pairs that she wanted and Dre ringed her purchase up at the counter, put them in a bag and handed them to her.

Enjoy the rest of your night said Dre.

You too Dre, so…how are things going between you and Gia? She asked.

Well I don't really know how she doing but I assume she's doing well, I only come through there to see my son or keep him for the weekend said Dre.

You and I should talk on your break; I have a private matter to discuss with you that I think you should know said Anita.

On his break Dre talked to Anita.

So what's good? Dre asked her.

Gia is abusing your son Darius said Anita.

What? Dre asked her.

I just recently found out and thought you should know, she got real drunk one night with me ranting and raving with how much she hates you and how much the baby looks like you and it pisses her off every time she looks at him.

I saw her handling him roughly that night because he wouldn't stop crying and smacking him to put him to sleep then she went on to say that sometimes she lets him get hurt so that you'd come over…I thought it was even sadder that her mom was right there listening and smoking a cigarette like she was use to her treating the baby this way said Anita.

Dre almost lost it as he rubbed his hands through his hair taking a deep breath. Man, you gotta be fucking kidding me; you gotta be fucking kidding me! He repeated.

She's a unfit mother and I never knew just how low she was, I want you to try to keep a cool head and not stomp her down…just get your son out of that house from both those ratchet scum said Anita.

Dre collected himself for a moment. Thanks, I really appreciate you for telling me this. Why would you gnark on family like that? He asked.

Fuck blood, that trifling bitch has been sleeping with my baby daddy for the last 3 months and she got hers coming trust and believe said Anita.

A little later that night, Dre's mom got home from work and saw Dre sitting outside on her porch.

She got out of her car and walked up to the porch and looked at him for a moment as he looked up at her.

Mom, Gia's hurting my son...you have to help me get him out of there said Dre.

It was only minutes that she came speeding up to Gia's apartment complex.

I'm about to go in and snatch her ass up and you take the baby and wait out in the car until I finish whooping her ass,want to hit my grandson I'll show her how it feel she said.

No mom, stay here...I got this said Dre grabbing her arm then got out and walked up the stairs.

Gia got a knock on her door while she was all over her cousin's man Brendan kissing him.

Who is that? She said getting up and looking out the peep hole but couldn't see anyone.

Who is it?!She said.

Pizza man! Replied a voice.

Pizza? I didn't order any pizza she said opening the door to Dre with a cold blooded gangster mug looking at her.

Dre what are you doing here-she said trying to close the door fast as he stopped it with his arm and pushed past her and glanced over at the guy on the couch: Stay out of this man he said looking around for his son and went into her bedroom.

Stop! What are you doing just barging in my place like this! You ever hear of calling before you pop up at people house yelled Gia storming after him.

Dre turned on the light to his son awake in the crib then begin gathering some of his stuff.

What are you doing Dre! She said.

Dre put the baby bag on his shoulder and picked up his son Darius.

Damn, you couldn't change him before you started your date... sorry ass bitch said Dre.

Let's go partner he said kissing his forehead then walked out past Gia who went after him.

Dre! Where are you going with my son! Dre stop! Dre! said Gia as he walked out the house and down the steps where his mom was coming up.

Yeah you stay right there child abuser, I should punch your lights out right now and I will so comon down bitch because the price will be right said Dre's mother.

Forget her, she got hers coming, let's go said Dre.

What?! Give me back my baby! yelled Gia as they both went back to the car and drove off.

Gia smacked her lips and went back up the stairs to her cousin Anita stood to the other end of the outside apartment hall with a stocky manly girlfriend of hers.

Girl, what you doing here? said Gia closing her door fast.

Bitch, I already know that he in there,I would fight you myself for being a trifling ass no good hoe but I'm pregnant so I bought back up and after she done whooping your ass out here you can go in there and tell him he next...but after I have this baby,I shall be digging mad hard and your lop sided ass,Kiki beat that ass commanded Anita and the muscular hood tough walked toward her.

I heard you like beating on babies, when I'm done with you you'll be going back to school to learn your abc's and 123's said KiKi.

Comon you manly ass bitch, what you got hoe said Gia putting her gang up

In the days to follow Gia would get another special visit:

Gia was in the mirror using make up to cover her black eye.

You caught me off guard that night bitch, but Imma catch you again and tap that ass she said to herself when she got a rang at the door bell.

Gia went to the door and looked out it to a guy standing outside unfamiliar to her then opened it.

Who you? She asked.

Gia Thompson? He asked.

Yes that's me and who is asking? She answered back.

Sign here he said handing her a clipboard.

I didn't order anything, what do you have a package for me or something she said signing it as he handed her papers.

You've been served he said walking off.

Gia looked at the court papers pertaining to child custody and rolled her eyes growling and slammed the door.

Soon there was a big custody battle regarding Darius, Dre and Gia met in court to fight for the rights of their baby and the child abuse charges but with Anita testifying on behalf of Dre's side as a witness to the abuse and treatment Gia committed.

Custody rights were awarded to Dre's mother to be legal guardian of Dre's son until he turned 18.

When Dre and his mother were leaving the court room she had a request for him.

You coming home with daddy and your new mommy said Dre kissing his son and holding him as they walked to the car.

I think it's time for you to come back home Dre, your son needs you there but don't you ever ever bring another gun in my house again or you and I will be in court do you understand me? She said.

Yes mam, I apologize and from here on out it's about taking care of my son said Dre kissing him.

Months down the line, Dre had his 18th birthday followed shortly after was his high school graduation.

I'm so proud of you Dre, I knew you could do it and I'm glad one of my sons made it to cap and gown, I never told any of you this but there was a special surprise waiting at the end of that ceremony she said holding his son and handing him a pair of car keys as he looked at her then out at the parking lot to his new car.

Now that's what's up said Dre.

Final Chapter: 38

The summer was just beginning and Dre was headed to the deep country just like old times, paying his relatives a visit.

Dre pulled up to their house and got out looking around taking in the memories, then walked up to the door and ranged the bell.

Erika opened the door and her face lit up with a big smile.

Dre! She said wrapping her arms around him and hugging him tight.

Omg, I missed you and I see you got a mustang out there said Erika.

I missed you too cous and yeah I think it compliments my personality don't you think? Dre grinned.

Yes it does indeed Erika smiled.

I see another pony out there and not the ones you use to take care of said Dre observing another car.

Yes that's all mine said Erika.

Very nice said Dre.

Thank you I know...come in smiled Erika as Dre walked inside.

His Uncle and Aunt walked in to the living room from the kitchen.

Andre, It's so wonderful to see you baby said his Aunt hugging her.

Hey Aunt Marylyn he said hugging her.

Nephew, boy have you gotten taller said his Uncle.

Yep and a tad bit wiser, how's it going Uncle said Dre hugging him.

Just fine here nephew, so how have things been in the city? Dre's Uncle Richard asked him.

Alright but I think it's time we sat down and talked about some things said Dre.

Soon they all sat in the living room as Dre talked to them about what was going on in his life.

I've been working, graduated high school and starting college in the fall…finally got full custody of my son and Gia is well somewhere haunting some other dudes life because I'm not in it said Dre.

Oh thankgoodness, I'm so happy about that. I knew that girl was bad news the first time I saw her said his Aunt.

I'm proud of you nephew, glad you held on to those important words I told you when you left here said his Uncle.

Yep I did, so when is the last time you talked to Trevor or have seen him? Dre asked them.

Well we haven't spoken to him in a long while said his Aunt.

I did hear that he works for Dave at his plant so I'm sure he's doing well but that's all I really know said his Uncle.

I think it's time we get to the nitty gritty of this conversation and why I'm here said Dre.

Alright were listening said his Uncle.

I know you know about the Trevor and I situation that was going on a while back and I think it's something that shouldn't be swept under the rug but bought to the forefront and since it centers around me then I should be the one to have my say on it said Dre.

I know a couple years ago that you think I was just a troubled kid showing up on your door step but I grew up fast, with no dad in my life to teach me I learned what I knew from the streets and with a baby I was soon stacked with more responsibility than any guy should have at my age at the time but I stuck in there and did what I could to provide and take care of him said Dre.

What happened between Trevor and I seems like it was the slightly older person taking advantage of the younger person but I'm not exactly all that innocent and that was not the case at all.

Truth is I developed feelings for him…I knew what I was doing and even though he refused my advances I still initiated it and even when I left here, I still didn't leave his life…don't get me wrong this isn't me coming out to you telling you I'm gay because were not having that moment, I still love the girls and rocking the boat with'um but hell…I came to find out I love the dudes too and I'm not ashame to admit it now that I love him… said Dre.

I still don't understand what this behavior is all about, or knew that you felt this way toward each other…a lot of findings still have me in shock said his Aunt looking at Erika.

You both were wrong for engaging in this activity in our home his Uncle.

I know and I apologize from the bottom of my heart for disrespecting your home, but you were the only family he ever known and all he ever had and you turned your backs on him…I've had to live with the fact that I'm responsible for him losing everything including you and that hurts.

So if you're going to truly blame anybody then blame me, but for him to have to suffer like this…isn't fair said Dre.

Well I didn't turn my back on Trevor, just saying said Erika folding her arms.

Despite everything that's happened, I know you still love him like a son just like he loves you.

So don't hold this against him, would you please forgive him and mend back your relationship, he's a hard worker and a good person and it would be a shame to spend a life time throwing away all those years aside like it never meant nothing said Dre.

I still love Trevor very deeply and think about him often said Dre's Aunt Marilyn.

So do I and I always will said his Uncle Richard.

Cool, so tell him that and I'm not leaving here until this family is made whole again, which is why I'm sticking around for a few days to make sure that happens and I want to see him but let that stay a surprise for right now said Dre.

I have his number we still keep in contact, dad here you go said

Erika handing him the phone.

Meanwhile at Trevor's new residence, he was outside hanging some clothes on the line and walked back into the house with the rest of the clothing pens in a can and put them on a shelf as his phone ranged on the table as he walked over and picked it up.

Hello said Trevor.

Hey Trevor, this is Richard…know it's been a long time but do you have a few minutes to talk? He asked.

Trevor sat down in a chair at his table. Alright Richard, we can talk he said.

Soon, Trevor drove to their house and pulled up outside then got out and walked over as Dre walked out the door and closed it standing to the front of the porch smiling at him.

What up pumpkin said Dre.

Big city, what you doing here?!said Trevor whose face lit up with a big smile.

Checking out some familiar faces down here in the deep and I guess I found another said Dre walking over to him and slapped five with him and gave him a long hug then Dre kissed him passionately and Trevor got really into it stopping them suddenly.

Eh, maybe we should chill on that, your people could be looking right now said Trevor.

Then they will see how much I really missed you wont they said Dre kissing him again.

Big city, still the aggressive Aires Trevor smiled.

You remember my sign? Dre grinned.

Yep, I been doing some star or zodiac research or whatever you call it…Aires is a fire sign which means your extremely passionate and hot headed, your the dare devil, the pioneer, rushing head first into something and going after what you want as if it's a trophi and your the one in the race car trying to win it said Trevor.

I am a sore loser that much is true, so if you thought that I was giving up on you, naw I just needed some time to get me straight I was always coming back for you bullboy said Dre pinching Trevor's ear.

I figured you might, I just didn't have the heart too after our last talk back then said Trevor.

Let's be real I always had the balls in this thing said Dre.

I was using them more though said Trevor.

Dre smiled. Yep and you used them well I might add."

Trevor just looked at him for a moment nodding.

Here we are, standing where we once met huh said Dre.

Yeah, looks that way, so you travelled all the way back down here said Trevor.

Yep, I had a couple reasons to come back said Dre.

I'm really glad to see you man, I know after everything that transpired and the last time we spoke- said Trevor.

All in the past homie, we both know how we feel so no need for those words, I'm thinking we can pick up where we left off…what you think? Dre asked him.

I'd like that said Trevor.

Cool, let's not keep the rest of the family waiting; I know it's been a while since they've seen both of us said Dre.

So How you been? Trevor asked him.

Good, what about you? Dre asked him.

Can't complain, I got a new dog…names Pal, golden retriever said Trevor.

Word, I have a pit-bull now…names big city said Dre as they walked up the steps and into the house.